Dying Young

MARTI
LEIMBACH

Dying
Young

DOUBLEDAY
New York London Toronto Sydney Auckland

Excerpt from "Cancer's a Funny Thing" by J.D.S. Haldane reprinted by permission of the Newstatesman Society, London.

PUBLISHED BY DOUBLEDAY

a division of
Bantam Doubleday Dell Publishing Group, Inc.
666 Fifth Avenue, New York, New York 10103

DOUBLEDAY and the portrayal of an anchor
with a dolphin are trademarks of
Doubleday, a division of Bantam Doubleday Dell
Publishing Group, Inc.

All of the characters in this book are fictitious,
and any resemblance to actual persons, living or
dead, is purely coincidental.

Library of Congress Cataloging-in-Publication Data

Leimbach, Marti, 1963–
    Dying young/Marti Leimbach.—1st ed.
      p. cm.
    ISBN 0-385-26724-X
    I. Title.
    PS3562. E4614D95 1990
    813'.54—dc20   89-17127
                                            CIP

ISBN 0-385-26724-X
Copyright © 1990 by Marti Leimbach
Printed in the United States of America
January 1990
      2   4   6   8   9   7   5   3
                    BVG

For my mother, Mary Leimbach.
And for Jay.

Dying Young

ONE

*F*inally, I see Gordon: dropping the screen door against the frame of his mother's side porch and checking his pocket for the key to his Mercury. He doesn't know that I am watching, that I'm sitting in my car running the radio off the battery, that I woke up at dawn just to see him—just to see what somebody like Gordon does at seven-thirty in the morning. The radio plays heavy metal—*Christian* heavy metal. The lead singer screams out, *"Jesus loves you,"* in a repulsive, stubborn way. I'm transfixed by Gordon, what he looks like, how he moves after only forty-five minutes of being awake, his mannerisms as he approaches his locked car, his confrontation with the layer of frost over his windshield.

He's got on blue jeans, a sweatshirt with the logo from a jazz festival across the front, an unzipped down-feather jacket, and a pair of duck boots with leather laces. His winter gear emphasizes the size of him. He works the ice scraper in swift clips over the windshield. Standing at his car door, outside a house so proper it could be in a photo essay of New England homes, he is a marvel of normality and I am so grateful.

Dying Young

With one boot propped on the carpet beneath the driver's seat Gordon calls, "Tosh, Tosh, come here, dog," and waits for Tosh, who bounds across lawn for the open door. Tosh scurries to the passenger's side and Gordon looks at his watch, then at the house, and makes leggy strides back through the screen door and into his parents' old gray and white colonial. On the radio the backup vocal team sings, *"God is above you, below you, beside you . . ."* while the dog and I stare through window frames into each other's curious eyes.

I feel that having Tosh notice me in my car is an omen that Gordon, too, will see me. Tosh begins to bark and I can hear the hoarse yowls from inside the car, see the fog of Tosh's breath on the glass and her smooth, pricked ears. She would like to play. She recognizes me from when Gordon and I took her to the beach last week and she probably thinks that I am here again to let her romp through the loose sand and retrieve a tennis ball from the ocean surf.

I decide not to look at her. I turn the radio way down, lie across the front seat, and wait for Tosh to stop barking. When Gordon shows up and quiets her, I think about how soothing his voice is—that even a bewildered German shepherd settles down to a voice so serene.

He says, "What's the matter with you, Tosh? Good girl, lie down, that's it . . ." and, weird as this might sound, I feel somehow comforted, as if he were talking to me. I imagine for a moment that my name is Tosh, instead of Hilary, relax my head against the vinyl of the passenger seat, and let the voice calm me. I wonder, not for the first time this morning, why I am sneaking around, what it is I am trying to bring about, and why anyone would force herself out of bed so early in the morning to watch a guy take the fifty yards from his house to the car.

It's not because I'm crazy and not because I'm in love with Gordon. And though I'm interested in what he presents to the world upon waking, at his puffy, early morning eyes and the slick way he's combed back his wet hair, there are easier ways to discover these characteristics in a man. It may be that I just wanted to start my day by observing someone other than Victor or myself, someone whose life is regular and who enjoys where he is and has come here, to Hull, Massachusetts, deliberately and will leave without incident.

I hear Gordon's voice, mellow and fading as he closes the car door. I listen as the car charges up. I hear the gears drop into reverse, then first. And before I've raised my head, I can tell from the sound of tires that Gordon is gone.

I think that at every moment in time you change your life—maybe not deliberately—but that something you do will forever alter the course you are on. If I had never answered the ad in the newspaper, I wouldn't have met Victor and fallen in love with him and I would never have moved to Hull. I wouldn't have met Gordon. Maybe I'd have found someone else and fallen in love with him and maybe he'd own a horse farm in Wyoming and that's where I'd be right now.

I was thinking about this yesterday while Gordon and I walked through the woods behind his house gathering branches for a fire. Our boots crunched over the icy path, the frozen, shredded leaves. We broke chunks of ice off the bank of a half-frozen stream. We pretended that they were icecaps melt-

ing into the Antarctic, that we were witnessing the slow destruction of the world—that soon Florida, Cape Cod, and Hull
would be flooded. We gathered a pile of wood, sat on the
redwood deck of his parent's house, and decided which
branches were dry enough to use.

"So that is your job—taking care of Victor?" he asked.

"No, it *was* my job. That's how we met. Then we fell in
love."

"People don't just fall in love, do they?" Gordon asked.
"Doesn't love have reasons?"

"I don't work for Victor anymore. I'm with him because
I want to be. It's got nothing to do with him being sick," I
told Gordon. Then I asked, "What kind of reasons?"

Gordon squatted on the deck and snapped a thin twig of
kindling. He said, "Would you like to come inside and make
a fire with me?"

It was that juncture of decision, that moment for changing everything. At first I didn't answer him. I wondered if he
was going to ask again but he said nothing. He looked up at
me and I pictured him bending by the hearth, pushing back a
log. I imagined the fire we would make with our collection
of damp branches: a low, noisy flame. I imagined making love
with Gordon by the fireplace, feeling the heat from the fire
against my thigh, my shoulder, one side of my face. And afterward, sitting up and staring into the flames, with Gordon
beside me or behind me, his face in my hair.

Finally, I shook my head no.

I am living within an unsettling stretch of indecision. Yesterday I refused Gordon when he offered and today I surround

him like a buried past. And yet I don't know that I want anything at all with him. I am Victor's girlfriend, a state of being that makes me proud and also anxious. I wander along hoping for a resolution as I fall into the lusterless routine of my days and nights. Nothing ever happens. Apparently I seem normal to the outside world. When I arrive at the launderette I am just another person with a basket of dirty clothes and a dollar bill for the Maytag. I appear not as a woman whose last hour has been spent huddling inside the cold shell of a car but as one who takes seriously the consequence of separating colors. The launderette is one of those coin-ops that stays open all the time; cigarettes from last night's clientele lie crushed across the linoleum. The walls are painted a bright lemon color except the front wall, which is entirely glass.

Today there are no other customers. Only me and the vending machines: a Coke machine, a candy dispenser, and a machine that sells various brands of laundry detergent, bleach, and fabric softener. On the far wall are two video games, one of which comes from the business Gordon owns, a company that develops video games and software for kids. The game is called Alien Turf and requires the player to enter a world of robot men who wield lasers and try to kill the player. Also deadly are the robots' pets, small creatures that look like bugs and circle around their masters, protecting them from enemy fire by zapping incoming missiles with their magic, blinking antennae. Interestingly, the robot men won't actually begin shooting until the player shoots at them, which I believe is a relatively new twist on video games.

I wait for the dryer to finish. I watch the gentle tossing of Victor's boxer shorts, my turtleneck, his black socks, my yellow ones. I think, How can I consider leaving a man while his clothes are drying in such an intimate manner with my own? The bright lights of Alien Turf blink at me, tempting me to play. I drop in a quarter and then another. I keep playing while the dryer spins. I've been killed twelve times by robot men of all ranks before the clothes have finished. I do a murderous job on their pets.

Lying to Victor is easy. He is a confident and tempestuous man—but trusting. I don't think Victor guesses anything about me and Gordon. Lately, however, I've noticed something in his tone that might be a hint of jealousy or suspicion, though I may be flattering myself. I'm no idiot. I've thought about this. You don't have to be Freud to know that using your car to stake out a potential lover is a sign that your current relationship is floundering.

But Victor sleeps a lot. If I were clever I could have an entirely separate life without his ever knowing it, which may in fact be what I have. It seems he is always just waking, rising from a nap, or yawning in either anticipation of or recovery from long hours of rest. It is as if he's constantly preparing for a return to bed. He will be rushed to finish something—a chapter of a book, most usually—before he has to go to sleep again. His life has been spent dodging the constraints of his disease.

For three months we've been living in Hull. We have a single, specific reason for being here: Victor is letting leukemia run its course through his body. I don't like Hull. Before we came here I searched the World Atlas for the eastern states of North America and found it, shaped like a healthy appendix and hanging off Massachusetts. Hull is quieter than Boston;

many of the winter residents are fishermen or retired. At any rate, they don't exercise their neighborliness on Victor and me. Victor admits Hull has its faults but claims it is a discreet place to die. And he is right. We live on the third story of a Victorian-style house situated on a narrow, partly paved street with a string of other houses whose windows are boarded for the winter. The rent is low off season, and Victor says the ocean calms him and, of course, the street is very quiet because no one lives on it.

We've shut ourselves away on this almost island. The peninsula swings north from its base and at the very tip is only forty minutes by ship across the Atlantic to Boston Harbor. But still, the link between me and the city where I used to live seems as tenuous as the thin neck of the peninsula on the map—as if any movement of the earth, any storm, any change of pressure, could snap Hull right off the coastline and place me forever among the unlived-in houses and back lots full of salt-rusted cars. I might someday look out our diamond-shaped window and see only the green and crashing ocean and no boats to take me home.

We live in a large converted attic room with sloped ceilings. It's only one room but it's a big one and has a separate kitchen. We rented it furnished and so we live within a strange cluster of odd decorations, unmatched chairs, and tables from various design schemes. Nice furniture, made from walnut and mahogany; the couch is stuffed with horsehair. But everything is in bad repair, chipped and splintered and cracked. I have the impression that at one time the furniture belonged to an entire system of beauty and opulence that has since fallen away. The roses on the chintz have faded to a rust color, as gloomy as the thrift stores and Salvation Army shops from where the furniture came and to where it will inevitably return. The closet smells of a mixture of mildew and moth balls, and also termite killer. It stocks a halogen lamp, a stack of army-issue blankets that we don't use, and Sterno tins. Also in the closet is a pile of pictures that were once on the walls. They're portraits, black and white, of somebody else's mothers and aunts and grandfathers. Regal-looking people, dignified in their high-buttoned blouses and stiff gray collars. When I took them from the wall I noticed that the spaces the frames had occupied were a darker shade than the rest of the wall. After I stacked them together and settled them in a closet corner, I felt strangely guilty, as though I'd violated some ancient code.

We have many vases which I occasionally fill with reeds and flowers. We have a brass-rimmed mirror with a distorted glass and wall lamps with tricky switches in the shape of key butts. There is a window with a view of the ocean, and a Queen Anne-style chair stationed for the viewing. And, of course, there are all of Victor's books, propped up on planks and cinder blocks that cover one peeling aquamarine wall.

*V*ictor is asleep when I arrive home, lying with one ropy arm bent over his face. I watch the easy rocking of the blankets as he takes each breath. I watch his sleeping face, his relaxed limbs. Then the alarm rings, filling the apartment with the lunatic sound of an electronic whistle. I reach over and turn it off.

"Did you set the alarm?" Victor asks. His mouth moves but the rest of him is entirely still. His eyes are closed and his breath is regular and deep. Yawning, he looks up at me, doing his best to focus without glasses. His eyes are olive-gray. Without his glasses they are so beautiful it seems odd that he can use such eyes to see.

"No," I tell him.

"Must be ghosts," he says. He wets his lips, reaches to the night table, and takes his glasses. "Get in bed with me."

I slide next to him. I taste salt and stale smoke in his hair. He is feverish; I have learned to judge temperature without a thermometer and I estimate 101 degrees.

"Where were you this morning?" Victor says.

"I did the laundry."

"At this hour?"

"I was going out for coffee anyway."

Victor kisses me and then smacks his lips. He says, "No, sweetie, you weren't drinking any coffee. Don't pull back, let me hold you. You're cool from being outside. I'm so hot I could melt you. I'm so hot you may just melt right out of my arms."

"I went on a drive. I went down to the water."

"You could have taken me."

"You were asleep."

"Coward," Victor says.

The breeze is strong against the window frame. I concentrate on the exact sound the glass makes against its pressure.

"Your breathing changed," Victor says. He runs his hand up my spine and scratches lightly between my shoulders. "I've been reading about how when people are lying their breathing changes."

The wind shakes the long arm of a maple branch against the window. The sound is like a knocking or a scraping. It ruffles the ivy on the side of the house, disturbing me, making me want to snap the rods of maple branches or send away the wind.

After a long pause Victor says, "Very early this morning I went downstairs to see if the car was still here. You weren't in bed and I had this strange feeling as if you'd vanished entirely. That you never even existed."

"Victor . . ." I say with apology.

"Of course, I would never get up and leave you that way."

"I wasn't leaving you, sweetheart."

"Sure you were," Victor says.

I get out of bed and go to the kitchen. There is no point arguing with Victor. I've been stupid to underestimate his intuition. I am angry and also ashamed. Still, I cannot listen to his carpings. There is only one way to maneuver in such a situation and that is through absolute denial. Instead of discussing Gordon with Victor I stoop among the lower cabinets in our kitchen, pretending I am looking for a pan. I make a lot of noise with casserole pots and Jell-O molds so that I can't hear Victor, who is ranting in the other room.

"Did you hear me, Hilary?" he shouts. "I am talking to you, could you pay attention for a second?"

I walk back to the front room and look hard at Victor. He sits up, folding the bedcovers at his lap, and returns my glare. I have a dishrag in my hand which I toss over one shoulder. He stares at me with unnerving constancy and I cross my arms. Victor takes a cigarette and taps the butt end against the night table. He puts it to his lips. He strikes a match and holds it a long time before setting fire to its end.

"I don't expect you're in any danger of winning the No-bel Prize," Victor says in slow and careful words, "but I do think you are intelligent enough not to lie to me."

"I'm not lying," I say. To myself I say, Keep your temper. Victor is struggling; Victor is having a bad time with it all. We worry apart and have learned the signs of each other's momentary panic. His illness has started to hurt him. There is a small amount of morphine in a desk drawer. Next to it is a prescription for more, a rather official-looking document with a doctor's difficult scrawl and hurried signature. It waits like a new page of a diary.

"Why do we have these flowers here?" Victor asks and touches the vase of carnations and lilies by the bed.

"Because they are pretty."

"Why did you put them here?" he asks.

"This might be hard to believe, Victor, but most people find flowers attractive."

"Well, I don't," Victor says. "I hate these flowers. They've been alive for a week and a half. It's unnatural for flowers to live so long. I would like them a whole lot better if they were dead."

Victor fills his hands with stems and dumps the shallow water from the vase into a puddle on the floor. Then he puts the flowers back into the dry vase.

"See how long you last like *that*," Victor says to the flowers. He reaches to the floor and lifts a bottle of rubbing alcohol. He twists the cap open and pours a drop of clear liquid against the stem of a pink carnation.

"Would you please stop torturing the plant life?" I say.

"Smell this," he says. He puts his cigarette between his teeth and holds out the carnation. "Can you smell it?"

Dying Young

I put my nose near the flower and breathe deeply. "It smells like flowers and alcohol," I tell him.

"It smells like hospitals and death," says Victor, pushing a funnel of smoke into the air.

We are silent together. Victor stubs out his cigarette and picks at something under his thumbnail. Then he folds his hands across his stomach. He looks at me cautiously. I go to the bed and sit cross-legged next to him, my torso making a shadow on his face. He is feeling fairly well today. When Victor feels well, he is more critical of me. Last week there was a big explosion over what books I read. He pulled his own books off the shelves, threw them on the couch, and said, "Read something decent for a change. Kant, Schopenhauer, Wittgenstein, Nietzsche! Lacan, Jung, Freud for godsakes!" The words I offered in defense spun away from him. I fiddled with my hair and waited for it to pass. Other days are much quieter. On other days, he stays in bed.

There have been many better times with Victor. Like when we sit up late and he talks about his life before he became so ill. He tells me about his childhood—the racy details of a life of wealth. Interesting stories, but interesting in the way even the most tired fairy tale would be intriguing if you were told it by someone who claimed it as true. I never believed about wealth until it was told to me by Victor. I never understood the inventiveness that comes with money or its distorting quality. The world was offered up to Victor like a giant Fabergé egg, like a present that he should continue to delight in and unwrap. He has a rich man's voice and stance. He has that impenetrable smugness; what, I guess, people call class. In the hours between 2 and 5 A.M. Victor has explained things that I never knew—about people for whom dreams live past childhood and the great differences between what I have taken as true and what exists as fact in a rich man's obliging world.

In normal circumstances, someone like Victor would never be with someone like me.

"Let me get in bed with you," I say. I slide beneath the sheet, feeling the warmth from Victor's fever, the damp spots from another night of sweating. Victor turns away shyly. I pull him toward me and kiss him behind the ear. I take some of his hair between my teeth and pull at it teasingly.

"I'm sorry," Victor says finally.

"Nothing's happened," I say, hugging him.

"How can you stand me?" Victor says. "Wait, don't answer that. You know, Hils, I get so angry at you and I don't understand why. I know this is crazy but—now don't get mad—but I just have to know why you forgot to get ice cream when you went to the store last time? Do you want me to lose more weight?"

"Of course not. I just forgot."

"Is that true?" He shivers the way he does when he has a temperature.

"Yes," I say.

"You're a good person, Hilary. Do you know I really think you are a good person?"

"You do?"

"Yes," Victor says. "And I'm good to you, too."

We begin to make love. But it is many minutes before I realize that this is what we are doing, so lingering is every action. It seems we are creeping toward making love even as we do it. Like a nonspecific act, like a gradual happening between us. It's as if we might stop altogether at any moment.

Dying Young

Victor's passion is slow, but persistent. We roll together like the images within a dream. As if gravity has been suspended, as if we are under water. We wait for our bodies to push toward each other of their own accord. We wait for the pulse of our love to reach its end.

Later, he is asleep again. I tread over the bedside collection of magazines and soda cans and newspapers. By mistake I step on the telephone, which has been dragged to the center of the room. The cord is tangled in all the junk on our floor. I follow the cord back to the phone jack, unsnarling it from chair legs, from within the pages of books and small mounds of dishware. I drag it from beneath a milk crate and nearly tip over a lamp while freeing it from behind the desk. I settle the phone back in its place on the kitchen counter and move the bouquet of carnations from the night table into the bathroom, filling the vase again with water.

The flowers look good on the sink. It feels like luxury to have flowers in the bathroom. I take off my clothes and hang them over a towel rack. I look into the mirror, sharing the reflection with lilies, admiring how the carnations bring out the pinkness in my skin. Looking into the mirror, I have to admit that though I may feel old I don't look it. I am plump: my heart has pumped twenty-seven years of healthy full blood. I have clear skin and nice, square shoulders. My hair shines like it did when I was seven and I have a smart-looking face.

Our shower is a corner of absolute functionability in an otherwise technologicaly compromised building. Every morning I revel in its never-ending force of hot water. It also creates a hideous amount of noise, making anything outside of its narrow dominion nearly impossible to hear. I'm shampooing my hair, lathering it up, when over the loudness of the shower water comes the colossal sound of two shotgun shots. I jump out of the shower, loop a towel around me, and yell to Victor. Then I go to where Victor is at the window. He stands in his underwear, balancing the nose of his gun against the window ledge. He has an antique double-barrel Remington shotgun that he calls the rat gun because killing rats is about all it's used for. He has the radio tuned to a country-western station. To the sound of a cowgirl's lonesome love song Victor pummels shells into the lawn three stories below.

"It is too early to shoot rats," I tell him. "It's really very early."

Last time he shot at rats two police cars and a fire truck showed up. I hoped that they would stop him but the police were impressed by the gun and the firemen cheered him on.

"I think I hit one!" Victor shouts. He pulls the shotgun inside and stands in front of me, his face animated. Next to him the gun is sleek. Its twin hammers are cocked up for the next round.

"You got one? Where?"

"Look," he says, pointing. "The stack of wood by the fence is where their house is. The bastards, they're probably *breeding* in there. I scared them out with gunfire. See that clump of fur? That's an impulsive fellow who decided to leave his shelter and brave it against the enemy's heavy artillery."

"That's mulch," I say.

"Mulch! How can it be mulch? My God, it *is* mulch," Victor pouts. "Damn it, I never hit anything."

Dying Young

"Can't we let the rats live just one more day?" I say. The breeze from the open window is cold. I am shivering beneath my towel.

"Rats smell and they carry diseases. Also they eat babies. You should be proud that I take an aggressive stand on such creatures. Do you really want to save any animal that feeds on small children?"

"The rats in our building don't eat any babies. They hardly eat anything at all. Really they are awfully malnourished rats," I say.

"I know what it is," Victor says, offering me the shotgun. "You want a turn. I'm always hogging the rat gun. Here, she's all yours."

"I don't want the rat gun," I say. "I want you to stop shooting at wildlife."

"Hilary, these are not animals you are going to see on a *National Geographic* special. Rats are vermin. Try to think of them as giant cockroaches."

"They have *fur,*" I say.

"You are hopeless," Victor says. He tugs at his underwear and goes back to the window. Balancing the butt of the gun against his shoulder, he squints down the long barrel and fires another shot into the air.

I take blue jeans off the radiator and pull them on. Victor cocks both hammers and fires twice through the window. The sound is enormous. I cover my ears and search for a sweater. The gun blasts again and I hear Victor yelling, "Near miss!" He fires once more and is sent off balance by the force of the shot. The Remington is a 16-gauge, a serious device, and Victor is not a polished shooter.

I stand at one end of the room, lean against the wall, and

watch him. To my right is Victor's desk, scattered with notes and open books. Across a monster-size Old English Dictionary is a spray of ink from a broken pen.

"Try not to hit any of the neighbors' children," I say to Victor.

"We don't have any neighbors," he says.

"Well, just be careful."

Victor raises his hand and salutes me. Then he turns back to his shooting. He kneels at the window and tricks back the hammer. It seems to me he hardly aims. He lets the shotgun kick his shoulder. He cracks open the breech and fills the gun with fresh shells.

"Look, that's enough, Victor," I say.

"They are just rats," Victor says.

"Come on, stop."

"Watch TV or something."

I go to the window and tap Victor. He ignores me, pivots on his heel, and takes another shot.

"I mean it, Victor. It's really bothering me."

"What are you!" Victor yells. He lowers the gun, his face red, his lips pinched, and frowning. "You want me not to shoot the rats; you want me to do what? Write a will?"

"Go to hell," I say. Victor stands, opens his mouth, and comes toward me. His angry face is foreign. I step backward, against the wall. He looks at me hard, turns back to the window, and raises the shotgun.

"Why do you do this?" I say. "I hate it. When you shoot things I hate *you.*"

"Look, it's just a little dissociation. If I were a Nyanga tribesman I'd dance around wearing the mask of a hornbill. But I'm a New Englander so I shoot rats," he says.

"Well, stop!" I yell at him.

"Why can't you shut up?" Victor says, aiming outside, aiming at rats, or aiming where there is nothing but empty sky, I cannot tell.

I lunge at the gun, pushing the barrel toward the ceiling. Victor twists away from me, struggling for the shotgun.

"What's the matter with you?" Victor shouts. His fingers are tight around the barrel. He uses his shoulders to knock me aside.

"Get out of the way!" he yells. He pulls at the gun, trapping my finger against the trigger guard. I scream and pull my hand away. The barrel slaps the window, sending glass in all directions.

"Are you done yet?" I say. A tear of melting ice slips through a fist-size hole and down the inside of the window's wooden frame.

"No, I'm not."

"Well, look what you did to my finger," I say, holding it for him to see. On one side of the fingernail is a swelling.

He puts the gun down and looks at my damaged hand. Then he takes a triangle-shaped shard of glass from the floor and, in a single stroke, digs the glass deep into his palm, splitting the skin into two pink ledges. A line of red forms in the pit of the wound.

"What are you doing?" I ask.

"Nothing. I'm bleeding."

"You're nuts," I tell him.

The blood oozes in thick droplets, making a half-moon across his palm.

"I'm leaving," I say, turning. I grab my coat, hoist it under one arm, and scan the room for my sneakers. At the door, I pull them on quickly, not bothering even to tie the laces.

"Hils," Victor says when I open the door. He walks to me, takes my wrist, and kisses it. "I'm sorry. Don't leave. Please don't leave. Stay with me. Stay and we'll make up. I'll do anything. I'll fix the window. I'll apologize to the rats."

I look at my wrist. Where he's touched it there is blood. Across Victor's mouth is a red smear. He holds his bleeding hand away from him. On the floor are fat splotches of bright red.

"No, I have to go. I have to get away. I'm making myself insane. I'm making you insane."

"Look, I'm not insane," he says. "I'm an asshole. I do assholish things—it's my nature. Why do you think I planned to pay someone to live with me? I didn't think it would be a picnic. You want me not to kill rats? I won't kill rats."

"No, go ahead and kill them," I say to Victor. "Kill them all."

I find Gordon at the harbor. He's in a boat—a twenty-two-foot sloop that was a gift to his father after Alien Turf came out last year. He bends over a pump, concentrating. Tosh lies on the dock, curled on Gordon's yellow raincoat. She bites her tail. Gordon balances on one knee, working the pump. His cheeks are blown scarlet and water has made dark spots on his duck boots. Tosh sees me first and stops biting her tail long enough to wag it. Then Gordon looks up at me and either squints or smiles, I can't tell. He turns off the pump and leans back.

"How did you know I'd be here?" he asks.

"Guessed."

"How have you been?"

"How have *you* been?" I say.

"How's Victor?"

I look over the harbor at the grainy blue sky, the lines of boats with their tarps on, the splintering pier.

"Oh, he's fine."

"He's asleep?" Gordon says.

"Killing rats," I say. "We got in another fight."

"Break anything?"

"Yeah," I say, "the window." Since we've been living together Victor and I have had several major household casualties resulting from our fights. So far we've chipped a corner of the mantel, put a hole through a closet door, ripped a lighting fixture from the wall, and torn the hose off the vacuum. I've catalogued these events for Gordon, who finds them funny but also sad.

"I thought about you this morning. I had this odd feeling—like you were on your way over." Gordon's voice sounds puzzled. He hesitates over each word in an effort to explain with precision. "In a way, I was expecting you."

I wonder if Gordon is playing with me and I get the urge to blurt out that he knows perfectly well I was parked outside his house this morning. Also, that he shouldn't make such a big deal of it.

"Coincidence, huh?" Gordon says. He smiles a cocky, boyish sort of smile.

I'm sure Gordon is not going to tell me that he saw me in my car. He's going to push me around about it first, see what kind of reaction he can get from me. He's going to make me confess and I could just rip his lungs out for this.

"Gordon," I begin. "It isn't what you think."

"Oh, I know, I don't believe in any sort of psychic power stuff," Gordon says. He reaches to pat Tosh. "I don't even think I can accurately say I've had a déjà vu. But still, without meaning to sound all hocus-pocus, I just wanted to tell you I was thinking of you."

I am an evil person: I always think the worst. In this way, Victor and I are exactly alike. Victor, too, would have thought that Gordon knew all along that I had been in the car and Victor, too, would have reached for that message within language that tells you someone is toying with you. I feel guilty because I don't think I deserve the good faith that someone like Gordon invests in me—I mean why should he be so honest and open and willing to see the good in me when I seem to be charging down his throat trying to peg him for one dirty deed or another?

We are in a booth at Cappy's Restaurant & Pub, one of the oldest buildings in Hull. It was a post office in the nineteenth century and a livery before that. Its most recent status as a restaurant resulted from the efforts of its founder, Cappy, who has made it a popular place with tourists in the summer. And right now, sitting at a table overlooking the harbor, I feel something of the optimism that accompanies the summer months. But it is November; I can almost feel the wind coming through the windowpanes of Cappy's restaurant.

Cappy has both the shape and texture of a hard-boiled egg. He's also completely bald, save a ring of steel-colored ropy hair which he coils along the top of his head. During tourist season Cappy is almost never around. He hires his son to run the place and then Cappy escapes to Martha's Vineyard. But during the winter months he is forever in his restaurant, which also functions as the town pub in the evenings. He keeps himself busy stacking crates of beer, mixing coffee beans, and talking to the fishermen who fill the handful of stools by the bar at lunchtime.

"What are you doing to your parents' house?" Cappy asks Gordon. He has his ex-wife's apron tied around him and a pitcher of coffee in his hand. "Here, honey, you have some more," he says to me and fills my mug. Across the front of his apron are the words, "Hot Mama."

"Just doing some repairs," Gordon says.

"Now? In the middle of winter?"

"They'll be back in the spring. It's easier this way."

"I thought you had a regular job," Cappy says. "I thought you built electronic doodads."

Gordon says, "I don't build them myself anymore."

"You should be out working, not lazing around at home," Cappy says. He winks at me. He reaches one hairless pudgy arm around behind him and pulls a chair from the next table. Cappy refers to all the houses in Hull as "home" even though he must know that many people with places in Hull think of their house in the city as their real home.

"I'm only here a couple of weeks," Gordon says. He has a plate of toast and is scraping some butter onto one of the slices.

"Well, it's good to see you here, boy," Cappy says. He reaches for the coffee pitcher and sloshes some coffee into Gordon's mug, even though it's still three-fourths full.

I notice for the first time that there is tremendous heat

emanating from Cappy, as if he had a furnace in his chest. Maybe that's what happens when you live in a cold climate long enough. Maybe you develop an internal heating mechanism—something you can sort of turn on and off, a survival strategy. Of course, Cappy is hugely fat. He may have to exert himself constantly just to remain upright.

"Where's Victor?" Cappy demands. "Why hasn't he been in here?"

"He hasn't been feeling great," I say. I forget if Cappy knows how sick Victor is. I can never keep track of who already knows, who is supposed to know and who isn't. Victor moved to Hull to be anonymous. And up until now we've been fairly anonymous. But what Victor hadn't counted on was that the winter inhabitants in a place like Hull are not altogether without their methods of amusement. Someone like Victor can stir up an enormous amount of interest and gossip. And when Victor gets in the mood he talks nonstop about how he is waiting for death, as he likes to call it. But I don't know if he has told Cappy. I have to play safe. Probably Cappy already knows that Victor is sick—but I don't want to bet on it and I don't want to tell him.

"He said he wasn't feeling too good last time I saw him," Cappy says. "Too bad. I miss having him around. He's a good talker, a real genius."

Gordon nods and pops the last bite of toast in his mouth. He watches Cappy with interest and, for a brief, weird moment, I feel the way a young mother might feel when the kindergarten teacher is telling her husband what a bright kid they have.

"Last time he was in here he talked about the prisoners

in the Nazi war camps. About what sorts of tortures they did to them and who was responsible and how they piled up the bodies in pits after they gassed them," Cappy says.

I look at Gordon and see that he has stopped chewing.

"Victor is fascinated by various forms of death and agony," I say.

Cappy continues, "He said these camps were pigsties and the Jews didn't have any water or medicine or food. And they made 'em work and beat them up and . . ."

"Sure, Cappy, we all *know* this," Gordon says.

"Yeah, but you don't know it like Victor knows it. He can use the German words for things. He can tell you the difference between one camp and the next: Treblinka versus Auschwitz."

"You must have taken notes, Cap," Gordon says.

Cappy sits straight. He reaches beneath his apron bib and touches a ball-point in his shirt pocket.

"I've been doing some studying since Vic was in here. I want to see what he thinks of this book I've been reading about war criminals. What's Victor think we should do about all the war criminals?" Cappy asks me.

"I wouldn't know," I say.

"Is he a professor or what?" Cappy asks.

"No," I tell him. Victor is not a professor. He doesn't even have his doctorate. He was a fifth-year graduate student— philosophy—when he decided to stop chemotherapy.

"Has he told you about how all the Jews joined together?"

"No," I say. In fact, he told me the opposite. He told me that in many of the camps victims would steal pieces of cloth from the SS officers' uniforms and sew them into their own clothes. Then they would try to act like the SS officers—giving orders, denigrating Judaism, even beating up fellow prisoners—until the real SS officers caught them at it and tortured them for mocking officers. He told me that story the day he became so nauseated from discontinuing his medication that he puked all over the front seat of our car and then in the bathroom and later in bed. He told it to me when I heated up a can of Campbell's soup for my lunch and he said the smell of it made him feel sick again.

"Well, what would happen, see," Cappy says, "is that even when the Jews had no food, no clean water, nothing to bathe in, nothing to cover their wounds with—even in the midst of living hell—they would share. You might give someone half your bread, or a cigarette, for example. He said sometimes a stronger man would work for a weaker one, that mothers who had lost their babies would give the milk from their breast to a man too sick to eat solid food."

"*That* I don't believe," Gordon says. "I bet they didn't even have any mother's milk. I bet they were too malnourished."

"What do you know? You build doohickeys," Cappy says. "Shut up and drink your coffee. Victor's a genius. Tell him, honey," he says to me.

Gordon and I inhabit a long and embarrassed moment.

"I don't build doodads *or* doohickeys. We develop video sports," Gordon says.

Cappy leans toward us, shadowing two thirds of the table. "They shared and suffered together. Nowadays, we don't do squat for anyone else, do we? We lie on our backs like dead lizards and watch the sun rise and set each day."

"Are we going to get a whole sermon?" Gordon says. But Cappy doesn't pay any attention. He's on a roll now.

"It's going to be the end for us," he says. "You know why? Something Victor said; he said nobody who was in those camps, facing death, survived without help. Caring was as essential to them as food or water or medicine or God. He said, 'Survival is a collective act.' " Cappy pushes his forefinger on the table for emphasis. If he were a judge, he'd be the kind that makes embellished proclamations and seizes every opportunity to use his gavel.

"Victor read that," I say. I don't mention that Victor has a T-shirt with that slogan on front. And on the back it says, "Keep Free Enterprise Free."

I look over to Gordon and want to protect him. Then I can't understand why I should protect him. He's not being attacked. No one has been attacked. We are just talking in the morning—such a normal thing.

"Doesn't matter," Cappy says. "If you ever fought in a war, you'd know he was right."

"Victor has never fought in a war," I say.

"That's right," Cappy says. "And he knows anyway. That's just it."

By the time we leave Cappy's I have lost my good mood. Sometimes as I'm driving down the road or maybe buying French rolls at the bakery, I imagine Victor standing behind me or sitting in the back seat or peeking through a window at me. It's as if he's with me all the time even though, lately, he's been in bed. It's like I carry his photograph around with me in my mind. At the strangest times his face is revealed to me. And as Gordon and I walk through the boatyard and back to where his boat is docked, I keep seeing Victor. I imagine him propped up on one of Cappy's bar stools, his thin legs crossed, a cigarette. I can see his curly hair shining in the gaslights. He leans back, taking in a lungful of air, and freezes, still-breathed, with his eyes narrowed. He begins to speak, the words flowing perfectly from his mouth, like well-directed children. I imagine him watching Gordon and me trudging back to the boat, his face gone red, his mouth turned down, the anger building in his chest. And in this way I let myself be judged.

"Do you have errands to do today?" Gordon asks.

I shrug and step around a pile of shoveled sand. "You want to get rid of me?" I ask.

"No," Gordon says. He stops at the dock and faces me. "No, I want to keep you. But I thought I'd ask you indirectly. You know how that works? I think to myself, I want to spend some time with her, but then I think, Well, she's probably got other things to do and will say she can't. So I ask you if you have other things to do. This gives you the opportunity to say something polite and understandable." Gordon takes in a long breath and lets it out. "So, Hils, do you want to say something polite and understandable?"

"I feel guilty," I confess.

"I am not asking you to run away with me—I just would like to know if you'd like to do something different. Would you like, for example, to do something fun?"

"I'm awful at making a decision," I say. I think of what Victor always says about how I cannot make a decision, the way he rolls his eyes and I feel like a four-year-old. "What is there to do that is 'fun'?"

Gordon laughs and I feel better. I even laugh a little. I shrug my shoulders and say, "Well, I mean it. I don't really know what is fun. Do you? I'm serious, Gordon, do you know something that is fun and that we could do?"

"Yes," Gordon says. "I think so."

TWO

*T*he ferry, which I have never been on, leaves from a part of the harbor called Pemberton and arrives forty minutes later at Long Wharf Pier in Boston. I've listened morning after morning to the foghorn on this ferry and I know its schedule from the timing of those long blasts. Gordon and I are on the eleven o'clock, standing on the top deck, which is deserted, and no wonder, the sea breeze is so strong that nobody in his right mind would occupy the rows of colorful plastic chairs that make patterns across the wooden floor. Gordon has his hands tucked beneath the sleeves of his sweater and I have the hood up on my parka.

We are sharing a bag of M & Ms, which we bought in the coffee shop before boarding and I am in charge of doling them out between us.

"Ahh, I want the brown one," Gordon says. "You take the yellow." He looks away and breathes the air greedily, enjoying it. Gordon finds pleasure in all aspects of the out-of-doors. He climbs rocks in the springtime, he's told me. He windsurfs on Nantasket beach. There was a documentary on television the other day, a special on people who hang-glide, and I almost expected to see Gordon out there, jumping from the side of a mountain and taking flight beneath the titanic wings of a kite.

"Don't you love New England when the sun shines?" Gordon says. He squints up at the sky.

"Sure, when it shines—which it doesn't," I say.

"It's sunny right now. Look at the sky, the sea gulls, the sun. Beautiful."

The sky is marbled by clouds. At the very moment Gordon says "Beautiful" another cloud obstructs the sun. "You spoke too soon, Gordon."

"Okay, but now see how dramatic it all looks: the steel of the guardrail against a background of turbulent sea, the gulls blending into a dark sky, the lighthouse way off in the distance, the wind. It's an adventure," Gordon says.

I look to the front of the ferry and think how strange it is to be moving toward Boston. I have wanted to go to Boston for weeks now, maybe months. Sometimes I envision the crowded streets of Back Bay, the lights along the Charles River, the Prudential Center, Copley Square, restaurants where I ate with friends after work, and I wonder what is happening at this very minute in the city. I might be standing over the hedge in the front of the house, shearing the unruly branches and pulling out the dried, dead leaves, and suddenly wonder, What are the colors of the Christmas lights on the Common this year and has the pond frozen solid enough for skating? Have the people in my old apartment discovered the loose kitchen tile? The tear in the window screen? Do the medicine cabinets still smell that way?

"Are you cold?" Gordon asks, and of course I am.

There's a chapped spot on my lower lip, a line of separating skin that I cannot keep from biting.

Gordon puts an arm around me and hugs my shoulder. "Would you like to go below? They have tables and it's warmer."

I don't move a muscle. I am as wary of the arm as a hospital patient is of an intravenous tube. I am so perfectly still beneath the weight of Gordon's arm that I might be mistaken for dead. I say, "Have some candy."

"Don't give me any of the red ones. I hear they cause cancer."

"They don't make red anymore. Besides, everything causes cancer," I say. I tug at my lip. It is so chapped that it stings. I turn to Gordon. I am looking straight at him now. "Once Victor and I ran through a pile of medical and nutrition books and some articles from the library and made a list of all the foods and the additives that are supposed to give you cancer. It took us a half week. I think it was four days, actually, and still we had a very incomplete list. Then we made a list of all the household products: things like shampoos and toilet cleaners. That took us two days—but by that time we were good at it. Do you know I'm still afraid to use deodorant? I'm convinced that it gives women breast cancer."

"Does it?"

"Who would know?" I say. "The fibers in this coat might be giving me cancer right now."

Gordon plays with the brown M & M that I have dropped in his palm. He turns it over and over, fingering the spot where the letters "m & m" are written in white.

"Bad subject," Gordon says.

I shake my head. "No, it doesn't bother me. Victor and I talk about it all the time. You don't smoke cigarettes, do you? At night I sit up late and smoke cigarettes."

"Never during the day?" asks Gordon.

"Usually not."

"You are a secret smoker," Gordon says in a teasing, declarative tone. He crosses his jaw, smiling a little, and I admire his looks. Gordon has marvelous facial expressions, all the more marvelous because they are so unrehearsed. He has a long mouth that curves differently at either end, radiant skin, and a beautiful, arched nose.

"Victor knows I smoke."

"I don't see how you can be afraid that deodorants will give you cancer and smoke cigarettes," Gordon says wisely.

"I once asked a doctor to tell me his best reason to quit smoking. He told me that thirty-three percent of cancers are attributable to cigarettes. You know what that means?" I ask and Gordon shakes his head. I give him more chocolate and say, "That means sixty-seven percent are entirely random. Besides, I'm not really afraid of deodorants. I just felt like saying that."

"What's it like," Gordon says shyly, "to live like you do? You know, I was at home last night and I guess I was watching a movie or something on television and a commercial came on—one of these ads for cereal. And I saw this young mother— maybe five years older than you—with a breakfast table ringed with children. There was a husband kind of knotting his tie, and all these kids, and maybe there was a dog. You understand the scene? Anyway, all through this commercial I thought, Poor Hilary, she doesn't have these things. She doesn't have a breakfast room or . . . you know . . . kitchen appliances."

"What made you think I'd want them?" I ask.

"Maybe you don't," Gordon says and laughs, embarrassed. "I'm just not quite sure how it is you live like you do— or why really. I mean what's it like to live like that?"

"Like what? Truth be known, Gordon, that apartment *has* a few kitchen appliances."

Gordon nods in a bashful way. "I'll fix your window if you want," he says.

"No, thanks. It's just a hole anyway. Victor will tape it."

Gordon takes his arm from my shoulder. He rubs his hands together to make them warm. He looks confused and somewhat doomed, as if he expects he is failing an important test. He props his chin with his hands and a sigh drifts from him. He seems so concerned and it both charms and baffles me.

"It would be easier for me to understand if you had known him before he was sick," Gordon says in a manner that suggests a long period of speculation. "Then it would make perfect sense. But you only knew him when he was already sick. You knew he was going to die."

I consider this. I say, "I always think that I can isolate events in my life—that I can keep them from affecting me. Victor dying, I don't know. I guess I'm fooling myself. Children understand this. They don't pretend that the television show or the story they hear before bedtime won't change the way they dream."

"How can you stand knowing that he is going to die?" Gordon says. His mouth is stiff, he looks at me steadily.

"Well, you know sometimes I don't think of him as dying at all. He has such a strong grip on life. Sometimes I forget what is really happening and I imagine that we have some sort of mutual project going—which in a way we do," I say. "Sometimes, I think we are having a baby."

"Are you?" Gordon asks, emphatically.

"I suppose not." I look across the ocean and realize that the gray shadows way off are actually some buildings and that we are finally nearing Boston.

"Don't you *know?*"

"I don't think I am pregnant, Gordon, calm down."

"Hilary, do you and Victor have sex?" Gordon's face is bent toward mine at an angle almost as if he were going to kiss me. But his face is so serious, so clinical. I imagine Gordon in a gynecologist's lab coat, a stethoscope slung around his neck and a plastic model of female genitalia on a bookshelf above his head.

"Yes," I say. "Of course."

"And you don't use birth control?"

"Well, no, not exactly. I have a sort of different perspective on things like birth and death than the average person, I suppose. For me they just happen," I say. What I don't tell him is this: it makes me sad to think of using birth control. You have to imagine Victor when Victor makes love. He's not Victor. He's someone else whom I might have loved for my whole life. Victor can only make love when he feels love—he can't fake it and he can't do it for some other reason. I've been with people who make love the way that they eat between meals. Victor doesn't have the energy to use sex as a filler. And all those things that add to desire—wanting to see our own body making love to someone else's, the little power struggles, the desire for control or the opportunity to be controlled—none of these will raise Victor's interest for lovemaking. They are his favorite themes for conversation but Victor's dick just doesn't work the way his mind does. It's controlled by something else, something sweet and internal—an inner Victor that I say a glad hello to once in a very long while. Now how can I, in the face of such a friend, remind us both that my life will continue beyond his and wear the precautions against any life he has left to give?

"I'm going to stand at the guardrail to watch," I say. "I want to see us approach Boston."

I walk between the aisles of benches and imagine briefly what this gray, wet deck looks like in the summer, the seats filled with people in cut-off jeans and boxy Hawaiian shirts; girls in halter tops, children with sunglasses too large for their faces.

At the railing I look out. There are large swells and isolated spots of water that whirl against the great pull of the ocean. A candy wrapper skids over the tops of waves and strangely I am delighted. Through the sound of the wind and the steady drum of the engines below deck, I hear Gordon's footsteps, as steady and inevitable as the ferry's approach to Boston. He stands to the right and slightly behind me, his eyes ahead as if he were judging the distance between where we are now and the many small islands that mark the beginnings of the harbor entrance.

I've imagined riding this ferry and seeing those islands, watching the jellyfish bob beside the boat, beneath the thin veneer of polluted water. I've had many daydreams about docking at Boston, listening to my footsteps make their hollow sound along the pier, passing the sign at Long Wharf that invites people to board the ferries. When Victor and I have had a particularly bad week—when he's been so ill he could do nothing for himself or when we've been fighting a lot or the car has collapsed and there's been nothing but sleet and icy ocean winds—I've often thought what a relief it would be to just board the ferry and go away. When I heard the low horn of the ferry calling its departure, I thought it might be beckoning me, that I could slip away to Boston, retreat like a fish into coral. Just go. But now, standing on board the ferry, watching the water pass beneath its sturdy hull, the sea gulls suspended like wind chimes in the air, I feel the goneness of a symphony at its last note.

"Have I said something wrong?" Gordon says.

"No, of course not," I tell him. "What could you have said wrong?"

But, of course, what could he have possibly said right? I've invested authority in Victor's words, not Gordon's. I've relearned myself according to a condition that exists between Victor and myself that has nothing to do with Gordon. What I want to hear comes out in whispers across a pillow in an attic room behind me. I'm missing someone miles back in a place I say I hate and often do. Gordon is silent beside me, and waiting. I'm aware of him in the same self-conscious way a foreigner in a train station is aware of his foreignness. Yes, I can go to Boston now, see the familiar sights and walk along streets that have a history for the nation as well as a personal history for me. But it cannot be how I imagined. Those streets are someone else's now. The Freedom Trail is lined with shops and office buildings; who thinks of the founding fathers while driving to work? A visit is only a visit. Gordon's hand on mine is only a hand. The sea's splash and the gull's caw are only noises and I am listening, instead, to someone who is silently sleeping in a bed that has become my own.

. . .

$\mathcal{J}$t's easy enough to be in a city you love even if it's with a man you hardly know. I pretend that all of Boston's peculiar charms—the cobblestone streets of Beacon Hill, the North End with its endless supply of fresh cannolis and bright bridal displays, the state house, Faneuil Hall—all that which designates Boston somehow makes a couple of Gordon and me, lends us a history together that we don't own. We wander the rows of vendor carts, talking about what sort of person would buy a marionette made out of shells, hair bands with antennae on them, aerosol cans of Love scented air freshener, or ashtrays shaped as crabs with googly eyes that bob up and down. We drop a dollar to a blind man playing a lap piano and singing "Georgia on My Mind." We buy a balloon. A slush puppy.

No problem imagining Gordon and I know each other well. We know the same street musicians, subway system, spots for clam chowder. I can fantasize that the rows of vendor carts are like shared experiences Gordon and I have. And, in a way, they are. He grew up in Brookline, in a comfortable neighborhood crisscrossed by tree-lined streets with stately names like Chilton Way and Linden Circle. I was top of my class at a third-rate high school but managed to get into Boston University, a private college, a great equalizer, where I studied science, though now I wish I had studied philosophy like Victor, who attended a much more prestigious university. But the philosophy department was out of the question for me. I felt I first had to adopt a new vocabulary, put the *r*'s into my speech, prove myself worthy of studying what someone like Victor naturally understood as his rightful domain.

Dying Young

I ended up a veterinary assistant in the suburb of Cambridge. I spent two years there, fixing cones over the noses of dogs who should not chew their stitches, holding cats for their shots, dropping fecal samples into solution, cleaning the cages of rabbits and kittens. I think I even remember seeing Gordon on the subway one morning. We could have met then, crowded together at the handrails, as the subway car rattled under Charles Street. Or in any number of the places we've passed today. Gordon could have been drinking beer at the Black Rose or standing next to me in a circle of people watching a break-dance routine, or picking apples from the carts at Haymarket on Saturday. He could have walked Tosh into the veterinary office, entered into the detergent-white animal examination room, where I spent—God knows how many—hours of my life sliding thermometers up the anuses of helpless, panicked pets.

We watch a mime outside of a brick building called The Marketplace. The crowd is dazzled by his invention of a transparent room in which he is trapped. He has on black and white clothing except for a bright lime-green cap. The mime is silent; and yet I feel like I'm eavesdropping. His quiet world of clear obstacles that trip him, trap him, send him into a quandary seems private to me, like nothing we should watch. I turn away finally, looking into the sky where the clouds are thin like antique cloth. The mime finishes his show and there is clapping. On his mouth is a painted line. Solid black. It raises as he smiles, collecting dollar bills.

.   .   .

We sit on a bench painted brown. The graffiti are all love: Frank loves Julie, Mimi wants Ben, T.J. plus S.K. There are phone numbers, awkwardly carved hearts, a happy-face sticker. We drink lemonade bought at a stand where they squeeze it fresh from the rind. It chills me to the toes.

I steal things. I'm somewhat worried that Gordon will reach inside my parka pockets and find the trinkets I've hidden: a tinseled pinwheel, a T-shirt with ducks and "Boston" stenciled in white across the front, a bag of warm cashews, an iron paperweight the shape and color of a cooked lobster. A part of me couldn't care less but a deeper and more badgering portion of my psyche labors with the fear that he will discover my secret and abandon me there on the sidewalk.

I've always stolen. There are things I cannot imagine paying for, I've so often stolen them. All my earrings, for example. I swipe spices in the grocery aisle. I steal magazines and Hershey bars. Fancy pens at stationery stores. I take things I don't want. It would make me nervous to steal something I cared for, something that could be missed. But gold chains dangling from a frosted plastic rack on a jewelry counter— who could miss just one? An electronic travel alarm clock so tiny you can lose it in your purse? I mean, why not?

I think about these, my crimes. I know it's wrong and I am ashamed; but as we turn the corner by a bakery I lift a key chain from a vendor cart.

Victor knows. I stole someone else's shirt from the launderette and, just my luck, the woman's name was sewn into the collar. I'll have a new gadget—a windup replica of the Flintstones' Dino or a design-your-own stamp set that he knows

I didn't want and he'll ask if I stole it. He'll notice the chocolate bar I'm eating and say, "A 'gift'?" and I'll nod.

This habit of stealing has embarrassed my parents for years—ever since my mother found an unexplained package of gum in my coat pocket when I was four years old. My father was bewildered by my later thievery—particularly my habit of stealing for others, which caused him some ethical dilemmas as he pondered the appropriate punishment for his grade school daughter who had stolen a gold lighter for her dad's birthday. Later, after the divorce, I stole from the two separate homes of my estranged parents, planting things from one apartment in the other. I put my father's favorite beer mug on my mother's cabinet shelf. I dropped my mother's address book into the mail basket on my father's desk top. I left his tie clip on her bookshelf, her nail polish in his medicine cabinet, his after-shave in the drawer of her nightstand. I wanted them to get back together but, instead, my father remarried. He even moved into a house, a real house, not an apartment. When I was in junior high school I stole a nightgown from my mother and hung it in the closet at my father's new house. His wife saw it and he called me, his anger exploding into the phone. Then I stopped visiting my father.

"Hilary?" Gordon says, and touches my shoulder. We're headed out to Faneuil Hall, stopped temporarily at a crosswalk. I shake myself back into the present and begin an apology for my distraction. Gordon doesn't want an apology. He wants instead to push my hair back behind an ear. He is sympathetic, allowing for my long silences as if they are a necessary condition to being with me—which I suppose they are.

. . .

$\mathcal{A}$t the Union Oyster House we sit on opposite sides of a wide table. We have chowder and beer. We play a game in which we try to land oyster crackers in each other's soup bowl. I miss a lot and he gets a lap full of cracker crumbs. Gordon asks me questions about my family, which I dodge, saying I am concentrating on the cracker game. Then he insists, so I tell him lies. I tell him I come from a huge family, all girls, and that my father does the weather on Channel 4. I tell him I went to Spain when I was twelve and, since then, have had a passion for paella. I tell him I spent winters in Bonaire.

"Oh, please," Gordon says, wrinkling his brow. He takes both my hands in his and says, "You knock me out with who you really are."

$\mathcal{W}$e go to the aquarium. My suggestion. It's not that I like fish so much as that the fish provide a means of escaping conversation with Gordon and I've been slipping into an inevitable cheater's silence. I feel that I either have to come out with it and confess my uneasiness over what appears to be a burgeoning love affair, or I have to be entirely silent.

I could say: "Gordon, you want to talk? Let's talk. Maybe we *ought* to talk. I feel myself liking you more and more and, as you know, I'm living with another man."

But that would be absurd because it's clear Gordon already is aware of my living situation, and I suspect he can draw his own conclusions about the implications of befriending a woman who is involved with someone else.

Dying Young

I could say: "Look, Gordon, we have to limit the romantic quotient on our relationship because I am not going to cheat on Victor."

If I say that, however, I will hate myself forever for being presumptive and defensive. For being precious with myself. It's not certain that Gordon even wants to sleep with me or that he would sleep with me if he did want to. Passion exists but passion can be resisted. He isn't asking at any rate so why should I jump the gun and tell him no before the fact?

And would I really tell him no? I might—I think I would—but what percent chance is there that I would say nothing at all, just begin unbuttoning my shirt?

When there are no accurate words or no words that are consistent with good behavior, I fall silent. Hundreds of words come to my mind as we amble past the aquarium tanks, all of them hopelessly inadequate. I spell out letters with my tongue onto the roof of my mouth. I draw P-L-E-A-S-E but don't know what exactly I am asking for, whether I want Gordon to take me by the shoulders and shake some sense into me, win me over with promises, with anything—or if I want Gordon to slink away like the gray tuna in the tank before us who has retreated from view and is currently inhabiting the space between two rocks.

Gordon always strikes me as exceptionally well balanced: he comes to an aquarium and he observes the fish. He studies the placards below each tank, taking in what Boston's ichthyologists have produced on the history of ocean animals. Right now he is reading the few paragraphs below what appears to be a preserved, prehistoric fish encased in glass. He's not like me, who arrives at the aquarium in an attempt to escape human interaction and then concentrates, with the power of one who is obsessed, on what might constitute the very next bit of dialogue exchange between us.

I breathe out heavily and decide to try to be *here* now, to be in the aquarium watching the fish, to read the explanation on the various types of salt-water game fish, to think aquatic thoughts.

If Victor were a fish, what sort of fish would he be?

The main tank, set in the center of the great hallway where we are, has a sea turtle, a swordfish, several eels, a large, flapping stingray, what I believe to be a barracuda, and a rather doughy-looking shark. Victor is way too thin to resemble the shark. Maybe the barracuda. I imagine Victor's face, if he stuck out his pointy, elfish chin and made his bottom teeth show, but still I cannot think of him as a barracuda. And certainly he is not an eel. The eels cluster together in one end of the tank. They have short, broad heads, scrawny long necks, gaping mouths, and eye sockets too large for their bubbled eyeballs that stare mournfully from behind glass. They look like monstrous tadpoles, like spirits trying to be brought back from the dead, like sea ghosts.

Victor is nothing like that. How could he ever be so ugly? How could someone like Victor ever look like that? Why do they put such hideous creatures in a tank for show anyway? Don't they know the eels look like death personified?

"Gordon," I say. "Why don't we leave?" Gordon is standing at the opposite end of the room in front of a wall full of smaller tanks.

"Go now?" Gordon says and looks at me. The fish in the

tanks by him are little and darting. From where I am standing they are just colors running together amidst bubbles.

The eel with the thinnest neck opens its mouth wide so that its neck shows tendons and even more length. The thing could be yawning, its mouth is so wide. Or it could be howling, the sound of a moan drowned by water.

*M*y feet are so cold on the ferry ride back to Hull that I tell Gordon we have to sit below deck. He agrees, taking my arm and leading me down the steps. We find a table by a porthole and Gordon says he is going to buy us coffee. He comes back with two steaming, Styrofoam cups and slides a packet of M & Ms my direction.

"Thanks," I say. "Open them for me? My hands are too cold."

Gordon takes my hands and rubs them between his.

"Poor hands," Gordon says. He rubs ferociously, then blows on them and rubs some more. "Put them over your coffee."

I do that. For a second I feel that almost anything Gordon told me to do I would.

Things seem to work for Gordon. His car works, for example. He has a startlingly clean engine and a chart of the exact dates and mileage of his oil changes. The innards of my car's engine no longer even resemble those of a car. If you opened the hood, not knowing that it was the hood of a car, you could only say that the vision of tubes and twisted metal and general grunge was "some sort of mechanical device." Gordon, on the other hand, can make things work; he can reconstruct his parents' house, fix a radio, make a car start, warm my hands.

Also Gordon seems to have straightforward and healthy social relations while Victor and I live in a sort of mass emotional confusion, never quite sure what things really are and always assuming that they are not what they seem most likely to be. The obvious is just too obvious for us. We have to dig deeper. We turn our words inward. Gordon takes everything quite calmly, always assuming the best, never reaching beneath the surface if the surface seems okay. That might seem superficial, but lots of times it's just correct. It seems to me that Gordon, unlike all the other people I have known, understands life as a fine condition and intends to live it as such. If at this very second Gordon should say, "Leave Victor and be with me," I would have to say, "Gee, why not?"

I melt M & Ms into our coffees. Gordon watches with great interest. He points into my cup and says, "Look, a drop of yellow."

Inside my coffee cup the candy has melted, leaving a yellow ring in its place. We look at the other colors: orange, brown, yellow, green, as they fade, leaving the sweetness of chocolate. All the way back to Hull I feel a tenderness from Gordon that is as invisible as chocolate in coffee.

At the parking lot by Pemberton Pier Gordon turns toward me. It's still early but already the sun has fallen back behind the horizon. There is the homey smell of fires burning in many fireplaces. The air smells like smoke and it smells like snow, though the ground is bare. Gordon leans against the closed door of my car, his arms folded in front of him. He stares into his elbow and says, "One time I was driving to work. It was morning and I was late. The traffic was clearing out on the highway and I took an exit ramp at a speed I shouldn't have. I hit a cat, an orange tabby."

He pauses now and looks pained. He makes circles in the gravel with the toe of his boot.

"So you hit a cat," I say. "So what?" Gordon looks away, his mouth hooked in a frown. Then he looks at me, breathes deeply, and begins again.

"When I got out to look I saw the cat was still alive," he says. "The end of her tail moved and there was a stricken look to her, a desperation. I had appointments I was late for. I should have taken her to an animal hospital or gotten a shovel and killed her. Anything. But I didn't. I went back to the car and drove away. Look, maybe it's not such a big deal but I thought about that cat every day for months. Every goddamned day. In my dreams I have rescued her a thousand times."

I imagine the cat, concentrating her shocked stare on Gordon's light eyes. I imagine the world as she saw it closing around her, evolving into a final, spinning panic. "Why are you telling me this?" I ask.

"Because I think I understand you. And because I want you to someday tell me things about yourself," Gordon says. He puts his hands on my shoulders as if he might kiss me, then doesn't.

I climb into my car. I pump the gas petal and turn the key, trying to trick the engine into starting. Gordon stands outside, looking wise, looking as though he cares. He is such an open invitation. I wonder if we will continue to be friends or if he'll vanish or hide or get smaller somehow in my life. I wonder if we will be lovers. I drive slowly on purpose out of the harbor parking lot, tapping the horn and waving to Gordon, who smiles and makes me want to smile, and then I feel bad because I cannot.

THREE

*T*he only other occupant of our building is Olivia Birkle, who meets me at the door. She's a lanky black woman, maybe seventy, angular and stiff like a paper fan. She's got her hair tied in a grandmother's knot at the top of her head. Crisp, coiled locks brushed back and held straight with hair gel. Her smile is wary, always wary, as if she were afraid you might do injury to her fragile sweet nature, as if something had happened overnight and you might not still be a friend.

But I smile fully at her and she relaxes, her wariness halts. Sometimes I'm good at making a person feel okay.

"Hilary!" she says and raises a hand. She makes my name sound like good news. "Come and talk to me."

She takes me by the elbow, walking her cagey, stiff walk into the first-floor apartment where she lives. She wears a clean, starched dress with a wide collar bow and pinstripes in blue and gold. We sit on her couch and she tells me how good it is to see me, how handsome my sweater is; she asks me about Victor and tells me what a hero he is for killing all the rats.

I don't contradict her. I don't tell her that it seems to

me he killed none of the rats but shot aimlessly into the sky.

She talks briefly about her daughter, whose beautiful teenage face shines from a photograph, decades old, on the fireplace mantel. She says the grandchildren are pretty as roses.

I finally slip out, holding up bunches of excuses as to why I have to leave. And she breaks my heart briefly at the doorway, singing a line from a song about God protecting young women, and kisses me so fast on the cheek it sounds like a match being struck.

On the way up the stairs I anticipate Victor's questions. He probably shot at rats all morning, ran out of ammunition, and then tried pelting them with stones. Maybe he even went into the yard after them. He might have tried smoking them out. I wish we had neighbors so that they would complain. I've thought of lodging an anonymous complaint with the state authorities myself. Anything. Mrs. Birkle was my only hope and she says she admires Victor's pursuit of rats, that it is a fine thing he is doing for the community. I think he better stop before he blows up someone's garage.

After rat homicide, my guess is that Victor slept all afternoon, ate a sandwich, felt nauseated, read an article, and watched the clock. He may have wanted to go somewhere today—to the market or just a drive along the coastal road to watch the ocean. He might have been feeling tender toward me, even passionate. Now he is probably angry. He will ask where I've been. I'll slice potatoes over the sink and he'll sit at the kitchen table, glaring at my back with a mixture of hatred and envy. He'll wish he could just go somewhere for an afternoon like I can without exhausting himself, without requiring a long recovery period. He'll eat silently, calculating his effect on me. When we go to bed I'll wrap my leg over his and he may freeze and move away. Or he may give in, fold up toward me like a kitten to its mother. We might make love silently or we might just lie like that, drifting in and out of sleep, reorganizing our limbs over each other, whispering, shelving our disagreements and accepting the simple things another body can offer. And in the morning, as if by magic, the anger will have sunk somewhere deep within us, almost gone.

As I reach the last flight of steps I hear sounds from our apartment: Victor's laughter, chair legs across the floor, the shrill exclamation of a woman. I'm startled by it—by a visitor in our apartment at all. My mind flips through the possibilities of who this person can be. Victor despises just about everyone. He growls at librarians who try to help him find a book. He is rude to postal clerks. He almost got us arrested once by screaming at the traffic officer who had stopped me for having an outdated inspection sticker.

Still, Victor is much finer than I am, much brighter, more graceful, more remote. Victor has a presence that few can rival. His great appeal is that he makes time count; he somehow reminds you that history is making itself there in front of you, that hours are weaving into your life and that you are designing them. This is a tremendous and powerful gift.

I stand outside our door breathing the musty smell found only in the oldest of houses and only when they are near the sea. I listen to Victor say something in ancient Greek and that is a dead giveaway because the only other person I know besides Victor who understands his references to the ancients is Estelle Whittier. She lives in Hingham, one of the more highly regarded areas south of Boston, where her glorious Tudor home is a wonder of prosperity and good fortune. And Estelle herself is a rare and startling person. She has crazy pink plastic sunglasses she wears when, for some reason, she is forced to go into the daylight. She lapses into German or Italian in the middle of speaking. She has a penchant for sculptured gardens and antique birdcages, in which she keeps feather-perfect professionally stuffed birds. I know all the stories about her, the various lives she's led with three different, now dead, husbands; the child she had who died in a most absurd and grotesque fashion—by putting his three-year-old finger into an electrical socket.

Victor adores this woman and, though I have no particular problem with her, I am baffled by his reverence. It may be because she reminds him of his family—very well-to-do old Bostonians from whom he is permanently estranged. Victor claims that he misses neither his father nor his money. That he hates the money. And that he hates his father.

Estelle has made a career out of marrying rich men. She coddles Victor in a maternal way. She stirs sugar into his coffee at restaurants, picks up his tab at bars. There is a bond between them that I don't understand but it is easy to imagine a baby Victor, with soft cheeks and fat, creased limbs, waddling through Estelle's enormous house. I can see him standing in front of a wall socket with his finger outstretched.

"Speak of the devil!" Victor says as I make my way through the door. He is wearing a tweed jacket with jeans, has his hair combed straight back, and is holding a wineglass. The alcohol shows in his cheeks and he is flushed a deep crimson, making his angular face somewhat demonic and ex-cruciatingly appealing. I see he has dressed the glass wound. Taped across the inside of his hand is a white bandage.

"Hilary, where have you been?" Victor says. "You know, it *is* Veterans' Day. I'm not sure how you thought I could celebrate the Armistice without you."

Estelle beams at Victor and says, "Ha ha ha," in her weird brand of laughter. Then she waves a hand at me, blow-ing a kiss. "Oh, my stars and glory, Hilary, you're blushing like a bride."

Estelle must have recently dyed her hair; the lamp shines off it and shows a pale pink color. She has lipstick to match and is draped in a getup I imagine she bought years ago on a vacation excursion to the top of a mountain somewhere in Latin America. The skirt, a bright-patterned wool wraparound, runs all the way to her ankles and she wears a matching pon-cho. She is such a tiny woman, as fragile as old lace and similar in her sad attractiveness.

"I hope you don't mind that I've barged in and absolutely stolen your man away," she continues. She has come with all her rocks—three fingers of each hand weighted with stones that are neither precisely cut nor set. When she waves a hand in my direction I wonder, not for the first time, how it is she does anything with those tiny, curled fingers that pack twice their weight in jewelry. "He is so *delightful,* Hilary, and so devoted to you. We were just discussing you, weren't we, Victor?" Estelle says.

"We *were* discussing you," Victor says, "as well as food poisonings, airplane disasters, and ozone depletion."

"He's *kidding!*" Estelle says. "Victor, stop being such a poop."

Dying Young

To me she says, "He's been glowing about what a wonderful woman he has in his life."

Victor says, "Hilary, I would kiss you but, if you don't mind, I think I will remain seated—you see, I am, now how can I put this without being vulgar? You see, I've been sick all day. Wretched sick, and it would be quite awful if, within the momentary delight of your welcoming kiss, I collapsed—suddenly, like a canary shot mid-song."

Estelle sits upright, her hands folded in her lap like a parent in a PTA meeting. "I'm so sorry, Hilary," she says, mocking herself through shy, downcast eyes. "I seem to have gotten your Victor drunk. I don't know what else it could be."

"Don't worry," I say to Estelle. "He's like this all the time."

I stand behind Victor, lean down, and put my arms around his stomach. "Hi, honey," I say into his neck.

"I'm not drunk. I'm trying to get some sound advice on how not to offend people with my charmless disease. People don't like to be reminded of their mortality—or mine, do they? They get rather taken aback when they ask you what you are planning to do for your summer vacation and you answer, 'Get buried.' "

"Oh, come now, Victor, you surely aren't going to be buried!" Estelle says, waving her wineglass. Her face is heavily made up. The lamp illuminates the penciling beneath her eyebrows and her forehead gleams. "How dreadful!" she says, and coughs. "What perfectly awful taste! Cremation is a far superior choice. I had all my husbands cremated! *Then* I buried them. I wouldn't hear of anything else."

"When they cremate, do they do it with or without the clothing?" Victor asks.

I cringe and try to think of something else to listen to. I consider dialing the weather report and listening to the tape, that too loud recording that repeats itself. I dump my coat in a chair and go into the kitchen to make tea. Victor will want something hot and loaded with caffeine within the hour. If he is drunk too long it scares him. He can only stand the oblivion of drunkenness for a short while and then he gets terribly afraid of it, as if he were likely to drown in the woozy, muddled feeling.

I have my own theory on Victor's reasons for drinking. I suspect Victor is testing the waters of death. He figures he'll blot out his conscious mind and render his motor control utterly unavailable. Then he can stew in the blankness of it all and imagine that death feels something like being drunk. Obviously, it's a rather compromised death state. After all, you wouldn't think that any amount of time in a bathtub would prepare you for a weekend surfing in Honolulu.

But Victor must get some results. Sometimes he gets very drunk and is silent in his armchair and I can almost feel his thoughts. I will be ready to call him on it and say, "Stop it, Victor. Stop torturing yourself. Death won't be like this anyway." But then Victor will turn to me, wearing an expression you might see in patients on emergency room stretchers. He'll beg me to make him a pot of coffee or strong tea. Then we will sit together with our kettle, staring at the black panes of the window, not even trying to make out figures in the night, the outlines of clouds, the moon. We are together, looking at nothing, holding our mugs of tea. Sip by sip, Victor comes back to me and after a while I point to the reflection off the ocean and Victor is able to nod and say, "Yes, it's beautiful." And then he is back to himself and ready to go on again.

I light the stove and hear Victor saying, "No, I suppose I shouldn't insist that I'm going to be dead any second. After all, I was scheduled to die months ago. Look! My head is full of hair. I've been off the chemo for ages and I'm anything but dead. Who would have thought I'd be alive? Hilary wouldn't have, would you, Hils?"

I lean against the kitchen counter waiting for the water to boil.

"Hilary!" Victor calls, and then he comes into the kitchen, his feet clumsy, the flaps of his jacket uneven. He gives me an enormous, sloppy hug and pushes his mouth to my ear. In his sweetest tone he says, "Oh, little darling, my precious angel . . ."

I kiss his cheek. I turn down the collar of his jacket. "You want tea, Victor?" I ask.

"No, no tea! Tea? Why tea? Why not wine? Why won't you get drunk with me? Come on!" he says and pulls me back into the living room. "Why can't my wife get blitzed with me?"

"Your wife? You two are married?" Estelle says, her eyebrows lifting. "What dears. How conventional and sweet."

"No, we aren't," I say.

"We're as good as married. What is in the sacred vow— ' 'till death do us part'? Isn't that it, Hils? Together until death do us part? Isn't that how it will be with us?"

I notice two empty bottles of wine on the coffee table, expensive labels that Estelle must have brought, wanting to please Victor. There is no way this woman, with her arthritic hands and manufactured teeth, could possibly have drunk a substantial portion of the wine. So Victor must have—which means Victor must be *very* drunk. And yet, when he lets himself be sweet, when he stands like this, with both arms around me, a leg behind my own, his face close, I really can't mind that he's drunk. I take in as much of him as I can. I squeeze his hand, I look into his eyes.

"I guess that's how it is with us," I say. Victor sloshes a kiss on my cheek and then takes a seat across from Estelle. He picks up a new bottle of wine and works a corkscrew through the top.

I sit in the chair by the window. I can hear the ocean as it forces itself against the sea wall. I wonder what can survive an ocean so forceful. What fish in the tank at the aquarium could suffer such an aggressive winter sea?

"Estelle, you are marvelously old, aren't you?" Victor says in a quiet and contemplative tone. He leans forward, observing.

"Not old enough. I look forward to *anciency.*"

"Good thing you didn't die young," Victor says. "Who would have been here to set an example of how to age with such panache?"

"Exactly," Estelle says.

"Look at the lines in your face!" Victor says.

"Victor!" I say.

"Oh, don't be a priss, Hilary, look at this woman's face. See how the lines curve on her forehead, making a series of arcs over her eyes? Isn't that spectacular? Imagine having all those lines, think of the work your face would have to do to become that way—the thousands of expressions, the years and years that it must take for just a single definite groove to emerge." Victor pops the cork off the bottle and pours.

"It is a pity," Victor says, "that I won't know how I'll age. Everyone else gets to watch as nature makes their body into something quite remarkable and I'm stuck with only thirty-three years of aging. That's not aging. That's not anything at all. What can you say about thirty-three? You've matured—that's your life's accomplishment. You've reached adulthood, have a full and working body; you are capable of killing someone or being killed. You can satisfactorily reproduce. I'm a salmon swum upstream, gasping."

Victor leans way over, his shoulder resting on the couch arm, his arms gone limp, and breathes in short-winded pants. He sticks out his tongue, rolls his eyes in their sockets, and makes rough, grating sounds from the back of his throat. Then he bolts upright again. Without pausing he launches into the next sentence, saying, "Salmon live until they are at their heartiest, bear young, and die right then."

"Oh yes! I saw that on Mutual of Omaha's 'Wild Kingdom'!" Estelle says.

"I don't have children. I won't even live to observe my son's oedipal complex! I won't be there to instill neurosis through toilet training. What a waste. What a horrible disappointment. I always thought I'd make such a distinguished old man. I counted on that."

"Is your father a distinguished older man?" Estelle asks with a certain painfully obvious interest that makes me squirm.

"Can we please not mention my father?" Victor says, splashing wine on his pants leg in an effort to bring a glass to where I am sitting.

"Dear, you will see your father again. And soon," Estelle says. "I know because I have consulted the cards."

In her purse Estelle carries a stack of ancient, hand-painted Tarot cards which both intrigue and frighten me.

"I have no doubt," Victor says and begins laughing as if something were terribly funny. "No doubt at all."

"And don't worry about dying," Estelle says. "The transition will be very easy for you. You are getting a lot of help from the other side."

"Here's to the other side," Victor says and makes a gesture with his glass. He drinks the entire contents in a single, emphatic swallow and then smashes the glass against the fireplace mantel. Estelle is startled and brings one of her small white hands to her chest. I look at Victor holding the long stem of the wineglass. It is topped with a jagged crest of glass. For a moment Victor looks as though he were raising a rifle to battle or declaring the departure of a round-the-world cruise. I think of Gordon at the front of the boat to Boston, his relaxed slouch over the railing, his forward-looking eyes and wind-whipped cheeks, searching the gray horizon, identifying the buildings in the small and crowded skyline.

"Victor, you're not going to start chopping up your hand, are you?" I say, eyeing the glass. I say it like I don't really care if he cuts himself, as though I think cuts are boring and also a nuisance. I say it like that but all the while knowing that Victor is very, very drunk and that even the smallest self-inflicted wound would make me panic.

"I'm not doing anything," Victor says. "I'm christening myself for the other side."

. . .

Dying Young

Death is painless, Estelle tells us. Death isn't really a death. There is no death—only a transition. Our lives are nothing but a series of bodily transitions. First we are babies, slaves to our bodies. We cry and teethe and puke. As children we seem to have mastered the body but puberty turns it all around and, again, the body slips away from us.

"Then there's adulthood and you feel in control," Estelle says. "But that goes as well. Being pregnant is a transition— we are not in control. Being old is the same way. My body is not mine anymore. Every time I look at myself I expect to see something entirely different. I look in the mirror sometimes and think, Whose arms are these with the fat hanging under them? Whose wrinkles are these around my eyes?"

"It's part of your character," Victor says.

"Only in the most remote of ways," Estelle says. "Anyway, death is one more transition in a long string of transitions, nothing more." She sips tea, leaving a half-moon of pink lipstick on the edge of the teacup.

It is late now; we are all tired. Victor says his head hurts. He leans back on the couch and offers an occasional yawn. The coffee table is littered with cigarette packages, crumpled napkins, glasses, and plates of crumbs. Estelle is in the very same spot. Her weird clothes make her seem more uphol- stered than dressed. It turns out that the clothing is from some indigenous people who live in Peru.

"What do you believe in, Hilary?" Estelle asks.

"You mean like God?"

"It doesn't have to be God. Just something. You must believe in something."

I consider this. People have asked me before. I once had a temporary job in a legal office in which nearly the entire staff was Quaker. In Harvard Square, all through the summer, there are people standing on crates preaching the ways of one lord or another. Sometimes I tease them, claiming that I cannot join their church because I am making up a religion of my own. Sometimes I ask if they would like to be a member in my new religion. Still, I have never really honed in on a particular belief system of my own. I guess I don't really believe in anything, though I am shy about admitting this. I turn to Estelle and shrug, not so much because I don't have an answer as that I don't have a ready answer. I can't give the name of a church or group with which I share any world view.

"Nothing," I say finally, and Estelle takes this in.

"Do you believe in life after death?" she asks. I have heard Estelle's many sermons about how we all have previous and future lives. Victor is forever making her recount the various lives she claims she has lived. The subject, to me, is somehow grotesque—and not only because Victor is so ill. It seems to me a form of denial, a weakness that has been glorified into a religion or philosophy.

"I don't believe in anything like that," I say. I hold a cup of tea, waiting for it to cool.

"Drink every drop of that last bit of tea and then turn over the cup," Estelle says to me, her voice crisp. "I want to read your leaves."

"You are going to read the future in the presence of a dying man?" Victor asks. He swishes his own tea around in its cup.

"Dear," Estelle says, "we've been through all that."

.   .   .

Dying Young

When Estelle speaks her head shakes slightly, the pink curls on her forehead move. She forms her words with a deliberate use of her mouth. Yet the words are soft. Estelle can talk for hours in this slow, distinct way. I find myself focusing on the white and yellow of her bottom teeth, on the pucker of her upper lip at the *r* sound of "Hilary." I've done what she's told me. I've finished the last of my tea and turned the cup over in its saucer.

"Hilary has a very good soul," Estelle says. "The leaves won't tell you that but I know it to be true. Victor, you've found a good one in her. It was ordained that she be with you when you pass over. You may have seen her through one of her transitions in a previous incarnation. Now hand me the cup, dear, and we'll read the leaves."

"I don't know why I'm doing this—I don't believe in fortunetelling or in fortunes and sometimes I don't really believe in the future," I say.

"Being with me makes you neglect the future," says Victor.

"When I was a kid I saw the Olympics on television. My mother said they come every four years and I couldn't believe I would live another four years to see the next one."

"Maybe you died as a child in a previous life," Estelle says.

"My poor little Hilary," Victor says sincerely.

"You are confused right now," Estelle says, peering into my cup. "You are rather scattered, it says so right here. But now look, there's a horse's head. Horses are very good, dear. See that head? Victor, can you see the horse's head?" Estelle tilts the cup in Victor's direction.

"No, what horse? I don't see any horse. Looks like a lot of tea grime to me."

Estelle's face is incredulous. "Well, dear, it's here plain as day. See its two little ears. And there is a rabbit nearby. A rabbit is good luck. Now, this horse is coming out of a barn stall—that's why we only see its head. You are emerging out of something, Hilary dear, you are beginning a new phase and it's a good one. Perhaps you've met a man?" Estelle teases. "A handsome man?"

"No, I haven't," I tell her.

"You're sure?" Estelle says, her eyebrows raised.

I look at Victor, who taps a teaspoon against the coffee table in an annoying, petulant manner.

"Yes," I say. There is absolutely no way Estelle could know anything about Gordon. There isn't even anything to know. Nothing has happened. There might be the kernel of a romance but there is nothing material to the relationship. There hasn't even been a first kiss or suggestive words; only unharnessed thoughts, pure imagination. Besides which, there is no reason to confess to any suggestion from tea leaves.

"Well, you have a really splendid future, anyway," Estelle says.

I feel as though someone has installed an electric fan in my stomach. I look at Victor and he appears slightly hurt. I try to conjure up something to say, something that will put him at ease. But all at once he is hard-mouthed again. He turns to Estelle.

"How upsetting to find someone as interested in the world as you, Estelle, wasting energy over specks of brown in a cup. It is distressing. No one can predict the future."

"Well, Victor, you certainly predict yours all the time, don't you?" Estelle says.

Victor sucks ferociously on his cigarette. "Death doesn't need prediction. Death we are sure of."

"All right then, good," Estelle says with an expression of a chairman of the board who has successfully completed an afternoon meeting. "We've accomplished something. Now, I must go. Hilary, walk me downstairs, if you will. Victor, my love, go straight to bed. Tomorrow afternoon come to my house—the two of you—for tea. Don't be late, tea is at three-thirty."

"*More* tea leaves?" Victor says. "I can't stand any more tea leaves."

"No," Estelle says and stifles a laugh. "We are quite through with that for you." She takes my arm and pulls herself off the couch. I walk her slowly to the door, listening to the popping of her joints as we negotiate the staircase, taking one step slowly after the other. By the second set of stairs she is more limber and for a moment I get a sense of a much younger Estelle. An Estelle who could be my age or Victor's. At the porch I deliver her to her car and she fires up the engine and takes off, speeding down our street. I wait until the car is gone and then trudge upstairs again.

Victor is in his boxer shorts, brushing his teeth. I stand next to him in the bathroom and take my own toothbrush. He turns away from me and I touch his naked shoulder. But he won't look at me. He stares into the wall and works the toothbrush around his mouth. I ask him what is the matter and he spits into the sink. I say, "Come on, Victor," and he wipes his face with the towel. When I get into bed he is asleep, or pretends to be asleep.

.   .   .

$\mathcal{T}$he ferry blasts six long notes into the morning sky. I've had a dream that a monster was found in the ocean; that they pulled it out and it sat on the shore until the wind tore at its gray hide, until its gills became exhausted and its huge eyes closed. Next to me, Victor is having a nightmare. He is pushing something away with his hand.

$\mathcal{V}$ictor is leaning over, his face above mine. When I open my eyes the first image I have is of an enormous fuzzy portrait of Victor, swimming above me. It is late morning; the sun forms a long rectangle over the floor. I wonder how long Victor has spent watching me sleep, what his thoughts were during those moments before I awoke, what he imagined I was dreaming. I reach to rub my eyes and clumsily brush across Victor's chin. He takes my hand and pushes it against the pillow. He runs his forefinger along my neck and over my collarbone, pressing at various points, as if he were searching for a certain part of me just barely beneath the skin, and all the while studying my eyes.

"You didn't spend any time with me at all," Victor says and pauses. "Yesterday."

"Last night I dreamt of a sea monster," I say.

"I felt well enough yesterday to spend the whole day with you," he says. He touches the skin over my voice box.

"And I wasn't here." I try a smile but it slips away from me. I concentrate on how I look to Victor, on how he might perceive my mood and the underlying opinions that make possible a mood. It's a sort of drama, a type of acting, for me to place within my speech and expression a power of benevolence, a sign of warmth and the projection of kindness. I try also to project a generosity to Victor, to dress Victor's expression in the clothes of intimacy and caring, to arrange the image above me as the image of a lover. I try every conceivable way of hearing his words as words uttered without malice, without intent, nothing but sequences of information.

"No," Victor says. "You weren't here." His glasses slip a fraction on his nose but he pays no attention. He stares into me as if I were the unpredictable contents of a petri dish, as if at any second something would come from me, a sign, a means for understanding, a new knowledge.

"And today you don't want to go anywhere?" I say.

Victor drops onto his left side and pulls my hand under the covers. He places my palm over his sternum and then moves my hand in a circular motion down to his belly.

"What do you have to do today?" he says. He holds my hand flat on his stomach. "Are you going to tell me?"

"Around five Cappy was supposed to take me to a tree farm in Scituate to pick out a Christmas tree."

"In November?"

"I have to claim it early or else there won't be one for us."

"Why go all the way out there?" Victor says. "Don't they sell Christmas trees in town?"

"Those are cut. The ones in Scituate are alive."

"What if I don't want a Christmas tree that's alive? Why would I want some tree living in my home? Sucking up my air?"

I give him a look.

"All right, fine then," Victor says. "It's just that you give me no choices, Hilary." He drops my hand and turns over. I rub the back of his neck, brush my fingers over his shoulders, and make my way down the length of his back. Victor is so thin that when he is naked his muscles and all of his vertebrae are alarmingly revealed. It is easy to see how each inch of bone adds to his total height, the formal way a shoulder blade fits itself into each side, the way the skin feels different across his neck, his lower back, along his spine: smooth on muscle, soft on fat, hard on bone.

"Do you remember when you first met me?" Victor says after a while.

"You were bald," I say. I put my hand in his hair, grabbing clumps and pulling gently at the roots. "And it didn't look right. I gave you a stark look, like some giant baby bird. I remember thinking you looked like an osprey."

"An osprey?" Victor says and makes a noise almost like a laugh.

"Yeah."

"At least you didn't say a pelican."

"No. Only an old person could look like a pelican," I say.

"When I was on the oncology floor there was nothing but old pelicans," he says.

I smile. I move so close to Victor that I almost cover him.

"I will never go back to a hospital again," Victor states with defiant satisfaction. "When you first saw my apartment in Boston, what did you think of it?"

"I was impressed. I thought you must be an artist because you had such a visual sense of things. There were no blank walls the way there are in other bachelor apartments. You had engravings, diplomas, African masks, antique candle-holders, a tray of glass candies. I liked your kitchen: the way you actually used your copper pots so that they were black-ened and each one unique. I liked the photographs of your relatives, framed in sterling. I liked the spoon in your sugar bowl with the silver angel perched on its stem."

"What about my books?"

"I didn't care about your books," I say.

"That's why we could never have been a couple in real life," Victor says. He waits.

"This is real life," I say.

"No," Victor states flatly. He lets out a sigh. "Tell me what you thought of me the first week you knew me. Was I interesting? Did you notice who I was or only that I was sick?"

"Who you were," I say.

"I weighed more, too."

"Not so much more. Maybe not more at all."

"You've seen the pictures. You know what I used to look like," Victor says.

"Yes," I say. I've sat in his living room in Boston with the pages of his life spread over my knees.

"Which of my friends would you have liked best?" Victor asks.

I think for a moment. Dozens of pictures go through my mind: groups of people celebrating at restaurants, pictures taken at parties, while fishing at Montauk, watching the tall ships come into the harbor. I've heard so much about the friends he's had over the years and how they met, or how they fell out of friendship, or how they left for jobs in other states, in other countries, that I feel I could speak intimately with any number of Victor's past loves, professors, childhood schoolmates, as if the time they occupied in Victor's life was the same time I have, as if there had never been a history in my life or in Victor's before we began making a history together.

"Gregg," I finally answer. "I would have liked Gregg."

"Gregg is a good guy; he will come to the funeral," Victor says. "You can meet him then."

Suddenly, I get the sense of *those* events, the things that will happen later, that will follow on a time line after Victor's death. All these smiling faces in all the albums stuffed with pictures will come to life at this one happening. I have an abrupt burst of—*what?* Not memory because nothing has happened. But I realize all over again that these people in the album really do exist in a history and there will be a future. The world revolves each day, sending us forward even as we dig in our heels and resist. I will someday see the faces from the photo albums and Victor will be gone.

"Don't talk like that," I say. "I don't want to meet Gregg."

"He's very handsome," Victor says. "You could do a lot worse than Gregg."

I imagine the photo albums falling from the shelf, a shower of faces.

"Victor," I say. "Can we get rid of the rat gun?"

"What? Sell it?"

"Yeah, or give it away. Or throw it away. Are trash collectors allowed to take guns?"

Dying Young

"We are not *throwing away* my rat gun," Victor says in a tone that lets me know he means it.

I look at his hurt hand. I put it in my own hand and feel that it is hot with infection or with healing, I cannot tell.

"You are too good-looking to have an injury. It's wrong on you," I say.

"Did you think I was good-looking? I mean in the photographs did you think I was good-looking?" Victor says.

"Yes. I think you are very handsome now."

"Don't kid me."

"I'm telling the truth," I say. When Gordon and I were walking down Long Wharf I had admired Gordon's carriage, the beauty of his walk, his long, fast steps that eat up the ground beneath him. But I had also a pang for Victor, whose movements are never so forward-directed. Victor walks tall, with perfect balance like a dancer, a celestial walk. As if there were a string connected to the sky and pulling him up to the heavens.

"I think you are beautiful," I tell him.

Victor takes a short breath and holds it. "When people ask you if you have a boyfriend, Hilary, do you say no right away or do you say, 'Yes, but he's dying'?"

"People don't ask me that question."

Victor turns onto his side and faces me. "I'm asking, Hilary," he says. "Do you have a boyfriend?"

"You," I say. I say it in a gladdened way but I feel awful inside, odious and foul.

"Only me?"

I nod.

"Sometimes, Hilary, I wish you'd give me another answer. I always feel like I've borrowed you from the world and that I must return you. But I never will. I'll make it hard for you. I'll make you ache this out with me."

I nod, not so much in agreement but to show I understand.

"Pretty thing," Victor says and puts his arms around me. "What have I done?"

FOUR

*A*fter my job as a veterinary assistant and before I answered Victor's ad in the Boston *Globe*, there was a brief time during which I lived with my mother. She has a mustard-carpeted two-bedroom apartment near Boston's airport. It's a shoebox shape and sits on the right bank of apartments in a low-rise building. There are four identical units above it and three below. I loathe Mother's "unit" but she is always reminding me about its extra bedroom and how I really ought to save my money instead of throwing it away on rent. So I moved in, designating a month as the uppermost boundary of my visit. This was, from the start, only temporary.

I had this vague hope of going to night classes, taking some upper-level chemistry, and reapplying to veterinary school—this time with the proper prerequisites: advanced chemistry and several years' apprenticeship at an animal clinic. I still had my usual doubts, nothing specific because I have never been deficient in any particular way, but I hadn't shaken that general gut-level feeling of being somehow inadequate for veterinary school, or any other elite institution. I felt, and still feel, as though somehow such activities are for others, that I am inherently underqualified and, as if from birth, excluded.

My mother assigned herself a regime of duties designed to accommodate my stay. Full meals, my laundry done, notes on my desk reminding me of the admissions deadlines for veterinary school. I got the best quilt, a new reading lamp over my bed, a brand-new cherry-colored toothbrush. An array of vitamin pills to be taken each day.

My mother's job at the mail shop requires her to apply the correct postage to every package or letter and to make sure they conform to Post Office standards. In the past nine years she has made only two mistakes. She gets up each morning precisely at seven and during my tenure in her clutches she insisted on advising me of the importance of a "good start" in the morning, though I never figured out what that good start entailed. She suggested that I keep my eye on the ball—whatever that meant. I really don't know what ball I was supposed to be keeping my eye on or, even more, what the ball looked like. I wanted to say, "Mother, I don't think I can even *identify* 'the ball,' " though, I said nothing. She cut out articles about women with distinguished careers and taped them to the bathroom mirror. The articles were inevitably accompanied by a photograph of an elegant woman with smart eyes and a New York face. It was always a woman I could never know; someone who, if she existed in the world at all, existed in a world different than mine or existed invisibly.

But the insistence of my mother was that I could, that I must, become one of those storied women from the magazine pages. She asked me what my career goals were, what I was aiming at, what my next "move" would be. She interrupted all events in order to discuss these "crucial issues," as she called them. She shook her head at me, scowling, when she caught me watching "Jeopardy" on TV. She stalked me while I was *in the bathtub* even, raving about what other mothers' daughters were doing, whom they had married, how glorious their children were. She asked what I was going to do, what my *plan* was. My mother also asked how I afforded the expensive perfume next to the sink, knowing all the while that I'd stolen it.

I figured I would live at home until the start of the next semester, that I could ignore her exasperated attempts at "improving" me at least that long.

About three weeks into my stay I was sitting at the table in the tiny kitchen with its space-saving devices (a coffee maker that hangs from the underside of the cabinet, a mini-fridge, and cupboards full of lazy susans), listening to my mother's bursts of criticism of how others spent their lives, suggesting that she could have done a better job with any number of the wasted years occupied by neighbors, ex-friends, distant relatives, as if her own sixty-four years were not a life at all. She paced the kitchen from sink to refrigerator and I knew that any second she would burst in with a diatribe of my failings; on every aspect of my being that binds me to the type of apartment we'd always lived in, near the airport, beneath the shaking sound of jets.

I was reading the classified section of the Boston *Globe* and hoping, with all the faith of one who prays for healing, for some answer to my own seemingly "wasted" life, and there was Victor's ad: small, neatly worded, and precise in its description. He was advertising for someone to help him through an illness, someone who wanted a place to stay and a small salary in exchange. So while my mother stood over me shaking an eggbeater and warning me that soon it will all be over, my life will have gone by with nothing to show for it, I decided living with anybody else, sick or not, had to be better than living with her. See how things happen?

And Victor, at this moment when our lives finally intersected, was one week home from a long and apparently traumatic stay in the oncology ward of Massachusetts General Hospital. He was reorganizing his life so that he could avoid forever any further medical attention. He was bored with working against the disease, and he was discouraged: every year he spent more and more time in hospitals. He explained this to his friends but they insisted upon his continuing treatment. They tried to persuade him, working their arguments to such crescendos that the nurses occasionally came running in, thinking something had happened. Their speeches didn't change Victor's decision, though their righteousness managed to alienate him entirely, until he would not allow any visitors at all.

What exactly Victor's thoughts were, as he lay in the hospital thinking about abandoning treatment, I don't know. But he explained to me once that he finally chose to discontinue his participation in being ill, to give in to the natural evolution of his illness instead of "existing as illness," as he put it. The many hospitalizations resulted in Victor's feeling that his body itself belonged to the hospital, to the white rooms and clear tubes and entourage of doctors whose stethoscopes clung to their necks and identified their status just as Victor's medical chart indicated his. There was finally a will to win, to beat out those white doctors and extract his body from their domain, even at the cost of his own survival. The point, as Victor will tell you, is that self-preservation only exists as long as one feels there is a sense of self to preserve.

After he left the hospital, Victor had his phone number switched and requested that it remain unpublished. He gave the alumni records division of the university an incorrect address and stripped the name from his mailbox. I can't truly know what it means to take such an action—a lonesome dive into uncertainty, administered with such an inventive will. But Victor had been sick for a long time. I forget just when it was decided he had leukemia, but it was sometime during college, when Victor thought all the world could be managed if one were persistent enough; when he felt sure that mutated blood cells were as conquerable as freshman physics or Sunday morning hangovers.

One night, while sitting by a beach fire made on Hull's shores, Victor and I pieced together these happenings that resulted in our coming together.

"What is so great about you," Victor said, "is that you don't try to control me. That you allow me to do what I want with my illness. My parents tried to control me my whole life. In fact, the only fights they had concerned which particular mode of domination they should pursue. My mother had the advantage because she didn't have to work. Also she had a great sense of humor; her voice had a sort of lilt and she always sounded as though she was on the verge of laughing. She had a wit that could get her almost anything, including my cooperation. Dad was always being yanked into attending meetings with lawyers or accountants. He had a very demanding job just maintaining what we already had. Money, properties, stocks, a very complicated trust—I don't know.

Dying Young

After Mom died he started drinking. He fought with his accountants and tax men. When I became ill he spent money like crazy—inane purchases. He bought a helicopter, for example. . . ."

Victor's father began barging in on his life, trying to get Victor interested in the house or the money or the parties they were invited to. He tried to get him to socialize with the right people in Boston, Marblehead, Hingham, which is where Victor might have lived had he not decided to cloister himself off from that world. Mr. Geddes would go into Victor's closet and measure his clothes so he could shop for Victor. He cursed the fact that his son's great love was books and he could not make accurate choices as to which titles to buy.

"It was wretched," Victor explained. "He always looked at me with these sorrowful eyes, and I knew what he was thinking. He checked my appearance for signs of decay. He stared at me strangely as if I might evaporate before him. I became tired of it and he ceased to have any effect on me. I just loathed him. Our falling out wasn't really a falling out. It was gradual and permanent. And he was more than insistent about my continuing treatment: he was like a drill sergeant. If I really wanted to stop, I had to expunge him from my life."

We were in sweatshirts and jeans, eating grilled chicken and throwing bones into the fire we'd made in the sand. It was a beautiful night with a soft breeze that blew on the fire so it rose high. Neither of us had expected to discuss anything serious but he told me about the old brownstone he grew up in, with its three floors of cheerless rooms, the ghostly attic that contained relics from his relatives who had passed through the house decades earlier. I looked into our beach fire and envisioned quite clearly the short, oak tables with surfaces large enough only for a vase of flowers or a lamp with dim butter light. I imagined Victor as a child, crawling beneath the intricately carved legs of buffet tables and dining-room chairs brought over from England. Victor, with his face pushed against painted glass, surrounded by lace curtains in dull white and ancient, frayed carpets over creaking floors. Victor, beneath cabinets of blue china, standing on his tiptoes, stiff and straight as a Staffordshire dog, while his mother explained the difference between place plates and dinner plates, the history of the water glasses, the demitasse cups, the handing down of precious objects from generation to generation. I dreamed of his mother's lilting laughter, her freckled English skin that Victor inherited. I thought of her squinting into the light, looking for spots on her crystal goblets, holding one up to the sun.

And I imagined Mr. Geddes, abandoned by his son, alone in barren rooms with their dusty end tables, angry at Victor's malignant blood. I thought of his having been "expunged," as Victor had said, and looked out over Hull's inky sea. I thought about the sand that loses out to the ocean's every splash, that permanence is always arrived at gradually, and that everything, even then, even by our happy fire, was always slipping away.

"I love to hear you talk," I told Victor. I leaned against him and felt his sweatshirt against the back of my neck. A beer bottle, too close to the flame, burst into six pieces. He wrapped his arms around my stomach.

"I can't express myself in words the way you can," I said. "Sometimes, in conversation, I don't feel like I have equal footing."

"In here," Victor said, pointing at my temple, "you are most eloquent."

Dying Young

. . .

$\mathcal{L}$ ately, I've been having this feeling as if somehow time is speeding up and wrecking things the way a tornado does—through a course that only it knows. This panic comes to me at odd times with a fervor and insistence that I can hardly describe except to say we are standing in one of the more complicated areas of Star Market, the specialty food section, and I feel as though my muscles are bursting through my skin, every vein is lifting itself above the surface of my body, and my heart has ballooned inside my chest, squeezing out my lungs.

Victor is unaware of my upset. He's in deep concentration over a choice of mustard. He scrutinizes the contents of two clear jars, comparing skillfully the ingredients and composition of each. Victor is always careful in selecting food, probably because he invests a great portion of time in cooking it and is a pretty good chef—though he has an insubstantial appetite.

A boy in an apron stocks chili cans on the far wall. The butcher stands behind his glass window and swaddles meat into neat, white packages.

I watch Victor select his mustard and I begin to feel a cozy sense of well-being. I feel safe, the way I feel when we cook dinner together, when I peel carrots over the sink and he spices whatever is on the stove. Those times—when Victor is in a good mood and he doesn't try to edify me about why democracy is a farce, or how the education system is damaging any hope for future progress, or why the environment will be destroyed no matter what anyone does—those times are why I can be satisfied with Victor.

He will tell me about events in his childhood, the evolution of accents in New York, or how the Hawaiians came to kill Captain Cook, and I will feel happy. Simply happy. Maybe this sort of thing sounds boring to other people, maybe most couples want to go out to dinner, not cook at home, and have friends they do things with. Sometimes I want that, too. But tranquil times with Victor are rare and cherished events worth wanting. Just watching him move about the grocery aisle, just watching him at all, brings me slowly back into myself, like a parachuter through miles of sky approaching a calm.

I touch Victor's shoulder and he smiles at me, then returns his attention to the shelf of various-sized mustard jars.

"I kind of like the idea of yellow mustard that comes in one of these squirt bottles," Victor says. "I've never bought generic mustard. But, you know, there's something very American about it. Maybe I ought to try to join the ranks of people who like yellow mustard."

"How are you feeling?" I ask. But really I am asking myself. How are you feeling, Hilary Atkinson? You are undergoing a rather acute anxiety attack, would you like a glass of water? Would you like to lie down?

"Fine. You know, even if I buy the regular mustard we should get another type as well, because I don't think I could actually eat yellow mustard. I just want it on the shelf as a sign of my willingness to eat it." Victor holds out several jars of mustard for my evaluation. "I am bewildered by all the choices. I submit to your better judgment," he says to make me laugh.

I'm smiling, feeling more at ease, almost generous. A woman with a thick pony tail and a tiny child perched in the front end of her cart drops a jar of mint jelly into her basket. Her child has sneakers with Snoopy faces on them. Tied around his wrist is the string to a blue balloon.

I'm about to answer Victor that we should buy all the mustards, all the chutneys, every variety of pickle or spice if it would please him. But I stop short, seeing a man with remarkably Gordon-like hair who is standing in front of an island of wine about seven feet north of the stock boy with the chili cans. He picks up a bottle, studies the label, and then puts it back on the shelf and takes another.

"Hilary, are you okay?" Victor asks.

"Yes." I say. The man turns his head and I recognize Gordon's straight profile, his longish nose that curves slightly upward, his heavy upper lip. Gordon is in a gray dress coat with a broad collar that fans around his neck, making him appear taller and giving his young face a certain classic fineness. "Let's go to the meat section," I say. I figure if Gordon is going to buy wine he might also get it into his head to buy specialty foods, which would put Victor and me directly in his purchasing route.

"What about pâté?" Victor says. "Sliced pimentos, pepperoncini?"

"I don't even know what that is."

I take Victor's elbow and wheel the cart toward the back of the store.

"This is no fun if you rush it, Hilary. You know I like grocery stores. You could at least allow me this one small pleasure. You know perfectly well what pepperoncini is!" Victor spins me around to face him. He gives me a stern look and shakes my arm as if he were disciplining a child. "Hilary?" he says.

I look over Victor's shoulder to see Gordon, who stares at me with his quiet eyes, one hand clutching a Bordeaux. For an instant there is this from Gordon: Why are you hiding? Then he looks away. He takes a second bottle from the shelf and walks in the opposite direction.

I set our groceries onto the conveyer belt. The jar of mustard is at the bottom of the cart; the awkwardness I felt in front of the shelves of mustard is many aisles of shopping away— but still I am nervous, the way you are when you barely miss having a car accident, or when you are speeding on the highway and pass a policeman who, for some unknown reason, decides not to give you a ticket. Not that I did anything, but that I could have been caught; not that I am a criminal, but that I could be criminalized.

I concentrate on the groceries, placing each item on the checkout belt and tallying the bill in my head as I work: yogurt, $1.69, shampoo, $2.15, frozen peas, 85 cents, tomatoes, 89 cents a pound ...

"Let me guess why you didn't want us to get pimentos and olives. Let's see ..." Victor says and fakes it like he's trying to think. He rubs his whiskers and winces as if it hurts to think so hard. "I know!" he says like he's made a discovery. "Your family was too *poor*. Pimentos and olives remind you of your deprived childhood. You gonna make my heart bleed over that again?"

"Victor ..." I load a gallon of ice cream on the conveyer belt, a can of chili, aluminum foil.

"Not Victah, Vict*or*," he says, correcting my pronunciation. "Say the *r*. Er, *er*, like an engine starting."

Dying Young

"Stop it," I say.

Victor stands behind the cart, watching with the same attention with which he might watch a chess tournament. I can almost feel the birth of a new criticism in his throat. As I nest a box of cheese wafers between dishwashing soap and Chips Ahoy cookies I wait for his comment. Victor side-turns and considers me from that angle as I fill the conveyer belt with boxes and cans and plastic deli tubs. I wonder what exactly he'll find wrong in how I look or what I'm doing. Will he say my hair is messy, that I have my shoelaces untied, that I am coldhearted and insensitive, that I'm too emotional? Victor is a genius at finding something wrong. I'm flattered by the necessity for hesitation in his insult.

"You are supposed to put the heavy things in first, like the laundry detergent and these cans of Campbell soup or the milk," Victor says finally. "Otherwise the eggs and the tomatoes are going to get squashed in the bottom of the bag."

I can't help it. I start to laugh.

"Go ahead and laugh, Hilary," Victor says. "You always have to do something nasty, don't you?"

"Oh, give it a rest, Victor," I say.

"You enjoy upsetting me, don't you?" he says.

"You started," I say, though I'm not sure.

"I gave you a suggestion, that's all. Suggestion: to put forward for consideration, to propose; to bring or call to mind as by association; to connote, to give hint of, to remind. Do any of the above definitions suggest—oops, there goes that *word* again—do they bring to your attention some sort of radical interpersonal warfare?" Victor says.

I get so disgusted when he starts like this, defining his

terms, spitting out anything that sounds authoritative. Sometimes he gives complete etymologies of the words he uses, sometimes he quotes from Plato. At times like these I consider what I am doing with this man, how awful he really is, and how little there is to admire in someone so mean and how I hope I never become like him. These thoughts quell my laughter for a moment and I stand straight-faced in front of him, waiting for whatever comes next. Victor's face deepens in color and he begins again.

"What is the matter with you?" he says. "Can't you see that I am only trying to offer you a piece of friendly advice?"

"Friendly," I say.

He gives me a long stare, the sort you'd expect from the captain of an enemy team.

"There's no point fighting with you, Hilary. You have to win. It's been ordained that ultimately you will win everything. Why are we getting carrots? You know I hate carrots."

"Because I like them. I think carrots are just great."

"Then you better eat every last goddamned one of them," Victor says.

Well, that one really sends me. I'm laughing, deep stomach guffaws, and turning around on my heel with my hand to my face. It's just too much; my laughter is calling attention from other store customers and I'm really in the throes of it when Victor takes my arms and shakes me hard. All at once I am humiliated and quiet. Housewives with babies pause at our checkout lane, staring with judgmental eyes.

Now, here's the thing: I would like to stamp Victor's foot, or throw something at him, or sock him in the stomach. I would like to do some sort of serious physical damage to him; really, I'd like to hit him in the mouth. But as soon as I think this, the instant I think of doing something harmful to Victor, I feel guilty and wrong and despicable because Victor is so ill and because lately he has been getting thinner; I've noticed, too, that the whites of his eyes are not so white and the skin beneath his eyes is purplish red. I'd like to protect Victor from everything, including his own diseased body. I'd like to lie myself flat against him and infuse him with some of my own health. The irony of our existence is so materially evident: I am a model of good health—bright red cheeks, clear skin; my lips aren't even chapped. I am no beauty, but I am as perfect and imperfect as the day I was born. For me to will harm to Victor is, in some ways, a worse crime than any other.

And Gordon, arriving at another register, unloads his handbasket and looks at me. His expression is ambiguous; I don't think he saw Victor shake me but he might have. He is utterly handsome and inviting and, of course, I am drawn and also hideously ashamed.

So I kiss Victor. I press against his angry lips and he takes a startled step back, releases my arms, and then slowly, sweetly, softens his mouth. Now it is Victor's turn for embarrassment. He pulls away from me and walks quickly to the exit door. I stand alone with two bundles of groceries. I am sorry now for this confrontation with Victor. I'm hoping that it will end, that Victor will forgive me my unspoken crime of willing him harm, of wanting to hurt him—though he could not possibly know what it is I think, though it is irrational for me to be sorry for something never spoken. I'm sure he knows and that I've hurt him. I am sure he senses Gordon the way birds sense a storm. I don't even look at Gordon, though I know he is watching me. I just want to disappear, for everything to disappear. I wish things between Victor and me had never begun, or that they would never end. And for a moment I construct the ultimate mental crime: I wish that Victor and I both would die—because it seems the only thing left and that we both deserve it.

FIVE

*T*o get to Estelle's house, we have to cross several bridges along the coastal road, pass a historic inn that is now a restaurant, the pinball arcade that is closed for the season, and a shop that sells all imaginable apparati for dart-playing. Then we wind our way behind a liquor store and take Route 228 into Hingham. Estelle lives atop a steep hill that requires dropping my old car into a low gear and hoping a lot. The car barely runs. Four hundred dollars, from a teenager who said his grandfather used to drive it. It is a white Oldsmobile with a mosaic of rust spots that makes it look as though it's been under gunfire. Over the left front wheel is a drawing of an enormous rat, done in indelible marker. There are stickers I still can't remove from the back bumper. The kid who owned the car spliced up bumper stickers and then recombined them into absurd messages. Everywhere I drive the people behind me read, "I Brake Arms," "Honk if you Dead," "Marines are Grateful for Contra Hugging," "Motorcycles are for Sailing," "Stop Jesus." I've peeled and peeled but driving is still an embarrassing proposition.

Victor looks nice. He has on an Oxford-cloth shirt, charcoal pants, and a paisley tie which he readjusts several times in the rear-view mirror before finally letting it rest undisturbed on his chest. He fidgets a lot, playing with the buttons on his shirt cuffs and bending the wire earpiece on his glasses so that they balance on his nose. He keeps getting his knee in the way of the gearshift. His blue blazer, in need of a dry cleaning, is folded in his lap on top of his overcoat. I suspect he has a fever, otherwise he would at least wear the blazer, if not the overcoat, but I don't want to say anything. It was enough that we got home and put the groceries away in peace. He didn't slam doors; I didn't grind coffee beans in order to avoid listening. Of course, we didn't really talk at all. He lay on the bed mostly. I took my collection of seashells from a jar in the kitchen cupboard and set them out on the counter. I know nothing about shells but I collect them on the beach and I keep them. I look at them sometimes and wonder what animals left them behind.

Victor becomes very quiet during the ride. He leaves his clothes alone; he puts his glasses into his shirt pocket and folds his hands in his lap. I don't disturb him to point out a flock of ducks landing in Weir River, their wings beating air and water. I don't ask if he thinks the noise the engine is making means I should take the car to the shop.

I steer between potholes, around slick patches of ice, brushing my hand against Victor's knee with each shift in gears. He sits loosely in the car seat, his head lolls against the window, eyes closed, and he worries me with his silence and his crumpled position. I could ask him how he feels but I know what he would say. We drive in silence—though it doesn't feel like silence, because there are a thousand things I can think to say and a thousand answers I imagine that Victor would give. Sometimes I feel I know Victor so well I could construct an entire conversation between us in my mind with complete accuracy. There are times, however, when I'm sure I don't know him at all, that neither one of us knows anyone truly and that our being together is just one of the accidents of life, as baffling as the fact that ice can burn you, that it can rain even when the sun shines, or that children can die before their parents.

"Here," Victor says. "It's this one on the left."

I drive through the tall iron gate to Estelle's house and make my way slowly through the sycamores that line the long pebbled driveway. The house is an enormous English Tudor, steeped in ivy, with a gray roof made from stone and a brick path that leads from two huge wooden doors. I know something about the house from the few conversations I have had with its owner. Parts of it were brought over piecemeal from Kent, England. The great beams in the kitchen and front hallway are from a sixteenth-century summer home and the roofing was done by several English roofers who spent a month living in trailers as they crowned the Tudor with rectangles of granite.

The house is based on a conceit that Estelle invented and reformulates on a regular basis. The idea is that the stone part of the house, the downstairs courtyard and simulated English pub, was the "original" part of an English country manor owned by a somewhat aristocratic family, around 1550. The drawing room, with a William and Mary double-dome walnut secretary and shelves of classic books, would have been added along with the south side of the house, when the (fictitious) family grew in number sometime in the seventeenth and eighteenth centuries. The furniture is relatively nineteenth century, though of course the fireplaces and doorways are studded with much more ancient iron fixtures, reminding us of the "origin" of the structure. Aside from the beams and roof, it is, in fact, entirely twentieth century. This house has become, more than anything else, a signature of Estelle. She has three husbands buried in the garden from three separate eras of her life.

And the house is sort of fun, after all. I marvel at the pebbled driveway; I like the way it makes the car rumble and toss. I like the shadowed, deep greens of the pine trees and hedges, the blanket of ivy that covers the enormous face of the Tudor in a gracious and casual way. I like the canopy of sycamores that leads up to one of the outbuildings, maybe once a carriage house, where I stop the car and listen, just to see if the atmosphere of Estelle's great house has a special sound as well as aura. I'm overwhelmed by its vastness, by its foreignness that exists even though it has been transplanted to familiar American ground. I'm drawn by its false conceit, the myth of its master and creator. I turn to Victor, who is staring at me, his hand beneath his chin as if he were considering something. He is alert again, straight and perfect in his beautiful clothes. He rubs his hand along the curve of his jaw.

"Can I tell you something?" Victor says. He lets out a long breath. "Can I tell you that if I weren't dying I would make a life out of learning how to love you."

Estelle, we are told, is waiting for us on the back porch. Our coats are taken and we are led through the enormous hallway beneath startling, ancient beams and film-screen-size walls that are hand-stenciled in pinks and peaches. Estelle is sitting on a glass-enclosed porch, frozen in her chair as if she were waiting for someone to take a photograph. She has redyed her hair to a cool lime, and tailors an expression of anticipation and amusement. On her lap is a project of paper flowers. She has a box of bright pinks and scarlets and a few of the completed flowers in front of her on the table. Two enormous dogs, of a breed I have never heard of, sit up nervously when Victor and I enter. They have drooping jowls and small pricked ears. Their mouths form wide, inverted V's. Estelle says, "Now sweeties, don't fuss. These are friends." The dogs are restless; one of them gets his feet under him to stand and is smacked across the nose. "Sit!" Estelle says sharply. "Annabel darling, can you remove these two rogues?"

Annabel stands primly in a gray and white uniform. She grasps a collar in each hand. The dogs' claws rasp the wooden floor and the tags on their studded leather collars jingle with the sway of their hindquarters. One of them turns its great, square head and regards me with casual interest before Annabel pulls them both through the doorway.

"Aren't you two *cute!*" Estelle says, ogling Victor and me. Her eyeliner, a shade similar to her strange citrus-colored hair, makes a crooked line along the lower ridge of her strong eyes and she wears obvious, poorly applied face powder. Yet she is enchanting. Her strangely painted face only adds to her charm, making her appear like a present waiting to be opened or a basket of Easter eggs. "It couldn't have been a better day for a tea, could it? We even have some sunshine! I thought we'd take our tea on the porch and enjoy the sun while it lasts."

"That would be lovely," Victor says. I cock my head in surprise; Victor never uses a word like "lovely." That is Estelle's word. He sounds ridiculous saying "lovely." Victor's sort of word is "horrid" or "wretched" or "acidulous" or "inane," but never "lovely." Why does he feel he should use her words now? I've made it an undertaking to adopt Victorisms in my own speech. I would love to be able to speak like Victor, not only to rid myself of my Boston accent, but also to have the words available to me, the way Victor does. It's not that he is perfectly expressive but that the presentation he gives the world reflects honestly his complicated personality. My conversation, on the other hand, is misleadingly simplified—my mind is stockpiled with unused words.

"How are you, Hilary dear? Sit down," Estelle says.

I sit in at the low table where a silver tea set rests on linen. There is a long tray of tiny triangular sandwiches surrounded by a galaxy of bright garnishes: radishes and parsley and orange slices in half-moons. They make me nervous, sitting on their silver tray so confidently. I hope my hair looks all right: I put it in a French braid. I ironed my skirt until it steamed by itself.

"Our Victor looks badly; have you been taking care of him properly?"

"I'm sorry?" I say, and cup a hand over my ear. "I missed that."

I am distracted by the lawn, which has an enormous garden and clusters of stone statues—a bird fountain, a little rabbit, an angel. There is an ivy-covered gazebo next to a frozen pond and a large, square maze, the sort of maze that the kings and queens in England had, with tall bushes separating the paths.

"You haven't been minding Victor. He looks awful, don't you, Victor? Victor, don't stand there like a goon. Sit down." Estelle is firm in her demands. She administers her instructions with casualness and expectancy as if her orders were those of an empress. "You are ill, aren't you? Would you like to lie down?"

"No, I'm fine. I'm warm, that's all," Victor says. There is a line of perspiration above his lip. "If you don't mind, I'll take off my jacket."

"Are you all right, Victor?" I say.

"I'll just use the bathroom. I'll be right back," Victor says, and shoots into the house.

"My, he *isn't* well," Estelle says. Her face grows soft with concern and, for a moment, I can picture Estelle as a mother or wife. This lasts briefly, then is gone. Again, she returns to her position of majesty in my eyes, her place among fables and places in the world I've seen only in the photo books and the pages of encyclopedias.

"He was fine a little while ago. Tired, I guess. He's always tired. We had a trying time at the supermarket."

"Tea?" Estelle says and fills a china cup decorated in the same colors as the flowers she is making. She pours delicately, raising the spout away from the cup. Then she clears her throat, gives me a wise look, and says, "The trouble is that if he is around someone with your youth and health Victor won't want to let you better him at anything. He'll want to do the marketing or whatever errands there might be just as though he were as healthy and capable as you are, which of course he isn't. You can't stop him, dear, his manhood is threatened. At any rate, it's too large a responsibility for you to watch over him."

I admire Estelle's long skirt, a woolen plaid that must be from Scotland or England. Also, the pearl blouse is quite beautiful, and almost makes her lime hair more bearable, as if it were naturally that color, the way eyes are sometimes violet or yellow.

"Don't you yearn to do other things?" Estelle says. She takes a crustless, round sandwich the size of a silver dollar from the tray and hands me it on a plate.

"Isn't that true for everyone?" I ask. I drape one leg over the other. I try to look *normal.*

Estelle says, "You are quite a remarkable young woman, do you know that?"

"Good tea," I say.

Estelle looks over my shoulder and smiles wide as pie. "Ah, our other gentleman has arrived!"

I look around and see Gordon, dressed in a tweed jacket and tie, a bottle of Bordeaux and some other liquor—something dark and regal—under one arm.

"I know it's teatime, but I brought some port," he says. "And some wine for when we are tired of the port." He kisses Estelle's cheek.

"You know what I like, don't you, dear,?" Estelle says, and puts her hand on Gordon's sleeve. "Hilary darling, I'd like you to meet my nephew, Gordon."

I am . . . astonished.

Gordon says, "I saw you once. Where was it? A supermarket?"

"Oh, right," I stutter.

I am feeling the way a goalie must feel when the ball is suddenly kicked in from nowhere.

"I didn't know you had a nephew, Estelle," I say.

"Oh, Gordon isn't really my nephew. He's just one of the old-timers here. I've known Gordon since he was a little boy on the beach. So he's like a nephew, more like a son really."

I turn to see Victor coming through the hallway. Estelle fixes a smile on her face and watches him until he joins us on the porch. I am baffled by whether she knows about me and Gordon. Could she know? We have had so little time together in the two short weeks he's been here. Where could she have seen us? At the beach? Was she sitting in one of the restaurants overlooking the shoreline watching us some afternoon as we ran with Tosh? Did she see him in my car at a stop sign? See us through one of the windows in Cappy's pub, or boarding the ferry to Boston? Did someone *tell* her about us? Did Cappy tell? And how would he have known? Is there really anything at all to know?

Victor comes in. Gordon rises and they shake hands.

"Do you know Gordon?" Estelle asks. "Hilary has apparently met him before."

"I haven't," Victor says and lends a brief smile. "How long have you known Gordon?" he asks me.

"We met once," I say, "at a supermarket."

"Ah," Victor says. "Shopping."

*T*he tea is abandoned for port. There's small talk, real dull. Victor asks Estelle where she got the interesting latten chandelier hanging in the front entrance and she tells him it is an imitation of the one hanging in the Berkeley chapel of Bristol cathedral. Victor also noticed, he says, the maid cleaning a collection of glazed jugs and jars. Was that Harvest pottery? Yes, Estelle replies and raises an eyebrow at Victor's knowledge. He places the period of some of her other antiques, shows some admiration for her acquisitions, and she seems mildly pleased with his flattery.

"Gordon, this is very good port," Victor says and looks into his glass. "But I hate port."

"Have wine, Victor," Estelle says. "There's wine."

Victor finds Annabel in the hallway and has her make him a scotch straight up. Annabel brings in a tray when she delivers it.

Victor says, "Annabel, how long have you known Gordon?"

"I don't know. A year?" Annabel says. She has a smile that wipes the slate clean of all other pretty smiles.

"I'd pay you more money than Estelle pays you just to have a drink with us."

"Annabel isn't a *slave,* Victor," Estelle says. She looks away indignantly.

"I don't drink," Annabel apologizes.

$\mathcal{N}$ow I'm pissed off. Victor is making friends with Gordon—or enemies, I can't tell. He compliments him on his dumb tweed jacket. Asks about his tailor, tells him that he's a fanatic for Alien Turf—a lie.

"I've been waiting for the right moment to buy a computer," Victor says, "but they're always coming up with something new."

"It's true," Gordon says, nodding. He holds his drink loosely, balancing it on his knee. His face is in a fog of Victor's cigarette smoke.

"And I think I need an operating system of even greater capability than the IBM personal computer."

"You can get a 386-chip, a multi-megabyte hard drive, a VAX . . ." Gordon suggests, bending toward him.

"I'm not sure I need a machine of my own, but really an entire universe of my own in which I can negotiate my own data sets, system networks . . . you know."

"Data sets are not a problem with today's technology. And everybody's networking."

"Of course," Victor says. He slams his palm on the table so the tea tray shakes. "You're right, Gordon, but it's all too slow. Frequent connection to nonresident galaxies can, for instance, lead to unexpected delays."

"You're razzing me," Gordon says.

"You have a way," Victor says, nodding at Gordon. "I like you so much I'll have a slug of your lousy port."

"I'm honored."

"You'll be sick," Estelle says, pouring.

*T*he view from the porch is amazing. We all gaze into Estelle's immaculate lawn. There are a few statues I hadn't noticed at first. A fake deer, fake-grazing by an artificial waterfall, now frozen, at the edge of the pond. There is a grouping of what Estelle calls "ground animals." That is, a chipmunk, a hedge-hog, a porcupine, a squirrel.

"Why not an anteater?" I ask.

"Or a guinea pig," says Gordon.

Victor turns to Gordon. "A guinea pig?" he says.

"*I* rather love the garden," Estelle tells us, after a tour of the house. We return to our seats on the porch and Estelle pours me a fresh cup of tea. I am nervous, so I eat, cleaning the tray of all its labored sandwiches.

"The garden is the only thing I could say I truly care for about the house," says Estelle. "Two husbands are under the azalea bushes. One is in the spot between those two firs. All ashes, of course."

"Location is key," Victor says. "I'd be humiliated, for example, if you stuck me beneath the bird feeder."

It takes a minute and then Estelle gets it. She shakes her head, clucking her tongue behind her teeth.

"It's sort of surprising to see a real English garden, isn't it? I've always been drawn to them. Perhaps I had one in a previous life," Estelle says. She's back to folding paper flowers. She tucks under one corner of a fuchsia petal and makes a crease with her thumbnail.

"It's beautiful," I tell her.

"Certainly is," Victor says. Annabel comes with another glass on her tray and Victor tells her to bring in the damned bottle.

"This house is full of surprises," Gordon says. "I'd love a house like this."

Victor glances outside and then focuses on Estelle. "I would demand that someone de-mortify the ground animals. It's absolutely criminal that you've turned them to stone like that," he says.

"Have a flower," Estelle says, and hands him a rose.

"There are mazes in palaces, aren't there?" Gordon says.

Victor says, "I think there's just tax collectors."

"You make fun of my favorite aspect of my property," Estelle pouts.

"Oh, Estelle," Victor says in his most resolute voice, "it's a lovely maze. I'm glad I've finally gotten to see one again. Very impressive. Very out of time."

"I had it planted twenty-five years ago. Whoever heard of a Tudor maze in the late twentieth century? It's like a whirlpool bath in Caesar's bedroom. Couldn't have it! But that's the glorious thing about the present—we can alter it. The maze exists!"

"I'm loving your Glenfiddich," Victor says.

"Gordon has gotten lost in the maze. Haven't you, Gordon?" Estelle says and pats Gordon's hand.

"Years. We're talking *years* ago," Gordon says.

Victor stares into the garden. He doesn't have to speak. I already know he is evaluating the difficulty of Estelle's Tudor maze. "It doesn't look *that* hard," he says.

"Only because you are looking at it from above, dear," Estelle says. "You can see all the pathways, so of course it looks easy. It's bound to appear simple when we're overlooking it. But once you get down there, enter between those green walls, you'll be quite lost, dear, I assure you."

"I don't believe it." Victor gives his drink a whirl in the glass.

"Well, go on then," Estelle says. "Try your luck. You seem to like to test the odds."

"I think I will," Victor says. He finishes his drink and puts it on the table. He takes a long look at the spread of maze across the lawn and I wonder if he's trying to memorize its paths. Then he tucks his shirt further into his pants and says, "Are you coming, Gordon?"

"I'll stay here and try to charm these two," he says, meaning me and Estelle. He puts his arm around the back of my chair.

Dying Young

"Admit it!" Victor calls, laughing. "You've poisoned yourself on that vile port." He punches Gordon's shoulder and Gordon makes a comic show of fending him off.

"Watch it," Gordon says when he comes close to rapping Victor's bandaged hand.

Victor opens the door leading outside and a cold wind pours in. As he closes the door he calls, "Off to conquer!" like a goodbye.

"Hilary, would you like some more sandwiches?" Estelle asks. I look at the tray I've emptied and with an urgent embarrassment I shake my head.

"Then some more tea," Estelle says. She takes the scattered heads of paper flowers and puts them in rows. Then she makes a neat pile of green straw-stems before seizing the teapot.

I look at Victor taking steady strides down the slopes of Estelle's lawn. The wind ripples the back of his shirt. He is not wearing his overcoat, or even his blazer. As he steps through the entrance to the maze I bolt out of my chair, knocking the tea from the cup Estelle is attempting to hand to me.

"Your skirt!" Estelle says.

I look down and see a long stain across my front. Gordon faces me with an expression I can't quite figure. But it could be pity, or it could be desire.

"Victor doesn't have his coat," I say.

"Oh, dear, so he doesn't," Estelle says. "Look at him, though, winding through the brush quite expertly! He's very bright, Victor. A very clever young man. I'd love to keep him, just to watch the way he negotiates the world."

"Where are the coats?" I say.

"Annabel took them, dear, now sit and I'll have her bring them in if you want them." Estelle rings a dinner bell.

"Bring Hilary's and Victor's coats, would you, Annabel dear?" she says.

"Mine too," Gordon says.

"You are awfully gallant," Estelle says. Gordon looks away.

Estelle says, "It is really quite useless for you to try to find him. Anyway, it was his mistake, to go out near naked."

I don't want to make such a big deal of it; I don't want to ruin everyone's fun. But it matters to me if Victor is cold. It matters to me when he feels sick. I don't really care how I seem to other people, if I appear overanxious. I mean I do care but I am so used to disapproval that it can hardly stop me.

Victor is at the southwest corner of the maze, skirting through a passageway between the hedges. I take a mental snapshot of the maze and try to hold it. I close my eyes and think of the paths and then reopen them and compare my mental vision to the real maze before me.

"That won't do any good," Estelle says. "Dear, I've seen many, many people do the same thing. I've had the maze for over two decades. Everyone tries to memorize it, to really know and understand it. They map it and still can't understand. When you get down to the thing, when you confront it with its mazeness, well, all that rational planning and mental work escapes you and you just run through it like any of God's creatures would—just like a mouse or a rabbit."

Outside the wind sweeps the parka hood back onto my shoulders. The sun is very bright and I have to squint as I make my way down the hill to the maze. The hill is so lush, unlike most of the dried and frozen lawns in Hull, and I think I feel the give of soft earth beneath my feet. Then I realize that the lawn is not a true lawn, but that it is some type of Astroturf, like what you'd put on a football field. The lawn, like Estelle's hair, is entirely artificial.

Gordon marches along beside me. He is so tall, he reminds me of some sort of spider, his legs are that long.

"Was it terribly obvious in there?" Gordon asks.

"What?"

"I can barely stand it," he says. "I want you so much."

We walk in silence to the bottom of the hill.

"Victor!" I call as we reach the maze wall. But the wind picks up my words and carries them away so that by the time I get to the second syllable I can't even hear what I'm saying. Gordon rattles the hedges along the maze wall in order to get Victor's attention. He calls Victor's name and I notice how strange it sounds coming from him.

Then I leave Gordon and enter through a part of the maze that might be the main opening, though I can't tell.

The floor is a confusion of dirt and pine needles and dead leaves. The hedges are high and thick; they are a shelter from the wind. I can hear Victor's steps not too far away and feel both relieved and rather foolish.

"Victor," I say, "I've got your coat and gloves here. Tell me where you are and I'll bring them to you."

He doesn't answer. Maybe the steps I heard were from Gordon. I wonder if Gordon is, in fact, really searching for Victor or whether he is making a play of it to please me. Then I put Gordon out of my mind.

I begin walking down the pathway, trying to peek through the tiny holes in the hedges for a glimpse of Victor's sleeve, the reflection off his glasses, off his watch. I look down to the base of the hedges, searching for his loafers, for a cloud of dust that he might kick up in the path. But I don't see anything. The wind increases and I hear loudly the sound of dry leaves and branches.

I try jumping high enough to see over the hedges but am unable. I close my eyes and remember the image I had of the maze when I looked at it from Estelle's glass porch. The pathways make squares and some of the squares come around so that they seem to be squares but actually feed into other pathways. They all have openings into other parts of the maze, except some lead to dead ends and some lead out of the maze and not into its center. Victor would be searching for the center and, of course, he would find it because Victor is the sort who masters any mental test, like puzzles, anagrams, and, I suppose, mazes as well. I have no reason to believe that I can work through a maze at all, as I've never done anything more than a simple crossword puzzle, and only then with help.

I feel angry because I can't find Victor and, once again, I am searching. It seems that in my life, and especially in my life with Victor, I am always going toward something, but never quite arriving. I come home and Victor is there on the bed. But he's never really there. It's as if, the minute I walk in the door, Victor's *thereness* evaporates. Whoever he was is replaced by who I think he is. And it's the same when I am home alone (which is rare). I might be reading or cooking. I might be trimming my toenails. But the minute Victor comes through the door I'm not there anymore. He displaces me like

water. I'm suddenly floating. We draw each other in and re-
volve around each other like moons. Last night, sometime long
before dawn, he got out of bed. He was feeling too sick to
sleep or maybe he was thinking about being sick, I couldn't
tell. I touched his shoulder as he stared into the blackness of
our window and his head turned. I watched his pale lips and
the way his eyes searched for me. He looked straight at me
but still seemed to be searching. Finally I found a means of
connection as I saw in his face the reflection of my own
panic.

"Triumph!" I hear, and there is Victor in front of me.
He's smiling a racy smile, like a sportsman or a gangster. He
throws his head back and laughs as if finding me there is
terrifically funny.

I know I look ridiculous: standing here in a tea-stained
skirt, my French braid gone loose and lopsided. I know he
must be laughing at how seriously I take everything, at my
hysteria over his jaunt through the maze. And though I'm sure
that my inclinations to bring the overcoat to him were well
founded and based on sincere affection and caring, I also
know that good intentions and "niceness" hold little currency
where Victor is concerned. And if I really thought these qual-
ities were worth while I would have nothing to do with Victor
at all.

"Well, go ahead and laugh," I say. "How do we get out
of here anyway?"

"What's the matter with you?"

"Here's your coat. I've had enough."

"What have I done?" Victor says and makes a poignant
gesture with his hands. "Hilary, what has gotten into you?

What's wrong? I was just going to tell you how beautiful you look. And what now? You're crying? You're so beautiful when you cry."

We find Gordon outside the maze, waiting in his patient way. I'm still upset, though my hysteria has settled down to a form of casual brooding. By the time we get back to the porch Gordon and Victor are laughing. Gordon is telling how he spent an hour lost in the maze when he was thirteen and how later he and his friends had races through it.

I sit down with a huff. I'm peeved; I look away from everyone. I demand a glass of scotch.

"Hils is having her scotch," Victor announces. "She hates scotch. This is a form of self-torture for her to drink scotch."

I'm suddenly so embarrassed, not so much by Victor's remark, but that my behavior on Estelle's porch should bring on such a comment. I am also mad because he's right.

I glance at the silver tea set, the delicate, rose-decorated cups, the various sorts of saucers, forks, and teaspoons, and realize how oddly juxtaposed my anger is to these artifacts of pleasantness. Estelle has placed a bouquet of her handmade flowers in a basket, where they are really quite beautiful. Victor sits straight; his thinness lends him a sophistication that other men, thicker men, can't have. Clearly, Victor is embarrassed by me, or rather, embarrassed *for* me because he never connects us as a couple so he never feels responsible for my actions. Estelle, however, looks quite pleased, as if she were listening to the call of a lottery ticket number and finding each digit precisely matches the one on her own.

"She's put off by you, Victor," Estelle says. She tilts her face toward the sun and stretches her neck like a cat. "Put off."

"Victor, let's thank Estelle for the tea. We should really go now. It's getting late."

"Go now?" Estelle says. "Why go now? It's just a fine afternoon and we are all enjoying ourselves, aren't we? Your mood will change, Hilary darling. You'll see."

Something in my expression makes Estelle change her mind. She says, "Well, if you really must."

Gordon stares at me—so obviously—that I would like to plug his eyes. Estelle arranges her skirt and reaches for her basket of paper flowers. "Won't you see if these go well by your window?"

I take the basket and thank her. I wonder, as Estelle settles back into her chair and begins a new flower, what it must be like for her to be here, in this big house, all alone. How is Estelle different after we all go home?

"Isn't that nice?" Victor says. "What an awfully nice thing to do, Estelle."

"Well, Hilary is a perfectly darling girl. Isn't she, Gordon?"

"Yes," Gordon says and nods at me. "She is. She is."

"Hilary, you look absolutely ridiculous standing there," Victor says. "Sit down and behave yourself. Have tea and try to act civilized."

I am going to kill him. I am going to kill you, Victor. You are a spiteful, horrible, scowling troll. I'm fed up. If you say anything more I will drown you in mouthwash. One more word and I'll take a vegetable shredder to your scrotum.

"Really, I think I'd rather go, Victor. Would you like to join me?" I say.

"Now that you mention it, I wouldn't. I think I'll stay and enjoy myself. Besides, don't you have an appointment to buy something?"

"You know I do. I'm going to buy a Christmas tree."

"Of course. A tree. How nice," Estelle says. She tells me she'll have Victor dropped off later and urges me to come back soon to visit.

I thank her again and nod at Gordon.

"It was a pleasure to meet you," Gordon says. He is grinning and tipping back in his chair like a high school kid. "It is very nice to know Hilary Atkinson."

"Don't forget the flowers," Estelle says and nods at the basket of paper rosebuds. Annabel appears at the doorway and Estelle asks her to lead me out.

I follow Annabel into the hallway and notice, all at once, that Victor is with me. I stop and look at him. He stands very close.

"If you want to leave, then go ahead," Victor says. "But you'll be hard pressed to prove I've done something unusually hateful in order to upset you."

I try to think of a response. I try to imagine myself as the mistress of this enormous house, as a woman who possesses authority, the way Estelle does. How wonderful it must be to feel the confidence required to wear pink or green hair and century-old trade beads from Mexico, to have power.

"I hate you, Victor. You're always such a pig. You were rude to Gordon."

"What do you care? Anyway, I like him. You're embarrassed because you spilled tea on your skirt. Am I right? Come on, Hils, am I right or wrong?"

Of course you're right, I think. See how much good it'll do you to be right.

"I'm going, Victor."

"Oh, go," he says and turns.

I follow Annabel through the hallway, through all the trinkets Estelle showed off to us during our tour. We pass racks of Spode china, a procession of Victorian drinking glasses on display by a window, an ancient clock by the staircase. I look at Annabel's back, at the crisp white bow against her gray dress. I think of how tiny her lower back is, what a nicely formed, athletic young woman she is beneath the dull gray cotton. And honestly, I think how nice *she* is, though I know she is only doing her job. What she doesn't do is make it at all apparent that anything unusual transpired between Victor and myself. Her gracious disappearance when Victor spoke in the hallway is appreciated double-much. She is sweet to me, ignoring that I am frazzled, that my skirt is wet and my hair has fallen from its careful braid.

"Annabel," I say and she pauses and turns to me. I notice her eyes, which are very deeply set and quite dark. She wears mascara and her lashes curl in spidery wisps. She is younger than me but not by so much. She might have been the younger sister of my college roommate, or someone I met in the bleachers at a ball game. We could have had coffee together and she could have told me about her boyfriends and her family. But as she is, leading me through Estelle's house, we are nothing to each other. We aren't supposed to talk really and now that she is in front of me I can't think of anything to say. "Annabel, thank you very much for all your work today," I manage finally.

"No trouble," she says and smiles that delicious smile. She begins to walk again. Her hair is long and dark beneath the pins that hold it in a bun. I can tell by her shape that she would be stunning in blue jeans and a T-shirt. In anything or nothing. I wonder how she and Gordon would look as a couple, or she and Victor.

"Hey, Annabel," I start again. "Do you live around here?"

"I live *here,*" she says, and points at the ground. "In this house."

"Are you happy here?" I say and then think perhaps I've said something wrong. "I mean do you like it okay?"

"It's a large room."

"Is your family from this area?"

"Brockton," she says. "I'm saving money to go back to college."

"I'm so glad to hear that," I tell her. "I mean about college."

A couple of steps later I say, "Is it hard working here?"

"Hard? No, no, not hard. I only work four days a week and the other three I spend in Boston with my boyfriend."

It sounds right that beautiful Annabel should have a boyfriend in Boston. There's someone to appreciate how carefully she brushes her lashes with mascara, so that they are long and full without looking fake. I am so pleased that Annabel gets off the ship at Long Wharf to receive a hug, that couples can care for each other in healthy ways, that young women are as beautiful as Annabel, that she has a large room, a small waist, an athletic step; that she has a pretty name like Annabel.

Dying Young

"Well, that's just really good," I say as Annabel opens the front door.

We shake hands. She has such delicate hands, the sort of hands I've always wanted, thin hands, hands with long fingers and oval nails. And she gives a proper handshake, a good, firm clasp. I shake her hand and then I get in my car and she waves to me. All the way down the long driveway I think of Annabel and I smile. But as soon as I've gotten back to Hull, onto the windy road that leads down to the coast and to the street where Victor and I live, I feel bloated on bad feelings for Victor. I think about how he is likely to punish me with silence, how unhappy he is with me, how unhappy I make him, how I've come to cause him to hate me in an effort to get him to love me, and how little control I have over myself and my affections. I wonder if I manufactured that scene between Victor and myself in order to bring on the inevitable destruction of our union even before its assumed end. I wonder, also, if I am willing Victor to be mean to me just so that I can justify an affair with another man, legitimize leaving Victor, validate a decision which one can never validate: because it is a private decision, because there is no right or wrong in interpersonal politics. And because our sort of relationship is one that, by its very structure, is lawless.

SIX

*A*s soon as I get inside the door to our apartment I unbutton my skirt and let it drop to the floor. The place is messy and cold. I charge up a space heater and find a pair of blue jeans and one of Victor's sweaters. I pace the apartment, thinking of what to do. I collect things I should put away, a breakfast bowl, a half-eaten Hershey bar, a furniture advertisement, an overfull ashtray. Then I can't figure out where exactly to put them so I dump everything next to the sink. I put Estelle's flowers near Victor's chair, imagining how they will look against the morning sun. I pace some more. I think about what else to do. I collect stray pencils, dirty teaspoons, plastic wrappings from pretzel bags. I fill a clay jar with matchbooks and unidentifiable keys.

I am perfectly alone; there is possibility for anything. I could go to the hardware store, buy four paint cans of azoorange and make our apartment into Mars. I could get a gallon of ice cream and a lot of Oreo cookies and cripple myself with food. I could buy chemicals and do irrevocable things to my hair. I could go through every personal item Victor has, seeking clues to his life before me.

But there are no new clues.

Dying Young

Victor lays his life open like a split melon. I know everything. For an hour I sit in Victor's chair by the window, just looking.

Victor keeps a pile of books in a stack by his chair. He has a small collection of first editions. Some are beginning to mold. I pick up a copy of Heidegger's *Basic Writings* and thumb through it, trying to decipher the cryptic penciled notes that Victor printed in the margins when he was still in school. I look in the front of the book and read "Victor Geddes. Please Return." Below is an address on Commonwealth Avenue. The street number is low, meaning it is close to Boston Garden. This must be the house Victor grew up in and where his father now lives.

Here are five things I know about Victor's father. He is sure that once something starts breaking it is doomed to break forever. This is why he would rather trade in his broken car than have a water pump fixed. He sits in a large den in his home, in front of a desk strewn with all sorts of documents, and constructs ducks and frogs and grasshoppers out of child's clay. When Victor was five, his father allowed him to eat spaghetti off the table with a straw. On her last birthday before she died, he bought Victor's mother a CB radio. When Victor was a child he left his favorite stuffed animal in the park and his father searched in the rain until eleven at night with a flashlight. All of these things Victor has told me.

I go to the desk and open the top drawer. I rummage through note pads, shopping lists, scissors with a broken blade, two unraveling spools of thread, a shark's tooth, a miniature Slinky, a brand-new disposable flashlight still in its packaging, and letterhead from the university where Victor was a student. I find the stack of letters Victor keeps in a rubber band and search it for a return address that matches the Commonwealth address. Mostly what I find are get-well cards from Victor's last stay in the hospital. There's also a wedding invitation for last September, the announcement of someone's baby, a change-of-address notice, and a lottery ticket. Finally I find something from Commonwealth Avenue. It's a small blue envelope with faint, round typed letters spelling out the address to Victor's old apartment in Boston. Inside is a folded onionskin page with a short letter from his father. The print is faded and riddled with typographical errors. The letter gives an account of Victor and his father's fight at the hospital after Victor announced that he no longer wanted to take treatment. Then it launches into a strident appeal to rationality and the limitless possibilities that hope can provide. Finally the tone softens, and there is a pleading for Victor to reconsider and call home with his current whereabouts. The last part reads: "Victor, for my whole life, whenever I was feeling unhappy I could think of you, of the joy you've brought me. Maybe the reason you won't continue treatment is because you haven't felt that same sort of joy. Couldn't you call me? Couldn't we try something new?"

I know for a fact that Victor never answered that letter and I'm dazed by his willful neglect. I dig through the drawer again, taking out a piece of notepaper—nothing fancy, just plain white—and write my own, brief message to Victor's father. I write,

> Dear Mr. Geddes, You don't know me but I am helping take care of your son. He is all right. Maybe he will call you—if I can convince him.
> —*Hilary Atkinson*

Dying Young

No, it is hardly a letter. But it lets him know that Victor is okay. He will be grateful for the short note, I know. And I feel somehow good and right as I fold it into a plain envelope, address and stamp it. I look at the packaged letter and feel proud. But then something happens; my confidence slips away from me. For a long time I sit at the desk and wonder if I should send it.

$\mathcal{M}$rs. Birkle calls me. Her voice is so tiny on the phone, a whisper from way off. She says, "I'm so sorry to bother you, dear, but if you could help me . . ."

I don't let her finish the sentence. I interrupt with a rush of assurances that I will be right there.

I get downstairs and she opens the door. Her smooth, sand-brown skin is puffed around the eyes. Slightly red. Her stiff lips are pulled tight into her mouth. She says, faint-voiced, "I burst the television."

Sure enough, in the living room is a toppled-over TV, lying face down on the carpet, surrounded by a scattering of smashed glass.

"Oh, I'm so sorry." My words come out staccato, like the signals in a Morse code.

"I was sweeping the carpet and got the cord of the television into the vacuum. I don't want you to cut yourself, but can you help me move it to the hallway so the men can take it away?"

I wonder what men she is talking about—the trash collectors? Does she think the trash collectors are going to come into the house and rid her of her disabled television?

"Sure," I say. "Sure, I will."

I go to the back of the television and position myself to pull it right side up. Mrs. Birkle insists on helping. She bends over the TV and I tell her, "No, go sit down. It's okay." I plead with her. I tell her not to exert herself. I tell her I've moved TVs twice this size.

"Is this a big television?" Mrs. Birkle asks.

"Yes," I tell her. "It's a huge television. A wonderful television."

I pull it into the hall, scattering glass and bulbs and wires. After I sweep up the last of the glass from Mrs. Birkle's carpet she puts a smooth, cool hand on my cheek. She disappears in the kitchen for a few minutes and comes out with a half pan of white fudge, begging me to take it.

*T*he last thing I want to do is go with Cappy to buy a Christmas tree, but finally I decide to get ready. I unbraid my hair and brush it out in front of the bathroom mirror. I wash my face and run some Chap Stick over my lips. Then I think maybe I'll wear mascara, the way Annabel does, and I hunt through the cabinet, find the mascara, and comb it carefully through my lashes. Of course, they don't look like Annabel's do. They don't sweep up to my eyebrows and they don't shadow my eyes. Still, I look better. I look good enough for some eyeliner and maybe some lipstick, too. But I don't own eyeliner or lipstick. I have a blunt-ended dove-gray pencil but no sharpener. I have eye shadow in a noxious green color that I got as a free sample. I have a small amount of blush—enough for one cheek. To hell with the face, I think. Go for the hair.

My hair is still suffering from its afternoon in a braid: a jumble of bends. I hoist it into a bunch and consider folding it into a bun. That would be too much trouble, though, and besides, the way the waves sort of swarm around my face adds something dramatic to my appearance. I like it enough that I don't brush it. I look into the mirror and try to imagine that my reflection is not a reflection but really a whole other person. I try to take myself in as if I were someone else, as if I were a stranger. I think, Interesting eyes, grayish with a brown splotch near the center of the left one. I think the splotch looks like a mistake, like a drawing in a coloring book in which the kid changed his mind about what crayon to use. But my hair, with all its waves, has some pizzazz. My hair is kind of pretty in its slovenly way.

I take off Victor's sweater and hunt for one of my own, a thin sweater that is not nearly warm enough but looks better. Then I switch my blue jeans for a pair of lined, wool pants with pleats and a belt. I turn up the cuffs and wear in-fashion socks. I get some shoes that make my feet look small. Put on a bracelet. I look in the mirror again and I decide that I look fairly good. Good enough to be doing something a lot fancier than buying a Christmas tree. I could be meeting friends for drinks, or visiting an old relative—or I could be going out on a date.

I pretend that the endless unlit roads of Hull are the brightly blazed intersections on Newbury Street in Boston. I stop at a convenience store and buy a pack of cigarettes and a lighter in the team colors of the Boston Red Sox. I smoke cigarette after cigarette, scaring up a flame from my new lighter. I'm dizzy on a nicotine high when I see a mailbox by the sidewalk. I stop, have about six thousand doubts about what I am doing, and then I drop Mr. Geddes's letter through the slot. When I hear the hollow sound of the closing mailbox door I think, Good job.

In the car, I take out a new cigarette, crack the window, and don't mind the cold. I turn on the radio and sing to the songs—loud. I beat the buttons on my radio, searching for some heady rock and roll. I thumb the tuner, trying to bring in the clearest sound. I pass the round dome of a lime-painted water tower, made gray in the shallow light of early evening. It's on eight legs like a giant octopus and I wave hello.

I know even before I get to the front of the restaurant and peek through the window what it is I am doing. When I come in, carrying a purse instead of a knapsack, holding my parka instead of wearing it, I turn to Gordon and pretend that I didn't think he'd be there. I smile; I call, "Hello."

"Well," Gordon says.

"Well, well," I chirp.

"You look . . ." Gordon gestures in a way that invites me to finish the sentence.

"Thank you," I say.

"Where's Victor?" Gordon says. "He's not still at Estelle's, is he?"

"I guess so. When did you leave?"

"A little after you. I offered him a ride. I like Victor," Gordon says, as if this fact surprises him.

I hear the sound of pans being stacked and remember Cappy in the kitchen. Through the triangular window of the kitchen's swinging door I see Cappy, apron on, sleeves rolled up. He's pulled a bunch of scarred baking pans from inside the sink and stacking them.

I'd like to sneak off with Gordon. I'd like to go to a

restaurant, a good one, and have something unusual to eat. A foreign restaurant. A restaurant where you have to eat with your hands. I'd like to drink too much, drive crazy through a snowstorm, any kind of event, anything to laugh over and recover from. And I'd like to do this with Gordon: sit across a table from him and later talk across a pillow.

"Estelle will bring him home later," I say. I look at Gordon, still in his tweed jacket, his hair falling just slightly over his eyebrows, and I feel like a child who wants to open just one more Christmas present.

"I'm here because Cappy and I were going to pick out a tree. I need his truck to haul it back. But I don't have to do it now," I tell him. "I could leave."

"Why wouldn't you want your tree?"

"Let's go to your house," I say. I blink purposefully and feel the mascara on my lashes, a featherweight that makes me think of Annabel. I look at Gordon and pretend that my eyes are the same shade of brown that Annabel's are, that when Gordon looks at me he sees someone who looks like Annabel, as animated, as cheerful. In this way, I begin to feel attractive. I begin to imagine Gordon with his shirt off.

*A*nd so we drive. I'm the passenger, so I have the awkwardness of silence without purpose. The driver can always concentrate on the road, or seem to. The passenger, what is his job? To be proximate, that's all, or to be entertaining. But I can't be the latter. I'm not interested in conversation. I don't talk because if I talk I am afraid that the understood agreement between Gordon and me will disappear, like a fog lifting, and we'll be placed back into the clarity of our separateness and the temporal limits to our affection.

And maybe Gordon is feeling the same way. Maybe he is thinking that he should be quiet now, that this is an act that will take place in silence like a true secret, never to be spoken even during its unfolding.

Gordon pops a tape from his cassette deck and boxes it back into its plastic casing. The motion of this is so abrupt in the capsule of the car that my stomach jumps. It seems almost like news, like something to be commented on, or at least acknowledged. But I'm steadfast. I look outside the window at the telephone poles flying by. For a moment it almost seems that the world is moving at the speed of these rapidly vanishing telephone poles and that Gordon and I are perfectly still, like stones in water.

We are a reckless bunch. Victor chooses not to take his chemotherapy. I decide on Gordon for an evening. Somewhere in the universe a man with children is choosing and unchoosing suicide. A baby, not wanted, is being born. A secretary is leaving her job to start a business she's always dreamed of. A teenage boy is picking up a guitar for the first time.

I could tell Gordon to drive me to the pier; I'd take the boat to Boston and from there a plane to, say, Phoenix and no one in Phoenix would know an ounce of my past. I could be a whole other person in the West. I could take up hobbies that I've never had before and pretend to anyone who met me that these were old hobbies. I could start being sexually promiscuous and play like I always have been so. I could say to men, "I don't like to call them 'one-night stands.' I consider every time to be a complete, all-consuming life experience."

Dying Young

. . .

When is the last time I made love with Victor? It was a week ago. No, it was six days ago. I remember being in bed, asleep, soundly asleep, so much that at first I kept falling *back* asleep. He pulled the covers down and was touching my breasts. He wasn't looking at me but staring down onto my nipples, watching the reaction from his fingertips and tongue. And then his hand was between my legs and I was awake but not really awake. Then he was in me and I was all of a sudden quite alert, on like a fire alarm, as he brought his face to mine and looked down on me and moved his hips slowly. "Baby," he said and ran his hand through my hair, "look at you."

Silently, I began to move with him but he reached down and held my pelvis and said, "No, don't do anything at all." He looked at me and kept looking at me, as if he were trying to make a mental snapshot, as if he were working on developing a memory.

I remember feeling as if the room had frozen, that the night was not getting blacker or getting lighter with dawn, that everything was quite stunned—that time began again at the moment Victor came, a silent, effortless orgasm. And when he fell to his side, his arm resting over my stomach, I wished he would climb back on top of me, that time could be stopped again, and we could go on, pivoting between night and morning, like a clock hand at midnight. You see, I always think of Victor as something I can't really hold, like water in my hand that will either evaporate or drip through the cracks between my fingers. But at that moment I felt as if he were a solid part of me, as constant as a fingerprint. That flash, when we were together, felt like I was Victor or Victor was me, and that we had, through our merging, shaken off one physical law and were capable of dispensing with others. Then everything was immediately reversed. Victor fell asleep. I stared at his sleeping face. I thought, Look at you.

Gordon reaches across the car and I'm startled, not so much by his touching me as that I hadn't realized the car was stopped and thought for a second that Gordon had simply abandoned the steering wheel and we would plow into the next telephone pole. But now I see that we are in a driveway, the same driveway I have watched him walk down many times in the past two and a half weeks. The car is off, the parking brake pulled up. Gordon sweeps my hair to one side and kisses the back of my neck. He has strong lips; I wonder if his kisses are making red marks on my skin. I wonder if he will kiss my mouth like that. I speculate: What should I do now? How should I touch him? Does he think we are going to do this in the *car?* There are a thousand things I want to ask him all of a sudden. I want to find out what high school he went to, what his friends' names are, his favorite books, how he spent, say, the last ten years of his life. I want to *know* him.

Somewhere there is a puppy wandering away from his new home, never to be found. A steamboat is charging up with passengers on board, waving. A new pilot is nervous at his first landing. At NASA they are on the verge of a discovery.

· · ·

Dying Young

I think that someday, after I die, I will go somewhere and be sitting across a card table from another dead person, playing hearts and saying, "When I was twenty-three I wanted to be a veterinarian but couldn't get into a vet school. . . . When I was twenty-seven I fell in love with a man named Victor and then met a man named Gordon. . . ." Sometimes I don't think I can ever tell a story of my life accurately because life is still continuing and there's no way to objectively portray it. I could try but it's like trying to pick up an endless plane of glass—I can't even get a grip on it. How should I know if I'm doing the right thing as I let the porch door slam behind me and enter Gordon's house? Maybe when I'm dead my soul will sit somewhere and map out everything I did and be able to tell exactly where I erred. Maybe in some other life—in one of the lives Estelle promises we all have—I will determine the secret to correctness, to doing things right, to knowing that one *can* do things right.

It's all really hard for me, making a decision. Decisions are just moments in time; there aren't any criteria for evaluation. With Victor, decisions are easier. I know he is dying, the medical authorities have promised it and Victor's own body shows the promise being gradually delivered. Victor has given me a scale. I know the ending.

But now with Gordon. How do I think his is going to end and what is changing now, as he pulls me on top of him by the record player? We listen to old blues songs from a stereo system so tall, and so glorious in its intimidating high tech, that it looms like a monument in the small bedroom.

His bedroom carpet is periwinkle. The curtains match the carpet and are held back with blue ties. The wallpaper is printed with monarch butterflies in rows. The room seems to deserve the laying out of a child's board game, pick-up sticks, or the construction of a house out of Lincoln Logs—not two people, peeling the clothes from each other, tossing together and refolding legs and arms. He is kissing me and I am an actor, performing with my tongue all the movements of a lover. And then instantly I *am* a lover. I'm tensed and reaching for the zipper on his jeans. I yank off my sweater with one quick pull over the head. I reach behind my back and unclasp my bra. I hear a moan and then realize that the sound is my own. Gordon says, "Hilary!" but I don't respond. Then Gordon grabs my wrists. He pulls my hands in front of him and I look at him. His grip is strong.

"Slow down," he says and lets go. Then he kisses me. He kisses my neck. We start again.

$\mathcal{T}$here's someone who often shows up in my dreams. A young girl, maybe eleven years old. Mousy curlicue hair that bobs as she walks. Tight-fitting square glasses, a chip in her tooth. "I think she is the daughter I will one day have," I tell Gordon. Our lovemaking has wiped me out. My speech is slow and slurred as if I am drugged.

"Tell me more," Gordon says. He is giving me a super deluxe body rub. I am face down on his blue carpet, listening to Peruvian folk music. It's an old album with scratches and skips but its condition cannot hide the long, sweet notes, the resonance of handcrafted wind instruments. A flute. A mouth harp. The aching sound of mountain isolation, of longing, of love.

"Well, in most of the dreams she needs some sort of help. She's lost in a city, for example, or she's in a car that has no steering wheel or no brakes."

Dying Young

In Gordon's hand is baby oil, an innocent clear bottle with a pale pink cap. He drops dollops of oil from the point of my shoulder to the top of my thigh. He smears it over my skin, pressing his fingers between ridges on my back.

"Does she have particularly strong dorsal muscles?" he asks.

"Oh, she's not *me*," I say. I turn my head and look at Gordon. He wears a pair of crisp white shorts. The muscles in his upper arms are stiff with the movement of his hands.

"Okay, okay," he says, "but she's always in trouble and needs *what?* Protection?"

"Not protection really. In my dreams no one can ever help her. She needs me specifically."

Gordon leans over. He kisses the rim of my ear. He rubs the back of my head with his chin. Then he wraps his arms under me.

"Does she need, just sometimes, Hilary, someone else too?"

SEVEN

I set the alarm for midnight but I needn't have. There's no way I will sleep before Victor comes home. I've spent hours now in bed, listening to the hum of the refrigerator, the space heater flicking on and off, the sound of jets rumbling through the sky. I'm reworking what has happened, going over everything. I'm trying to make sense of it. I'm trying very hard.

I came home a little past ten, feeling sore, guilty, ravished. I had my underwear stored foolishly in my pocket. Four inches of snow fell, big flakes. I stood for many minutes, ankle deep, waiting for the wetness to seep through my shoes so I could pretend to Victor that I'd been on a long walk. I stepped around Mrs. Birkle's broken television and went noiselessly up the stairs. Outside our apartment, I pushed the door open a fraction, listening for his breathing. But Victor wasn't home. I stashed my clothes in the back of the closet and, in the shower, ran a soapy washcloth over every stretch of my body. I washed my hair, my scalp, my ears. I scrubbed myself numb. Standing in front of the mirror, I studied my face for whisker marks. I dabbed on Victor's after shave and then slapped it on my stomach and thighs.

Dying Young

I wore a pajama top and a pair of Victor's boxer shorts and waited in bed, listening for the occasional groan of the foghorn at Pemberton Pier. I wanted Victor right then, very badly. I wanted him as people want shade in Morocco.

Sometimes wanting Victor feels so primal that I cannot remember a time when he wasn't part of my deepest self, when he didn't occupy a place in my mind as he does now, when my every thought wasn't balanced by whatever his opinion might be, when I couldn't look for him inside myself. I am ashamed of this about me, ashamed by there being a crack in my construction, an incompletion that makes possible the entrance of someone like Victor. And that this crack could also generate the desire for Gordon. Strangely, also, I am thankful.

Late, very late, I hear his key in the lock, the whine of our door opening, and see the shadow his body casts across the pine floor.

I want to be reassured that nothing has changed. I know something has changed, of course, but only in the sense that some information has been brought to the surface. I'm the same person as before I made love to Gordon but now that I have actually done so the person who is me becomes more apparent—as if I brought myself to my own attention. I no longer have to maintain an image of myself as a good and martyred soul—I'm not. I have made my way toward something more real for me, toward a gray area, a mire of ambiguity, some mass of confused emotion that is mine in a way that being the faithful and good lover to Victor was never mine.

Victor glides his thin body through the narrow space of the front door. He hushes the creaking floorboards and pushes the door gently back. He holds his shoes. He's all the way into the bathroom with the door closed before turning on the light, allows himself only a trickle of water for brushing his teeth. He knows to be quiet. He knows to be considerate.

He must have an understanding that something has happened. He's not up to date about me and Gordon but he's got an inkling. I feel it's all over the apartment. Big lights. Gordon and my relationship being advertised like a New York premiere. I feel as if there's an atmosphere of it, like we're swimming in it. I'm screaming my confession in every breath, in my sweat. There's that code between lovers, a language that you can speak but cannot find a grammar for.

Victor drapes his blazer over the desk chair and drops his pants around his ankles. Unbuttoning his shirt, he watches me. He crawls beneath the covers, smelling of scotch and snow.

I have this curious feeling: I want to tell him. My thoughts are so full of the phenomenon of my cheating that I think I must just blurt it out, that the words will come from some force of their own, as if they know their own importance and insist on asserting it.

I make room in bed for Victor.

It is very dark and I can hear the ocean. Victor's chest expands and shrinks next to mine. He knows I'm awake. He kisses me and then puts his head against my shoulder.

"Are you disappointed in me, Hils?" he says.

It's happening again, that voice inside him coming out, the sweet voice that I hear so occasionally, the voice of his lovemaking, of his confessions, the voice he uses when he reaches back in his memory and tells a story of his childhood, the voice I search and prod for and cannot find until it is given.

He reaches over, sweeps my hair onto the pillow, and hugs my shoulder.

"You must think I'm *trying* to make it harder for you. That I want to exhaust myself, to drink, to go out in the cold just to hurt you."

He's talking about our fight at Estelle's house. For him, nothing more than this has passed since he last saw me. For me, the words spoken those many hours ago are almost forgotten. They are replaced with images of the drive to Cappy's, of my sweater coming off over my head, of Gordon beside me, catching his breath, an awkward drive home. I have to think hard to remember the other scene: the maze, Victor in his shirtsleeves, trying to find him and feeling humiliated. Yes, I can remember it, but it seems as innocuous as running a traffic light when nobody else is on the road.

"I don't do it so I'll leave you faster," Victor says. "I don't do it to get sicker, to spite your efforts, to make fun of the vitamin pills, the balanced meals, the rest."

"I know you don't," I say.

"I don't want to die, Hilary," he says.

I hold him very closely. I feel his breath on my neck. I rock him. I want to hide him in the depth of me. I want to hide us both.

In the middle of the night, at a moment when I could still have been dreaming, I hear Victor say, "What do you think of Estelle's philosophy?"

I don't open my eyes. I don't move. I remain nearly asleep, letting Victor's voice enter my thoughts. I wonder how long he has been awake, turning over Estelle's theories of past lives, her bold assertions about the futures we will all carry with us into eternity. She has told us she was a farmer in England and that she rode the fence lines of her property on a bay horse called Franklin. She told us that in another life she had been a beautiful woman. A "vixen," she said, a female Casanova. She asked me, in all seriousness, who I had been before and what I could remember.

"I don't believe it, Victor," I say to him, but tenderly. Outside the wind roars so strongly that it seems to shake the house walls.

"You don't think you had any previous lives?"

"No."

"Well, guess at it," Victor says. He loops his arm over my chest and pulls himself toward me. "What do you think you *would* have been?"

"Maybe I was a corn husk," I say and kiss his hair. "Maybe I was a planet no one's found."

I sleep a wretched sleep, have nightmares I cannot remember except in snatches, and wake to the sound of the doorbell.

"My God, someone is at the door," I say.

Victor opens his eyes slowly. He is as white as the pillowcase. I'm startled by the sight of him.

"Victor!"

"What?" he says, without moving his head. Even his freckles look pale, as if they've been bleached. The bones in his ribs show through his back and he is stock-still.

Dying Young

"Nothing," I say. My mouth drops at the sight of his yellow eyes, the ash-gray skin around his temples. "I'll get the door."

I get up. I feel dizzy. I look at Victor. His face is sunken into the pillow. The only color he has is his coppery hair that shines in a sort of macabre brightness like blood brightening a soldier's white chest.

I'd forgotten we even had a doorbell—that's how long it's been since I've heard it. I find a pair of blue jeans, start to put them on, and then realize that they are Victor's. His jeans are too tight for me; hard to imagine but it's true. I can button them, but barely. I get a T-shirt and a sweater and pull my loafers on. On my way out the door I glance back at Victor, who has shut his eyes again.

I go down the steps; the draft on the stairway is refreshing. The hallway is flooded with light from the windows. So much white light.

When I open the door there is Gordon with winter-red cheeks and a stack of firewood in his arms.

"Are you nuts?" I say. The wind sweeps against me in one cold slap.

"I thought you might want some wood."

We stand there, him on the porch and me shivering at the door.

"Okay," I say, "come in." I let him lead the way up the stairs. I watch his boots take the stairs, one after another. I admire his breadth of his shoulders.

"I wanted to see where you live," Gordon says.

"I live with Victor."

At the landing I say, "One more flight."

The door to the apartment is open a crack. I say, "This is it. Wait here. Let me see if Victor is up yet."

"Did I come too early?" Gordon says. He's slightly out of breath, his face flushed; his arms, braced against the wood, look burdened. Gordon whispers, "I had to *see* you," and wrinkles his forehead.

I slip through the door and find Victor, lying in bed, blindfolding himself with his hands.

"I must never drink again," he says. "It can't ever, ever happen. Why do you let me drink, Hilary? You know how bad it is for me."

"It might not be the alcohol," I say.

Victor moves his hands and looks at me, a little surprised. "Who was at the door?" he asks.

"Gordon. He's standing in the hall right now with a load of wood."

"Oh," Victor says. "What does he want?"

"To give us the wood," I say.

"What? A gift? Oh. Oh, then I should get up," Victor says. He leans on one arm and starts to rise out of bed, but the arm gives. He props himself up on one elbow and waits. He appears to be concentrating. He doesn't move. "Hilary," he says finally. As if he's made a discovery he announces, "I don't feel well."

*A*n hour later Victor is still in bed. But he has on a flannel shirt and is sitting up. Gordon is at the foot of the bed, a plateful of breakfast on his lap. Close to the fire, I can feel the heat from its shadowy blaze. This is the first time we have used the fireplace since we've lived here. It's also the first time I have made French toast—Victor's favorite—in many weeks. I used real French bread that I bought in a bakery and I have to admit that it tastes pretty good. Victor can't eat. Everything makes him sick this morning. He says even his toothpaste comes all too close to being food.

"Okay," Victor says to Gordon, "now let me guess what you were doing, say, Fourth of July a decade ago. Let's see, you are, how old? Three years younger than me. Ah! Just a baby! You were ... now let me think ... on the esplanade watching fireworks."

"Of *course* I was on the esplanade," Gordon says. "That's no guess."

"Okay, you were on the esplanade *with* someone." Victor wrenches his brows together, thinking. "... with your sweetheart who, many months later, you discover had hoped you would take her to bed that night—but you didn't."

"No, I did," Gordon says. He leans back, raising a finger. "I did and it was breathtaking."

"You remember? That long ago and he remembers!" Victor says. "It *must* have been breathtaking."

I hand Victor a glass of orange juice and he looks at it as if it were radioactive.

"We made love behind the Boston University boathouse, on the boardwalk that connects one end of the bike path to the other. The fireworks were going off. A skyful of grand finales."

"Wow," I say. "And I get excited if we do it in another room."

"We don't *have* another room," says Victor.

. . .

$\mathfrak{I}$ go to the fire and use a thick piece of kindling to turn over a log. Then I sit cross-legged blowing onto the flame, feeling its uneven heat. I think to myself that summertime is over-rated, and that there's nothing better than a home that smells of oak wood in the morning.

"Your turn," Gordon says to me. "What were you doing Fourth of July ten years ago?"

I think for a moment but I can't recall exactly what I was doing. "It was the year before I started college. I was in Mexico, which explains why I can't remember the Fourth so well. I mean, July the Fourth is just another day in Mexico."

"What were you doing in Mexico?" Victor says.

"Long story. See, my mom and dad had been separated a long time and were finally getting a divorce. My mother—okay, she's a crazy woman—sent us to live with our dad. He's a mechanic and he got asked to work at some car race in Mexico so he left us with this other woman who was blind and who had a farmhouse on the north shore. Her name was real long. It sounded like an operation, so we called her Mrs. C. She came from the South and had one of those singsong voices. She made fun of how we talked. She sat my little brother down in the kitchen and made him say, over and over, 'Hot buttered popcorn' and 'Park your car in Harvard Yard.'"

"My God!" Victor says. But you can tell, sort of, that he thinks it's funny. "Hut budded popcon," he imitates.

"I'd kill her," Gordon says.

"Oh, look, you couldn't kill her," I say. "She was in her late sixties and blind and she had this husband, actually this *ex*-husband, who lived in the top floor of her house. I guess when they divorced she couldn't get the guy to move out. He just stayed and stayed. Mrs. C. needed all sorts of equipment just to get around. She had a cane, a walker. She had a stuffed animal, a hippo named TuTu that she sat on the coffee table and spoke to. She had like a busted hip, pinned together but barely, after her ex-husband pushed her . . . well, okay, that's what *she* said. . . ."

Gordon coughs on a crust of French bread. "He pushed her?" he says.

"They fought all the time. She wanted to charge him rent."

Victor says, "He pushed her down the steps for a rent check?"

"Who knows? Anyway, she thought he ought to pay rent. She said why should he get to live in the house for free? The courts declared the house *hers.* At least once a day she'd climb up the stairs and hit him with her cane. And he retaliated; I liked him actually. He would rearrange all the food on the refrigerator shelves, replace her soap with a bar of wax, pull the volume knob off the television, that sort of thing."

"Oh, come on!" Gordon says.

"You're making this up," Victor says. "Well, what happened? Why did you go to Mexico?"

"Well, see, that's just it. One day Mr. C. died."

Both Victor and Gordon find this remarkably funny. Victor's eyes are pulled wide open. He hoots and turns to Gordon, who is laughing into his sleeve.

"And Mrs. C. came down the steps all upset and made my brother go and check. He died in his sleep."

Gordon stops laughing. His face takes on a puzzled expression and his mouth forms a short line. "How sad," he says.

"Well, at least she had her house to herself finally," Victor says. He looks away and pushes his jaw to one side, as if considering the privileges of solitude.

"No," I say. "She said she couldn't stand to live there anymore. She sold the house so we had to leave. Oh, we could have gone to my mom's apartment and stayed there for the summer. But my father was in Mexico and my brother was fourteen and really into cars so we went to Mexico."

"Extraordinary," Victor says.

"You ever hear from Mrs. C. again?" Gordon says.

"Did you ever find your dad?" Victor says.

"I heard that Mrs. C. moved to Montgomery, Alabama, and, no, I didn't see my father."

"How did you kids pay for a trip to Mexico?"

"Just did," I say.

My brother was a rich little teenager. He sold pot in the bathrooms of a dozen different junior highs. Now he sells pot in Arizona. He's rich and he's trash. He has a wife named Sarah who rides horses and—this is despicable—they get the horses stoned, too.

"You must speak some Spanish," Gordon says and I nod.

"I never knew that," Victor says, bewildered. "I never, ever knew that."

Second round of French toast and Victor is finally hungry.

"One for me, too!" he calls.

We've consumed the whole morning talking. Victor's face has a lot more color to it and he looks . . . *happy,* happy in a way I haven't seen him before. He looks sort of, I don't know, at *home.*

I follow Gordon into the kitchen, noticing with admiration the straight, long lope of his walk. I show him where things are in the kitchen. It's a tiny kitchen, with four warped cabinets, a gas oven that is decades out of date, a fat white refrigerator with interior walls crusted with ice, an old-fashioned can opener. It shares a wall with the room with our fold-out, our desk, our window. It's narrow like a girl's shoe.

Gordon whirls the eggs into milk and soaks a slice of bread. Then he tosses it onto the griddle and lets it sizzle in butter.

"Are you still sorry I came?" he says, looking with concentration into the iron pan.

"Who says I was sorry you came?"

"Oh, come on, Hilary, I can tell." His voice is low and forceful and correct.

I say, "I'm very happy you're here. Victor *likes* you."

"Victor likes me. And I like him. And I like you."

"Why did you come here?"

"I wanted to see how you lived. I couldn't imagine how you could live with him before. I kept thinking, What's that pretty woman doing in a depressing old house with a man like that?"

"What do you think now?"

"I think we are all in trouble."

There's a sputtering sound from the frying pan and Gordon quick-flips the bread. The cooked side is spotted brown and yellow, perfect.

Gordon says, "I keep thinking about last night . . ."

"Shhh!"

He whispers, "It's like I have a movie projector in my head. I keep thinking of you."

"You still think of someone who you spent an hour with behind a boathouse in Boston."

"I married that woman," Gordon says. "I'm married to her now."

Things start to make sense. Of course he's married. Why shouldn't he be married?

"Where is she?" I say.

"She left me," Gordon says.

Then Victor comes into the kitchen.

"Look," he says, smiling. "I'm up."

And there he is, a little wobbly standing there, steadying himself against the counter. Gordon reaches for his arm but Victor ignores him. With effort he becomes linear.

He says, "Bad hangover. Mule trains, pneumatic drills, Vietnam in my head."

In Gordon's basement there is a small room with dark paneling and a single yellow light bulb. He calls this the "sea room." It has shelves of sea things. There's water skis, diving masks, flippers. Five fishing rods lean against one wall. On the far side are two life preservers, a stack of dirty orange life vests, a tackle box, a crate to keep hot things hot and cold things cold, an array of fishhooks with feathers and bobs in bright colors. Above the door is a stuffed fish, a tuna, that Gordon caught last year.

At home Victor is reading. When I left the house he made a noise like a goodbye while turning a page.

I am nervous near Gordon, but intrigued. Everything in

the sea room fascinates me like the contents of a rare museum. In a cedar case lined with velveteen is a diver's watch. The watch has a thick black strap, a brightly illuminated dial, and a bubble of sturdy glass. Surrounding the dial are marks with numbers that Gordon tries to show me how to read.

"All these numbers have a specific meaning," he says, turning the watch in his hand.

A wet suit, royal blue with a stripe of yellow, is crumpled in one corner.

"This is like a shell," I say, touching the wet suit. It feels to me like the skin of something vaguely human.

"You don't call it a shell," Gordon says.

I imagine Gordon in his wet suit, breathing in stored oxygen, battling the great curves of waves and then sinking into the cold ocean and finding peace in its blank greenness.

We go to the beach to collect clams. They are huge, the size of your hand. When the tide is out they line the beach. Sea gulls puzzle over them, picking at the open ones, the dying ones. They fly high above the waves, dropping the clams against rocks, making huge piles of broken shells. Gordon and I take only the shells that are tightly closed. We toss them into a plastic bucket.

"Here's a razor clam," Gordon says, showing me a narrow, rectangular shell. "See the hinges? I've never eaten a razor clam. Hey, did you know that kelp grows faster than any other plant life?"

We pick clam after clam. The bucket is heavy; its plastic handle bends with the weight of ten clams.

"I have some shells at home," I say.

"What, a collection? What sort of shells?"

"Not a collection. Just some shells."

Gordon bends over and takes two shells from the sand.

"This," he says, showing me a tan shell the size of a half dollar, "is a moon shell. Some time ago a moon snail wound this cone. Each one of these turns here is called a whorl."

"I have one of those at home," I say. "I just didn't know the name of it."

"There's other species that look kind of like this. There's the immaculate moon shell, for example, which is smaller and shiny white. There's spotted moon shells and lobed moon shells. I'll have to come over look at your collection sometime."

"It's not a collection. I only have a few."

"Yours are undoubtedly the most beautiful shells ever found on Hull's shores," Gordon says, teasing. He holds out his hand. "Here, have a periwinkle."

I pocket the shells and Gordon puts his arm around me. We walk against the strong wind of the ocean, stepping just outside the spray of waves. We pass more shells, some of which Gordon explains to me. He tells me that snails can feed on other mollusks by drilling a hole through their prey's shell with a special tooth called a radula.

We see legs from lobsters, from crabs. A crab, nearly dead, shuffles meekly with one leg.

"This lobster claw probably belonged to a five-year-old lobster," Gordon says, showing me a thumb-sized claw.

"A now dead lobster."

"Or a one-handed lobster."

At his house we make love and this time it feels like love. In a tub of fresh water our clams spit out their sand.

At four o'clock the daylight has already crept away. We boil the clams in a large pot and watch them open like blossoming flowers. We carve them out of their shells and chop them finely. We soak them in spices and lemon.

Later, again in bed, we eat the chowder we have made.

Gordon and I go walking amid crunching snow. Inside my boots, I've wrapped my feet in plastic bags to keep them dry. Gordon's hands are shoved deeply into his pockets and he has his ski cap pulled close to his eyes. His boots are high, pushing his jeans up so that they bag at the knee. Our breath comes from us in short bursts of fog.

We cross two mounds of park land, two glacial drumlins connected by a thin strip of pathway over the bay. We are surrounded by water; we can see the narrow peninsula of Hull and the ocean beyond. There are pine trees and bear oak and dirt paths that cross over and around the hills. Gordon has a long stick he walks with. He taps it against the toe of his boot and sometimes he lets it drag behind him in the snow. He explains about types of oak, the difference between black oak and white. He talks about scrub oak that can produce acorns at a younger age. He talks about the unique vegetation of seacoast areas, about the marshlands farther inland, the effects of hurricanes.

"Hull was founded in 1644 but the Indians had it even earlier. They called it Natascot," Gordon says. "Isn't it weird to think that there used to be Indians here and now there aren't? That this whole area was called Natascot and now it's Hull. I couldn't even think about calling it anything else."

I imagine Hull with no houses, no roads at all. Just endless ocean, pitch pine, a vast expanse of white sand. I think about something Victor told me, that despite whatever they're saying about the greenhouse effect, sea-water temperatures might be lowering again and, maybe in only a few more centuries, the planet will begin experiencing another ice age.

"I make a connection with a place I live and there's no way to change it," Gordon says. "My wife felt so awful about our separation, she offered to give me the house. But I *had* to move out. I couldn't live there. Every corner screamed her name; I'm telling you, I could smell her in the paint."

"I understand," I say. I think about how strange it seems that anyone before us could ever have lived in Victor's and my apartment, or that anyone could ever live there after we have gone. I think about an ice age that existed fifteen thousand years ago and that everything we understand as civilization is taking place during a relatively short time between glacial periods.

"Did you live in the same house the whole time you were growing up?" Gordon asks.

"No," I say. "My parents both got new places to live when they separated."

"Another example of what I'm talking about," Gordon says. "What do you think split them up, if you don't mind me asking? Sometimes I wonder how it is that people can break up after so many years, so many life experiences together."

"I had a sister once," I say. "She died when she was four. Some sort of heart disorder. I was an infant. I didn't know her. There I was sucking bottles while my parents watched their firstborn become unable to run, to walk. After she died they left her bedroom exactly the same. They didn't put away the toys or clear out the drawers or even go in there for three and a half years. When I went to nursery school they finally made it into a laundry room."

Dying Young

"That's gruesome," Gordon says.

"Oh, yeah," I say. "I'm not sad about it because I never even knew her but I'm sure it led to the eventual ending of my parents' marriage. Or rather, the way they handled it kind of ate away at their marriage until there was nothing left."

"Something like that, Hilary, it's very hard. . . ."

The earth is getting colder every year. According to Victor, the climate seven thousand years ago was warmer than today.

"They didn't even remake the bed," I tell Gordon.

"What was your sister's name?"

"Janice," I say. "It was Janice's room."

EIGHT

We're in a place called The Tavern where I've never been, downstairs in the poolroom. I'm a shark. I let Gordon and Victor make bets on who buys drinks, knock a few balls around. They're an even match, Gordon and Victor. Gordon stands over the table, his body making a forty-five-degree angle at his hips. He stays in position through the whole shot, smacks them hard, and gets a lot of rebounds. Victor's better at a side pocket. He holds his cue in a peculiar way but he pokes them in with consistency. He's got careful geometry and he tucks his chin when he shoots. I watch them until I finish a beer. Then I say, "Okay, let's get some real betting in."

I'm wearing a skirt this cold night. Real cold. Snow. Mrs. Birkle gave me a pair of boots—old-fashioned witch boots that creep just past the ankle. I went downstairs, trying to give her my little black and white television. But she wouldn't take it. She shooed it away with the back of her hand and giggled into her dress collar. She rejected the TV but insisted I take a pair of boots. To her they are just old hand-me-downs. To me they are vintage fashion.

The boots look too good to be on me.

Dying Young

I've lost some weight. I can't stand eating when Victor is dropping pound after pound. Gordon says I look fine. He says now I'm more than slim, I am svelte. I was in his shower yesterday afternoon and he said, "There's nothing better than naked you."

I take a pool stick from the rack and angle a few pretend shots. I chalk up the stick good and bait Victor with some teasing about what a great player I am.

"You want to bet some real money? Fine," Victor says. "I'll bet."

He walks over to where Gordon is sitting and finishes his beer. "Hilary thinks she's a pool queen," Victor says.

He racks them up and I make a weak break. I miss as often as I can. I want Victor to win this one easy. He stays ahead the whole time by at least five balls. He shows off, taking the harder shots so I can catch up. He does one shot with the cue behind his back. He tells me I shouldn't drink and bet.

"You got me," I say finally as the eight ball drops into a corner. I let out a long sigh and say, "Let's up the stakes. Double it. I've got cash." He gives me a look like I'm crazy. When I ask if I can break he says, "It's your money."

Victor collects the balls and divides them stripes and solids. He rolls the triangle down the pool green and shakes them into place. He stretches his arms over his head, cracks his knuckles. "I thought you said you knew how to play this game?" he teases.

I wop out a doozy of a break, sending two balls in. I'm stripes, with a table full of shots. I slice a thin one into the corner, sending the cue ball around the table to catch a couple straight shots at the corner. Victor's balls are nested in a

clump and mine move with delicate precision into the corner
and side pockets. It's six balls before I miss. Then Victor cops
one. Then me. Gordon drinks beer and watches with a curious
expression. He's pleased at every shot I make. He smiles a
little when Victor misshoots and grazes a number thirteen—
my ball—sending it directly into the corner pocket. I'm mer-
ciless. I want to win. I want to show off for Gordon. I take
Victor two games in a row. A slaughter. An embarrassing
skunk.

We go upstairs. There's a country band doing a slow
Hank Williams number. Victor turns to me, elbows bent, open
palms. I lean into him and dance with my head on his shoulder, eyes closed. He squeezes me hard and sways his hips. We
dance closer and closer to the band, right next to the speakers
so I can feel it against my neck. The music is so loud the
floor seems to vibrate with it. Victor kisses my ear. He says,
"You shyster. You tactician."

$\mathcal{V}$ictor finds a group of video machines and asks which of
them are Gordon's. Gordon points to one called Space Cham-
pionship Wrestling in which the player has to wrestle an alien
version of Hulk Hogan. "It's a dumb game," Gordon tells him.
"Don't play." But Victor insists and spends forty minutes popping quarters.

Gordon's sitting on a bar stool emptying a beer into a
tall, iced mug. He gets it too high in the glass so the head of
the beer curls over the edge. He slices the foam with a finger
and licks it clean. He says, "Dance with me."

The band does oldies, but it is eclectic. They've got a
guy who strums the country tunes and a girl singer, maybe

nineteen, in a slinky tube dress and eyes the size of dominoes doing Grace Slick and Marianne Faithfull. She belts out "White Rabbit" in a fierce, growling voice. Gordon and I position ourselves in the middle of the floor, making room for ourselves amidst the many couples. We start dancing in awkward steps, not sure how close to hold each other.

He says, "Now, if I hadn't ever made love to you, if we were, say, on a first date and there were no Victor, how would I be dancing now? Would I be this far from you, or this? Would I have my hands on your hips or on your shoulders?"

"Shoulders," I say.

"Oh, yeah. I guess I would." Gordon smiles. He moves his hands. He looks up at the ceiling and makes an exaggerated sway to the left. He says, "I would be afraid of offending you. I would be anxious about what you were thinking of me. I would be less drunk, more cautious . . . eager to please."

"You don't have to come out with us if it upsets you," I tell him. But secretly I am grateful. Never, *never* have I seen Victor more willing to be happy than he has been these past five or so days that Gordon has been part of things. They sat up last night playing cards. Victor bought a box of cigars with a label from the Dominican Republic and they filled the room with the damp smell of cigar smoke. Gordon wore a baseball cap turned backward on his head. Around three in the morning they moved the game to the kitchen so that I could go to sleep. Toward dawn, when I got up to go to the bathroom, they were still at it. The coffeepot steamed on the stove top. An enormous pile of chips lay across Victor's end of the table.

"Who's upset?" Gordon says. "I'm just telling you about what I wouldn't do if we were on a first date."

He turns me sharply and digs his chin in close to my

neck. "I would not, for example, pull you up against me like this and sneak a feel of your nipple."

"Gordon!" I look up at his grinning, sly face. He stares over the top of my head, smiling.

"Don't worry," Gordon says. "We're hidden by the crowd."

"I don't want to dance anymore," I say and stand away from him.

"Ahh, Hils, I'm sorry . . ." he begins.

"No, it isn't that." I look across the room to Victor, who is bent over the video game. The bar is done in heavy paneling with red velveteen chair cushions and carpeting. The lighting is so dim Victor is only a shadow. "I just don't like the song," I say.

I tell Victor I am going for a haircut. He sits in his chair, a book resting on his knee, and reads with a frown. He is wearing a pink and white striped shirt that billows over his shallow stomach and brings out the scarlet in his cheeks. His fever paints him rosy. His disease lies.

"Did you hear me?" I say. "I'm going out."

"What?" he says without looking up.

Sometimes I think that books are for Victor what teething rings are for babies. I can remember many months ago, when he had more energy, I would doze off after our lovemaking while Victor switched on a reading lamp.

"I'm going to get my hair cut."

He nods.

"Want to come?" I ask, but Victor shakes his head.

He says, "While you are out can you pick up a few things

for me? Carrot juice, celery, kelp pills, seaweed"—he looks into his book—"and liver."

I sit on the floor and lace my boots all the way up, tuck in my pants. The long underwear beneath my jeans makes my legs feel clumsy and stiff. Twisting my hair into a wool cap, I wish silently for spring.

"And brown rice, too," he adds, raising his finger.

"What do you want all that for?"

"New diet. This is one of those natural health books. I am devising my own cure for cancer." Victor looks a little embarrassed. He turns to me, explaining, "They say the success rate is highest for patients under forty. That makes me a sure winner."

"Let me see that," I say. I take the book from him and read the table of contents. Chapter One: Understanding Cancer Cells. Chapter Two: The Chemical Properties of Cell Reproduction. Chapter Three: Slowing Cell Growth. Chapter Four: The Diet. Chapter Five: Thinking Health. Chapter Six: Taking Control of Your Disease. The title of the book is *Thinking Your Way Out of Terminal Illness*. It is authored by two doctors. They claim that their book has helped thousands of people. The photograph on the back cover shows them smiling in their lab coats, glossy and optimistic like two people together at a wedding. As if cancer patients and cancer deaths had never touched their jeweled lives.

The first two months I was with Victor, I had to dissolve huge vitamin pills in his soup so he wouldn't know he was taking them. Now he reads health books. He wants seaweed.

"Where'd you get this book?" I ask.

"Gordon gave it to me."

"Gordon?"

"Yeah. He called yesterday and said he had a book for me so I said, 'Bring it over,' and he did."

"How long did he stay?" I ask.

"I don't know. A couple minutes. He just dropped off the book."

"And that's what you talked about? The book?"

"We didn't talk. He popped in, had a look around, gave me the book, and left. He had the dog with him and didn't want to leave her in the car. He asked about you and I told him you were taking a bunch of skirts to the dry cleaners. Isn't that where you were?"

On my way into town I think about Gordon giving Victor that book. It is hard to believe Gordon would find a book like that at all credible. Of course, it is like Gordon to uncover the optimistic in even the most hopeless of circumstances. But for Victor to place any faith in such a book is more than bizarre. I don't think I've seen Victor read a book that was still in print, let alone something like *Thinking Your Way Out of Terminal Illness*. He must be feeling very sick, that's all.

Gordon gave Victor a book. Now they are friends enough for that, for book-giving. Gordon has been fixing the roof on his house. Every day we can hear his hammer pounding if we listen for it by our window. Victor told me he'd always wanted to have a house, to learn how to repair it. He said he likes to hear Gordon's hammer. It's so steady, it sounds like a heartbeat.

Of the list Victor gave me I find liver, celery, carrot juice, and a bottle of kelp pills at the pharmacy. I cannot find any seaweed. I go to many different stores, asking cashiers and managers where I can buy seaweed. Hull is surrounded on three sides by beach but one cannot buy seaweed here. I get superstitious for Victor. I imagine that everything in his new cure book is totally useless except the one remedy, the seaweed that I cannot find. I imagine that the seaweed is the catalyst that triggers the proper mixing of chemicals to combat cancer, that without it the cancer-fighting properties of carrot juice, liver, and kelp remain dormant and useless. I fret, go to more stores, but remain defeated. The back seat of my car fills with grocery bags, none of which contain seaweed. My parka pockets are stuffed with cans I have shoplifted: baby shrimps, caviar, kippers, tiny mushrooms in clear jars. I might not have stolen them except that I ran low on money and did not want to stop long enough to go to the bank. I bought a cheesecake for Victor, cashews, and peanut butter. I bought him Encare, A *"De-Licious Milk Shake with over 1,000 Calories"* that comes in purple cans. I bought him chocolate.

I go to a men's barber shop. It's cheap and they do a good job. I sit in the broad cushion of the barber's chair. The man with the scissors also owns the place. He makes a comment about not usually having young women customers. He picks my hair up in bunches and lets it fall against my shoulders. I've told him to bob it four inches above the shoulder, at the place where my backbone meets my skull. I hear the quick whisper of scissors behind my neck. I feel the barber's fat thumbs behind my ear, at the corner of my jaw, against my scalp. My hair tumbles to the floor, clumps of honey brown and blond. Against the tile, it looks foreign, like somebody else's hair. I think of it being swept up later, a nest of brown in the dustpan. I think of it mixing with other people's hair. I imagine green trash bags, ballooned with hair. Hair in the garbage truck, the smell of hair burning in a dump pile. I imagine my scalp: a perfect, smooth eggshell.

The barber sprays on water to get a more even cut. He combs out the wet strands. He takes his scissors and touches them quickly all over my head. His scissors are like a hummingbird, they move so fast.

I imagine piles of mannequins with no hair; chalked outlines of people's shapes on sidewalks, their heads a smooth white line.

"Don't move," the barber tells me. His accent is from somewhere else. With effort, I keep perfectly still, balancing my head exactly between my shoulders. I wince with every scissor sound. The scissors are just above my eye. I remain still. The barber's fingers are flat against my forehead. He scowls in concentration. He props my chin up with his thumb. He takes away the scissors and rolls my head forward, backward, from side to side.

At last, he is finished with me.

I need Gordon. I need him so I go to him. I drive my car through town, pressing into a low gear to climb the hills. When I am within several blocks, I roll down the window and listen for his hammer. But there is no hammer. Today, there is a saw. It buzzes through the air, protesting as it is pressed to wood. It sings all over Hull. I listen to it, my window down and the air chilling my face, sweeping back my freshly cut hair. My hair smells of perfumes, blunt cut, like mown grass.

Free from the weight of its former length, the curl ripples through in waves.

When I reach the driveway, Gordon's saw gives one long wail and is silent. He balances its metal body against a pile of wood. His smile is like a ticket home.

This has been how long now? The days fall away, marked by visits to Gordon. There is Gordon, and there is absence of Gordon. Tuesday, no Gordon. Wednesday, Gordon over for dinner, Victor and he on either end of the couch, like two dolls. Thursday, Gordon under a quilt with me. We scrambled together, wrestling. We made lunch together. We made love. Today, a Friday, makes the second complete week.

Already things are different for us. Already there is change.

Gordon waits until we are inside. Then he kisses me. He stands in front of me and examines me as if I were his own reflection. He undoes the first four buttons on my blouse and puts his hand inside. He runs his fingers over my breasts, my collarbone, my neck. He gives my hair a tug. He cocks his head and raises an eyebrow.

"I cut it," I say.

He pushes my shirt off one shoulder, then the other. He moves back a foot and takes a look. His eyes wander over me. He looks at my stomach, my breasts, my face. As if I were a painting.

You can't see the ocean from Gordon's house. There's a short lawn and then a vast blanket of woods. Always there is a vague

rustle of leaves and branches, of sticks, of icicles. We wander
along the wood's narrow paths, through patches of pine needles and snow. We hold hands. The branches of pine trees are
weighted with snow, drooping. We move slowly, in heavy,
booted steps. Everything is still, frozen, set.

I am ready to hear now about his wife, about his family
in Boston, about any children that may exist. I want to hear
about them, imagine them, even care about them. I'm not
really a competitor. How could I compete, living as I do in
this uncooperative way? Devoting myself to a man whose needs
are not even his own but belong to the stranger that has
become his body?

Gordon know this. Already my life has been open to him.
Like the woods, it is full of interest and repetition. My life
hibernating with Victor.

Gordon squeezes my hand. He's watching me. Every couple of steps he glances my way. He will tell anything about
himself, every last detail is available to me if I ask for it. He
will allow me my hibernation. He will sink into my life without harm. He will be Victor's friend, if that is what is required,
and he will be mine.

All this has been agreed upon quite silently.

$\mathcal{V}$ictor looks through his window and admires the snow, made
shiny and slick by the heavy afternoon sun. He says he wants
to go tobogganing and phones Gordon, recalling his number
from memory. Gordon agrees and Victor and I layer ourselves
in socks and long underwear. Victor is excited as we drive to
Gordon's house. He turns on the radio and thumps the dash-
board to the beat of a soul station. He says he feels really

good, that his blood is stronger, almost normal. He climbs out of the car and pulls me down the walkway to Gordon's front door. When we pass the woodpile and the yellow silent saw, I feel almost as if I have already confessed, strangely relieved and also half sick. Gordon opens the door, wearing the same clothes that he had on this morning.

"Excellent! Let's go!"

Victor, then me, then Gordon, one behind the other and clinging. The toboggan is down the hill like a raft over a waterfall. We are laughing and yelling. Our faces are wet with snow.

"Watch out!" Gordon calls. Victor steers the toboggan around a sinking in the snow. Still, it sends us off balance. My stomach contracts as we lean with the skid. Our screams rise, the snow moves under us; it swells like a wave over the edge of the sled. Gordon's arm is tight around my rib cage. I am clinging with a fury to Victor. The snow is huge and blinding and flying. Then we are straight again, sleek and fast. We curve to the right, over a small hill that we hadn't realized was a hill until we were right upon it.

I feel my voice rising inside of me as we fly over the hill. The sled seems out of control. Victor swerves to the left, then the right. My face is showered with snow.

"Don't worry!" Victor yells. The toboggan gains speed. "I'm a toboggan genius!"

Then finally we start to slow. Everything is quiet. I listen to the smooth hum of waxed wood over snow. The pine trees, the bushes, the stone fence that marks the field, all in focus.

. . .

At Cappy's we sit at a table beneath a framed map of the eastern seaboard that shows the water depths from Florida to Maine. The fireplace is near us and the flame roars and spits as we drink hot rum toddies. Well, Gordon and I drink hot rum toddies. Victor has grapefruit juice. When Cappy served us, he looked at Victor's juice and scowled at it as if it were cod liver oil before putting the glass on the table.

Victor unlaces his boots and pushes them under the table. He rubs his feet and leans back, eyes shut.

"That was good," he says. "I don't remember the last time I went tobogganing."

"Me either," I say.

"Do you realize that it must have been twenty years since I've done that?" Victor says.

"Is that how long? Twenty?" says Gordon.

"I can't believe it. For twenty years I've been missing out. Every winter I kind of thought I was missing something, you know? But I never knew what."

We talk like that for a while. Gordon tells about when he got lost hiking in the White Mountains in New Hampshire. Victor says he took a former girlfriend to Nepal and hiked for days in various depths of snow. He describes the taverns with their small rooms that you could rent for fifty cents a night, the huge plates of steaming rice. He does an imitation of an old Indian woman who cut a lock of his hair because she wanted to keep its fine redness in a glass jar by her window.

We order another round of drinks. Cappy brings them over and sits with us. He is wearing blue pants, a white

T-shirt with a V neck, and an apron with a splotch of something yellow across the bib. He must have been cooking. His face is beaded with sweat. The man is a human furnace. I wonder what Cappy does in the summertime when the weather is hot. How does he survive? Then I remember that he gives the pub over to his son in the summer and goes to the beach. I imagine him flat on his back, his belly like a balloon rising, threatening to lift him over the beach, over the waves that crash beside him, delivering him into the sky, up to the sun. Cappy as a spaceship. Cappy orbiting the planet.

"What's the matter with you, Vic?" Cappy says. "You look like hell and you're not drinking. What are you, sick?"

"No," Victor says. "I'm getting better. I *was* sick. I was very sick."

Victor laughs. I look at Gordon, who is looking at Victor. So I look at Victor, too.

"What was wrong with you?" Cappy says.

"I'm telling you. I was sick," Victor says. He sips his juice. "I had this horrible disease that was going to kill me. I was a goner."

"Well, what happened?" Cappy says. "What made you better?'

"It was this," Victor says and points into his glass. "It was juice that made me better. I owe my life to the grapefruit."

"Wise guy," Cappy says. "When are we gonna talk about the war again? I've been reading about Nazis. I read a book about how the U.S. knew where the death camps were and wouldn't bomb the railway tracks."

"Is that true?" I ask.

"Says so in the book," Cappy says.

"Yes, it's true," Victor says. "We didn't want to save the Jews. Well, that's not right. Our politicians didn't want to save them. World authority didn't want to save them."

"Oh, come on," Gordon says. "I don't believe that."

"You don't believe it?" Victor says, his eyebrows raised. "Which part don't you believe? That the government was aware of genocide or that the government was unconcerned? "

"The second," Gordon says.

"No wonder you are so happy," Victor says and taps Gordon's glass with his own. "No wonder you're so fun to be with."

$\mathcal{V}$ictor puts on Bach and says he's going to rest. I tell him that's a good idea; Gordon and I will cook dinner. I make fettucini while Gordon sautées mushrooms and stir-fries broccoli with ginger. We pretend we're gourmet chefs and talk with French accents. We tease each other and dodge spatters of hot oil. We anticipate our feast with tastes of everything. We have blueberries and chocolate. We have dinner candles and wine. I bring out the pasta, a mound of steaming white. Gordon follows me with the vegetables and sauce. Victor is too tired to eat. He lies on the bed, face down, fully clothed. I take a plate over to him but he shakes his head. I return the extra plate to the kitchen, where it waits and grows cold.

I say, "Victor, can I do something for you?"

He groans and says, "Just eat your dinner."

Gordon and I sit at the table, in front of plates of too much food. I blow out the candles and switch on a small lamp. We try to eat but we both watch Victor. Gordon rises from the table and goes to take Victor's shoes off. I roll pasta over my fork and then set the fork down. Gordon looks at me and then at Victor. We get up and go to the bed. I kneel on the mattress and, gently, I turn Victor over. He mumbles something; his hand brushes my shoulder. Victor is so thin that turning him is effortless. The way his pelvis sticks out makes me think of a young girl's.

I look at Gordon and suddenly feel pornographic.

Gordon steadies Victor and I gather the bottom of his sweater and then pull it over his head. We unbutton Victor's shirt. I hesitate, feeling shy about Victor's naked body in front of Gordon—as though it is me he is undressing or some part of me that he had not yet seen. After a long moment I look down at Victor and then, quickly, as if suddenly in a hurry, I unclasp his belt. Gordon unbuckles his watch. I unzip his jeans; Gordon rolls off his socks. I drop his pants onto a chair. Gordon lifts him like a child as I turn the blankets down.

A gray day, a Saturday. The church bells are chiming; deep, lingering notes.

Victor is in bed, not reading, not sleeping. "Someone is getting married," he says.

NINE

*G*ordon's bathroom is a veritable pharmacy. There are hundreds of prescription bottles, half full with tiny tablets and capsules in pastel colors, like yellow and lime and pink. He invited me over for the sole purpose of this cabinet and these bottles with all their possibilities. This, because Victor's been hurting more lately. Every day, handfuls of aspirin.

Gordon is helping me decide which ones to take. He uses the toilet seat as a chair.

"Metolazone?" I say.

He shakes his head. "For Mother's blood pressure." he says.

"Aldomet?"

"Father's blood pressure."

"Hydrodiuril?"

"Also Father's."

"Clonidine?"

"Menopause," he says. "Mother's."

"What are these white ones here?" I say, holding out a fat jar of chalky pills.

"Those are good," Gordon says, nodding. "Back-pain medicine. I used to snort it when I was a teenager."

"How strong is it?"

"Made my nose bleed," he laughs. "When my mom found out what I was doing she threatened to have me sent to a drug rehab center."

I pocket the pills and hold out another bottle. "What about this? Mellaril," I say, showing him.

"Most definitely." Gordon says. "My wife's antidepressants. Take both bottles of that."

In fetal position I wake, surrounded by empty bed. No Victor. I bolt upright, sending the sheets flying. The window is open. Freezing air. Two space heaters burn full tilt, but to no effect.

I catch my little toe against a table. I stampede the kitchen looking for Victor. I hurl the bathroom door against tile. I open the front door and look down the empty staircase. Re-entering the apartment, I approach the window with dread and anticipation. I cringe at the thought but force myself to look for him on the ground below. My eyes tear up from the wind. Two dogs, both black, jog the beach, stopping occasionally to pee on kelp. I hear a sound behind me and pull my head inside.

Victor shuts the door and tugs at the fingers of his gloves. Pinned under one arm is a newspaper.

"Damn you," I say to Victor. The wind flies through my hair, whipping it across my neck. Victor walks to where I am and closes the window.

"I burned the toast," he says.

. . .

I'm arranging my seashells along the edge of the sink. I wonder if shells age and grow brittle. I wonder if they change color or get thinner with time. I take a magnifying glass and look closely at a gray-toned scallop. Victor walks in, digs under the sink, and comes out with a patch of felt and some sort of cleaning liquid in his hand.

"I'm polishing the gun," Victor says.

"Does that mean you're going to be shooting?" I say, squinting through glass. The shell is full of colors. The edges are dark like a fishtail and the center is lilac-gray with a cloud of pearl. "Because if you're going to shoot I'm going to do my ears a favor and go somewhere else."

"No, just oiling and cleaning," Victor says. I move my magnifying glass over the line of shells on the counter. At the outer edge of the glass I spot an ant, a little red one, dead on its back with stiff, hinged legs curled into the air. Beneath my magnifying glass its pincered mouth looks dangerous and large.

"What are you looking at?" Victor asks. I move away from the ant.

"Nothing," I say. I gather my shells together, putting them back in the Kleenex box where I keep them.

"Honey, don't," Victor says, touching my hand. Across his chest is the gun's long barrel. "I was just asking."

He takes me into the other room and sits on the couch. He pulls me down next to him and then kisses me full on the mouth. He cups a palm beneath my chin and we kiss a long time.

"You know the golden era of the shotgun is really over,"

Victor says after a while. "During the late 1800s and early 1900s things were better. Seasons were longer, bag limits higher. But nowadays there isn't much point in an old double barrel like mine."

"What are you saying?"

"That I ought to get rid of the gun."

"What are you going to do?" I ask. "Put it to sleep?"

"I thought we could dig a hole for it out where the rats make their rancid little nest and just kind of bury it. It'll be a private affair. You, me, the rodents," Victor says. He looks down at his hands. The hand he cut weeks ago has healed now, leaving a wide scar the shape of a half-moon.

"Bullets, too?" I say and Victor nods.

Outside the morning sun is blinding against the snow. Victor digs into the ground with the edge of a rusted shovel. I slam at the dirt with a hoe, pulling clumps of dark soil, unearthing rocks. The snow has made the topsoil soft but hacking a few inches under is hard work. Besides, the wind is going at a pace that makes me thankful for things like goose down and long johns.

"It's freezing out here!" I yell over the wind. Winters in Hull are always windy, I've learned. Some months the peninsula is either dead calm or high winds with no in between. And you can go from falling tree branches to tranquil, foggy air within hours.

"You think *this* is cold," Victor says. "Scientists in the Antarctic work in temperatures fifty degrees below zero. One breath taken through the mouth can crystallize the lungs. Laughing is to be strictly avoided. So next time you're complaining about the cold, think of how people in the Antarctic feel."

I look at Victor. He's caging a smile behind his serious mouth. He lays the gun into the trench we've dug and packs it with dirt.

"Is the gun very valuable?" I ask.

"It's a collector's item," Victor says.

"Maybe we shouldn't have buried it?" I say.

"The gun made you anxious, right?" he says.

I look at the long line of dirt and think if anyone ever found the old Remington they could never figure out how it came to be buried in the backyard of a broken-down house. I nod and tell Victor that it bothered me some, yes.

"Then no more gun," Victor says, kicking the gun grave with his toe.

I study Victor's expression, his round eyes, his half grin. He has a scarf wound around his neck and a deer-hunting cap pulled low on his brow. He is moving toward me in slow motion, wrapping his arms around my shoulders, resting his lips against my forehead. There is only the loud howl of wind and Victor's soft breath. Victor is holding me, maybe thinking nothing, or maybe worried that I might leave him.

I wait in my car for twenty minutes and still Gordon hasn't arrived. I look over the dock, over the green water of the bay. It has frozen toward the shore in broken blocks of salt water. A crane rests next to a line of boats that have been pulled up on the shore. Its clamped jaws are like those of a sleeping animal.

I listen to a radio talk show in which people call and

give their opinion on UFO sightings. One man says he's seen a UFO, the same UFO, several times. A woman calls, claiming she's heard aliens in her brain. Some clown phones in and says he's the alien in question and would like to be released from the inside of this woman's mind. Another guy calls and says if we don't clean up the air we will have to construct a dome over the entire earth and no aliens will be able to land. The woman with the alien in her brain says that's a good thing. I turn off the radio and sit in silence, glancing occasionally through my rear-view mirror for a glimpse of Gordon's car.

Finally I see him in the distance, making turns down the hillside and into the dockyard's gravel parking lot. He's full of apologies as I get in his car. I tell him I didn't mind waiting. I tell him about the talk show and about the guy who made fun of the lady with the alien in her head. I tell him sometimes all I want to do is watch the swirls of ice in the bay or look out over the high, dark waves of the winter sea. All I want to do is sit by myself for a while.

Gordon kisses me and drops a tape into the cassette player. "First we feed the pet. Then we'll get on the road," he says as the high whine of a violin fills the car.

Tosh is a smart dog; she knows we are talking about her. I hear the thump-thump of her heavy tail against the seat cushion. I crawl over the seat and sit in back with her, talking to her, rubbing the soft hair beneath her jaw. I say, "Well, how are we today, Miss Tosh?" and she puts her front paws in my lap and reaches to lick my face.

We go to Gordon's house and I admire the job he's done laying tile in the kitchen. The tile, a sort of creamy beige, has been fitted perfectly across several feet of counter top. I'm impressed by the work. It requires exactly the sort of patience and precision of which I am incapable. Gordon explains that he still has to put on the glaze to make it shiny and easier to clean. He also says he wonders why he spends so much time on a house which is not his, but his parents', who never saw anything wrong with the old counter top, or the front door lock, or the downstairs bathroom sink, all of which Gordon replaced. They were actually angry when they heard he'd trimmed the long beard of ivy that reaches skyward from the chimney base. But Gordon says he doesn't worry about them. He knows what improvements the house needs. Probably his parents won't even notice a difference when they return in the summer.

In the living room, propped up on the coffee table, is Mrs. Birkle's color TV. I made Gordon take it from the hallway and he promised he'd work on it.

Gordon calls me to the kitchen. He spoons dog food into a gray bowl. He smiles and nods at the large windows that overlook the woods. Outside, two bluejays chase each other.

"Such a fuss," Gordon says.

We feed Tosh, who is grateful but who gives us a deceived stare as we're leaving. I look at the living room's bay windows as we pull from the driveway and see Tosh's face pushed through the curtains.

It's a long drive through the south shore; we are going to buy a Christmas tree. I unlace my shoes and put my feet directly beneath the heater. Then I settle back and look at Gordon, whose tall head nearly grazes the top of the car. Gordon's hair, grown slightly long, sweeps back from a cowlick on his forehead and falls to one side in a casual, tremendous way.

The Christmas tree farm is the same one Cappy told me about over a month ago. Cappy has to be down there today to pick up some machinery for his pub, and we agreed I'd meet him. He's going to take the tree back for me in his truck.

Gordon said he wanted to go. He said meet him by the docks, which meant he didn't want Victor to come, not that there's been any trouble with Victor. But I think Gordon wanted an excuse to spend the day with me alone, away from Victor, who is usually the most prominent and vocal member of our threesome.

And I suspect Gordon has something he wants to tell me—which, in fact, turns out to be the case. He begins by switching off the tape player. He begins with a sigh.

"Okay, Freddie is an artist. A sculptor. I met her at a show."

I picture his wife, Freddie. In my mind she wears an ivory-colored coat, swooping calf-length. She wears a ruby pin and the latest in ethnic jewelry: a long Mexican necklace, made from iguana claws

"She works in clay. She does these little clay *things*," Gordon says. "She's over a foot shorter than me. She never liked to hold my hand when we walked because she said it made her feel even shorter."

I picture white clay sculptures with round embryonic shapes and Freddie over them. Freddie with little bones, tiny hips, feet that are pumiced, painted, and small. I picture Gordon and Freddie walking Tosh on a spring night.

"What color hair?" I say.

"I guess you'd say brown, but with red, too," tells Gordon.

I see a blossoming bush of mahogany. I see a delicate white neck and sunglasses in tortoiseshell.

"We had a place—Somerville. It was one side of a Federal house."

I imagine a living room converted into a huge studio. Inside, Freddie wears one of Gordon's pajama tops, a pair of black stockings, and ankle socks that glitter. She kneels beside a glass table, her work spread out before her. Her hands are wet in clay.

Gordon admits, when I prod him, to a rivalry with Freddie's sculptures.

He says, "She had them sprawled over the floor, drying on newspaper and torn grocery bags, on sheets that were not old yet. On my shirts. I don't know why, but it used to be that all that bothered me."

Freddie has freckles and he promised to marry her one Independence Day as she cleaned the splinters from his knees.

"I have a daughter named Raleigh. Not really mine," he tells me. We curve around a tree branch that has fallen in the road. It has rested there so long that snow cozies around it, leaving bare roadway beneath.

I imagine Freddie shaping an elephant, a bear, a collection of ducks, and a tall giraffe with an elegant neck. I see her tiptoeing past the sleeping child's crib, adorning a table with these, her new sculptures.

"Here's a picture," Gordon says and flips his wallet my way. Beneath frosted plastic Raleigh beams at me. Thick black hair and dark, high-arching eyebrows. She's got her teeth and extra chin fat and a pale dress with puffy sleeves.

"I came home one afternoon and there he was. Raleigh's father. Also an artist. I've seen him at the shows. He does massive paintings. He gave one to Freddie and I didn't even think about it. It hung over the fireplace for five months and I never knew. So there he is in my living room and I say, 'What are you doing here?' He says he's picking up some of Freddie's sculptures for a show. I say, 'How'd you get a house key?' and he stares with surprise into his palm as if the key had been put there by ice fairies. Then Freddie came in, carrying a bottle of wine."

I picture her so pretty, a rainbow of a woman in a rose-colored dress, smelling of apricot soap, her hair swinging cleanly at her shoulders. In the doorway, the bottle of wine rolls from her hands.

"So you left her?"

"No. I made a lot of money on Alien Turf, joined a hiking club, learned to cook Szechuan style, walked for hunger."

"So things were okay?" I say.

"I don't know. We had all the trappings of a normal life. Freddie sculpted like before. I took the baby on strolls through the park. I had a lot of money all of a sudden so I did, you know, dad stuff. But no, it didn't work out. I got a lover. She got a lover. A new guy, a doctor named Bert. I got another lover. She moved in with Bert. Bert has this enormous mouth," Gordon says. "He looks like a Great Dane with that mouth."

When I ask, he says he misses his daughter, whom he considers his daughter despite her biology, most of all.

We pass neighborhood after neighborhood of large estates with Dutch doors and perfectly shoveled flagstone walkways. I wonder what Gordon's house in Somerville looks like and picture Gordon and a dark-haired child shaping the round head of a snowman. In my daydream, the child bounces at Gordon's knees, asking to be picked up, and Gordon lifts her high into the air, balancing her chest against his broad, flat hands. Raleigh is way above him, laughing, flashing her dark eyes. But then she's lifted from him by some invisible force, some law of nature that pulls her away. And she drifts backward through the treetops toward a lavender horizon, soundlessly screaming and reaching for Gordon, who remains hopelessly grounded next to the frozen snowman, watching his daughter's agonized face.

"Here's an imitation of Bert," I say to Gordon. I have my back against the door and my bare feet in Gordon's lap. I pull at either end of my mouth with two fingers.

We pass a cider stand, a horse farm, a water treatment plant.

At the town center we drive beneath ribbons of Christmas lights. In the pharmacy window twin candy canes rock according to the rhythm of a metronome. Hanging from a street lamp, an ornamental Santa shakes in the wind.

Out of nowhere, Gordon says, "I bet you wouldn't love Victor so much if he were healthy."

"I don't think you'd be so friendly toward him if he were healthy," I defend.

"I wouldn't *have* to be so goddamned friendly!"

"Oh, quit," I say, turning away. The sun casts its last efforts against a mackerel sky.

"Sorry," Gordon says after a while. He pulls over to the side of the road and yanks up the emergency brake. He turns toward me, hands wild around his face. "I honestly like the guy, you know that? I want to speak openly to him, to comfort him, to help him get through what just has to be torture for him. But when I get into a conversation with Victor, all I can do is make jokes and talk around his questions."

Gordon lays his arms and head against the steering wheel. I toss his hair with my fingers. I switch on the hazard lights and wait. He reaches over and pulls me to him, his grip hard around my back.

"Am I no longer human or is there some reason to think that what we are doing is okay?" Gordon whispers into my neck.

I'm puzzled and suddenly very likely to cry. I want to cry over our wretched and complicated lives, how unbearable it is to be at an age when every horror—even death—can be soothed by something sexual. I want to pull Raleigh from the sky and place her in Gordon's arms, for him to see and hold on to. I want to declare that no, we are not doing anything wrong. How could we know how to act with everything running by us like spilled oil, making our every frantic step a useless repetition? For many weeks I haven't felt human at all, but like a ghost. We are all three ghosts, running between our houses, forging a place for ourselves but all the time living quite against the grain of a world made fantastic by our lies.

. . .

When we turn off the main drag the road gets worse. We pass several county trucks that have partitioned a portion of the road with blinking lights. They are clearing some tree branches and a bank of ice that has fallen. A mile up is a wooden sign that says "Breathstone Farm." Tacked against the wood is a cardboard square with "Live Trees" stenciled in Magic Marker. The gravel driveway is rifled through with potholes and deeply entrenched tire tracks. It's been raining and the snow has melted into dirty mud. Gordon's car tosses over the long drive.

We park in front of a high pile of snow and mulch that, mixed together like that, has the appearance of an enormous scoop of chocolate chip ice cream. The parking lot—if you can call it that—is slick with mud and flooded with puddles. It has a few trucks and a golden Mercedes with a wreath strapped to its front grille. The Mercedes has mud splattered in circles over each tire. Next to the Mercedes is Cappy's pickup with an explosion of dried mud across the door.

There's a shoveled walkway leading from the parking lot. We head toward a red and white striped tent and a string of white lights marking a square field of trees. The field is lit with floodlights. The snow shines especially bright against the contrasting green. Beyond are hills, crowded with pines. The air is deeply scented with Christmas.

The walkway is slick, the ground made soft with the weight of many customers. Gordon's duck boots are good enough for this sort of terrain but I'm feeling rather stupid in sneakers. They sink, nearly coming off every step. I have to sort of slide forward, like a kid on ice skates for the first time, and am relieved when we finally reach the tent.

The tent opens wide as a garage and inside a large, bearded man sits at a picnic table and bites the end of a pipe. The pipe smoke lingers in the air above his head. The man gives us a captain's salute and says, "You here to buy a tree?"

"Yes," I say. "We're meeting someone."

"Cappy?" he says. His hands are bark brown, lots of scars. There's a blotch of purple over a thumbnail. "He's at the barn. We got a lame horse he's looking at. I'm Walt."

Walt invites us to join him at the table. There's a heater hooked up to a generator and I warm my wet feet.

"Cappy says you're a veterinarian. Is that true?" Walt asks. His long, furrowed face gives the impression of a pilgrim. He's got steel-colored hair that is long in back and he has stiff, pilgrim lips.

"I worked for a veterinarian for years. But, no, I'm not a veterinarian," I say. I have the familiar urge to lie to him, to say I am a veterinarian. This is something I have wanted to be for years. Forever. But I don't know anything about animal medicine. I know only how to take directions from someone who does.

"You want to look at my horse? I bought him three months ago. Lame ever since."

Emerging from the field of brilliantly lit trees is a small family, undoubtedly the owners of the Mercedes, looking not like a family but like an advertisement for families. The father carries a white fir over his shoulder while his daughters touch the flapping branches and inspect the ground for pine cones. A beautiful woman with soft, enormous eyes admires the tree her husband carries. Several feet behind is a young boy, maybe thirteen, with an ax in his hand and workman's gloves stuffed in his pocket. He balances the ax against the short end of the picnic table and makes change for the Mercedes family from a wad of bills.

"Do you have ones for a five?" he asks Walt. Walt checks his billfold and counts out four crisp one-dollar bills. Then he produces a palm of shiny silver and from it the boy picks quarters. "Thanks, Dad," the boy says and then walks off with the Mercedes family. Mr. Mercedes, the father, turns and waves at Walt, who nods his head and says, "So long." Walt watches them leave, taking long puffs from his pipe.

"That man has come here three years to buy a tree. Each time he's got a new wife. I don't know why he comes here. Our trees are live, I tell him. But he always wants us to cut one down." Walt shakes his head and sends a stream of pipe smoke into the air. "You gonna have a look at my horse?"

"I really don't think I can do anything for your horse," I tell him.

"No?" Walt says and leans back. Some tobacco settles in his beard and he flicks the brown leaves from his chin with the back of two fingers.

*T*he path down to the barn is wet and extremely uneven from where horse hooves have sunk into the mud. I study the ground, maneuvering away from the deepest mud, and pick my way toward the stable.

"What happened?" Walt says. "Forget your boots?"

Dying Young

I own many shoes and the dressy boots that Mrs. Birkle gave me, but I don't own a proper pair of work boots. It shouldn't make a difference but, for whatever reasons, my inadequately dressed feet contribute to my feeling even more ridiculous for thinking I might help this man discover what's wrong with his horse's leg. Gordon makes his usual fast strides and Walt ambles along at a decent pace while I sink and swish and curl my toes, hoping that I don't pull out of the thin sneakers. Then I see Cappy, balancing through the mud.

"Hey, hey," Walt says as Cappy approaches.

"What are you doing here?" Cappy says to Gordon. He has a beer tucked in a coat pocket.

"I gave Hilary a ride," Gordon says.

"She can drive, last I heard," Cappy says. He faces Gordon and takes a swig from his beer.

"I know she can drive," Gordon says icily.

"Oh, yeah. I guess you do," Cappy says. He turns to me and says, "Where's Victor?"

"Home."

"Someone cut your horse's feet too short when they put on his shoes," Cappy says to Walt. "You got some butcher for a blacksmith. I pulled the shoes. Let the old boy stand in mud for a while and he'll be okay."

This is the sort of advice that a veterinarian can sometimes give and sometimes not. The sort of sound judgment that is administered after years of knowing. Cappy, a pub owner, is already decades beyond me in such knowledge.

Walking back to the tent, Cappy leans a heavy hand on my shoulder and bends low to my ear. "Estelle told me this morning something about Victor. Tell me it isn't true."

I slop through the mud. I yank an ankle from the mud behind me. I confirm what he has heard about Victor and watch Cappy's face grow more sour. I stare at the ground as he shakes his sad head.

J use the bathroom in Walt's house and walk a gravel road back, carrying a flashlight. The sky is sapphire. Beneath the gleam of a floodlight, I can see Cappy, Walt, and Gordon at the truck. My new Christmas tree is pitched on its side like an accident victim. At the base of its trunk is a bandage of white cloth.

The tree is so big that they have to rearrange the stuff in the truck. Gordon stands on the truck bed, pushing his shoulder into a waist-high aluminum barrel that barely budges.

"Push it on back!" Cappy yells to Gordon. The barrel begins to move, I hear the sound of metal scraping metal.

"Get down then, Gordon. Walt, give me a hand with this," I hear Cappy say.

Walt takes a pair of gloves from his pocket and pulls himself onto the truck.

"Get outta the way there, Gordon," Cappy says.

"That's okay, I can do it."

"Why don't you just come down?"

"I said, it's fine."

"I bet Victor's wondering where she is. You know, your friend Vic." Cappy says.

"Go to hell," Gordon says and vaults the edge of the truck.

Dying Young

When I enter the bright circle made by floodlights, Cappy pretends he doesn't see me and he doesn't see Gordon.

Gordon switches on the headlights and winds his way out of the drive. His face is glum and he sinks down in the car seat. I sit next to him and lean my cheek against his upper arm.

He says, "Cappy was the first person I told I was getting married. My parents were at the summer house and we called but there was no answer. So I called the pub and Cappy answered. We told him and then we told my folks."

"Does Cappy know Freddie?" I ask.

"Sure. Sure he does. Everyone knows everyone. I want to stop and have a drink. Would you mind if we stop somewhere?"

I want to say no. I want to say that I've been away from Victor for too long and that it's time to get home. But I can't say that. Not after how Cappy treated Gordon. So I say, "Yeah, let's have a drink." We take the dark roads for a few miles and then see the lights of a town center. It's Christmas, all right. Every store front is looped with colored lights. On a grassy area by a circle of small shops is a life-size Santa Claus and twelve brown reindeer. A gathering of spotlights make the shadows across Santa's face deepen and I am reminded of Walt, his grooved face and his handsome young son. I wonder what sort of personal life Walt has, whether he has a wife and, if so, whether they are happy. I just can't tell anymore with people. The Mercedes family had seemed perfect to me and, of course, that couldn't be the case. Not with three wives in three years. Walt seemed happy enough but, again, I could be wrong. If I saw Gordon and me stepping from Gordon's car, two young people holding hands beneath Christmas lights, wouldn't I think they were happy?

TEN

*I*t's late when I get back to the apartment. The moon is high and I trudge up the steps feeling tired. Then I stop and listen. There are noises from inside our apartment. As I climb the stairs I hear something being pushed along the floor, a heavy *thwack* of books falling, and the creaky sound of wooden drawers being opened to their widest.

At first I think, Okay, our apartment is being broken into. There's a burglar inside and I better turn around and get out now. I better call the police. Then I think the burglar probably has Victor up there and that he might have shot Victor or tied him to a chair. I can't leave him there—anything could happen to him. Victor's the type who would hassle a burglar. Or *burglars.* He would taunt them with snide comments or just sit with an angry, powerful expression. He wouldn't be intimidated by their guns. He'd say, "Hey, I'm a dying man. You think you scare me?"

I hear a crash and take three stairs at a time. Then I stop and go down a flight. I think, If there really are burglars in the apartment, what could I do for Victor? Then I continue up the stairs. I face our doorway, with its tiny green wreath that I hung just yesterday. The lock isn't broken. Still, I open the door half expecting three men in black leather. But there are no men. There's only Victor standing with his hands on his frail hips.

In the center of the room, at the foot of the bed, are all of our possessions. There's a mound of clutter—an umbrella, milk crates, an extension cord, stacks and stacks of books, a hair dryer, an open suitcase, newspapers. He's emptied his desk drawer into a plastic trash tub and there's a duffel bag stuffed with clothes.

"What is *happening?*" I say, but already I'm about to cry. It's clear what's happening. Victor is moving out, moving us both out. I almost don't want to hear the answer. I don't want to have to hear his words, his voice telling me he knows where I've been and that for me to have an affair . . . *to have an affair now* . . . well, how could I? He paces the room. His blue jeans look huge on him and he's trembling. I'm careful to keep my eyes on him. I watch him closely, the way a trapeze artist carefully tracks the movements of his partner. I hardly breathe for watching him.

"You have to tell me," I say, though in my mind a voice is yelling, No, Hilary, don't let him speak. Don't let it start.

Victor doesn't answer me. Instead, he ducks into the bathroom. The light is off and when I rush in I almost trip over him. He bends over the toilet bowl, heaving. His shirt has a broad run of sweat from collar to midsection and with every heave I feel his ribs rise sharply, seeming to break through the skin. I stand there, hands across Victor's wet back, feeling his body rack and stiffen. He loses strength and kneels onto the floor, one hand still gripping the sink basin.

He begins to talk, but his words are choked. He says . . . nothing. He reaches one hand behind him and grabs my ankle. The whole room smells like the farthest-down cement bottom of a subway. I'm bending over Victor, my face near his hair. When I get close enough I can smell the usual smell, the Victor smell, beneath the vomit and sweat.

"Nothing's . . . coming . . . out . . . anymore," he says. He puts his arms across the seat of the toilet and rests his head. I brush my fingers over his damp hair. Near his hairline the curls are flat against his forehead. A drop of sweat makes its way down the side of his nose.

"How long has this been happening?" I ask. I put a towel to his mouth and let him cough into it.

"Hours."

I picture Victor alone and sick all afternoon. I feel my insides have been punched out, leaving a hollow space, like a building under construction that has only its most skeletal structure. I feel like I'm a vandal; I was those three guys burglarizing the apartment; I have Victor bound to a chair, his mouth bleeding from where he's been smacked with a gun.

Then I see that Victor's mouth *is* bleeding. I position the towel so that light from the other room shows up its color. There are rust blotches. They frighten me. They are awesome and terrible like the perfect funnel of a tornado on the horizon. I wonder if I should tell Victor. Should he know that he has blood in his vomit? Then I think how frank Victor is about his disease, how really his sort of rational approach to illness is the saddest and most cynical aspect of this all. Besides, I don't have to tell him there's blood. He knows it. He must be able to taste it. He's probably wondering if he should tell me.

Dying Young

"God damn you, Hilary," Victor says. He reaches his arm and grabs a bunch of my hair, pulling me right up to his face. "You are supposed to be here for me."

I'm wild with a need to respond. I want to say everything to him, to fill him with words of comfort and soothing. I want to break myself open for him, let him see inside me, everything I have for him, all the words I can't deliver.

"You are supposed to take care of me." He speaks slowly, with effort, with deliberateness. I nod and press myself against him. It is many minutes before he has the strength to rise.

When finally he is in bed, the covers folded over his chest, he closes his eyes and I sit for a while, holding a wash-cloth against his forehead. He's calm now, his face relaxed. I think how beautiful he was the night we kissed for the first time, standing by the dock at Long Wharf. Someone had launched a toy boat, a schooner, and we watched it tackle each long wave. I think about our promises, both spoken and unspoken, and what more might have been. I wonder if we would ever have had children, for example. And then I feel strangely perverse because, in truth, I'm glad we have no children. I am glad that I don't know his parents or friends, that there will be no one to comfort when he dies. Because I don't think I can comfort one more person. Not now. Not after this.

When Victor is asleep I tread lightly into the kitchen. I'm very hungry but the only thing ready to eat in the refrigerator is some sort of complicated rice and beet salad that is part of Victor's new diet. Other vegetables, too—weird stuff, like rhu-

barb. There's half a stick of black licorice still in its wrapper.
A peeled onion, a doughnut, a hard-boiled egg in a custard
dish. I look for something very simple, something like peanut
butter. I find a jar behind the vitamins in the cabinet and have
a hard time loosening its broad lid. I pour myself a glass of
milk, drink the whole thing down, and fill the glass again. I
spread peanut butter on toast and eat quickly, standing over
the sink. I eat as if someone were going to take it away from
me or as if I am doing something wrong.

The bathroom reeks, so I clean it. I am quiet. I use only
a thin stream of water to fill the sink. Then I add ammonia. I
scrub the fixtures with a brush I find in the cabinet. I use my
nails. Everything is very old in this apartment. The toilet has
a webwork of tiny cracks at its base. They are clustered and
intricate at the bottom, like leaves of dried coral. I scrub
closely, trying to clean the blackness from these cracks. I
push harder and harder against the porcelain. I am breathless
over the toilet bowl. The ammonia is strong. The brush tumbles from my fingers and I sit down hard on the floor. I watch
bubbles of soap glide down the toilet seat.

I dry my hands on my jeans and assess the damage Victor
has done to the apartment. The bathroom is stripped—nothing
but naked white porcelain. Even the toothbrushes are gone.
But when I look at the pile of our possessions stacked on the
floor, I think, Oh, good, something to do tomorrow. I also
think that I'd kind of like to throw them all away. There is a
strange corruption in my nature that makes me feel a mild
satisfaction any time I lose something. For example, one time
an airline lost my baggage in Newark. Well, that should have
made me mad. But actually I was thinking of how free I felt,

with just a knapsack and a wallet. No other possessions at all—just me. Then they found my stuff and had a van bring it around and that was okay too.

Very little in the pile Victor made is mine. A polo shirt and a sweatshirt with the neck ripped out. A Henry James novel I never read. Some Magic Markers. I don't have many things. When you move as often as I have, you eventually lose everything you own.

I go to the pile and pull out the portable black and white television—the one I have been trying to get Mrs. Birkle to borrow and she just won't—and balance it on a milk crate so I can see it from the bed. I want to sit with Victor, who's sleeping. I can sit with him and watch TV—that's a good plan. But I don't know what I want to watch on television. I really don't know any of the shows. What I want to watch are shows that no longer exist, shows I grew up with. Simple stuff. "The Dick Van Dyke Show" would be good. Maybe there will be a special on wildlife or a late night movie. But when I turn it on it's the news and they are doing a panorama of winter scenes from all over the United States. There's a blizzard near Chicago. They show a street studded with abandoned cars. They show a quiet, perfect snowfall in Maryland countryside, the farmhouses cozy and inviting. And, of course, the contrast comes from shots of the Florida coastline where the ocean's cool waves are hundreds of sunbathers' welcome deliverance from an afternoon's heat.

Now they have a report on a parachuter from Southern California. He hooked himself up with a camera so that he could film his descent from ten thousand feet. The newscaster explains in his solid, punch-card voice that when the parachuter jumped from the plane he had forgotten to attach his parachute properly. The parachute slipped off within a few hundred yards and the man fell all those thousands of feet, still holding the camera.

As I watch the report, my stomach crumbles. The worst part is that they show the film footage, the film from the camera the parachuter held through the fall. You can see the perfect beginning, the beautiful shots of Lake Elsinore from a parachuter's perspective, shots of the other parachuters free-falling from the plane, floating in space beneath the halo of a parachute. You get a sense of the awe of drifting through the atmosphere, a different sense of space, of vision. The camera pans down to the ground, to the earth. And then there is a sudden jerking as the parachuter realizes he has no parachute. His hands wave in front of the camera; he angles it up at the people who are yelling and pointing from the black hole of the plane's open door. Then he looks at his feet. At the earth swinging lazily below. Then, mercifully, the news channel switches back to the anchor.

Victor stirs in his sleep and then mumbles something. I switch off the television and lie on the bed beside him. The smell of him is strong. I'm glad he is awakening even though I know it is good for him to rest. The film footage has scared me. I'm shaky and nervous. I press against Victor and his arm falls over me.

"I guess I have some decisions," he says into my ear. "I guess it's all really happening."

"It could be you just have a flu," I say. "Like anyone."

Victor grunts. "It isn't the first time this has happened. This is just the worst time."

Dying Young

I have the parachuter's film inside my mind and am playing it over and over. I see his desperate hands waving, the sudden blue, all the world a sky.

"It could be something you ate," I say. I speak loudly into his ear. "You don't *know*." I circle my hand over his upper arm and squeeze hard. Hard enough so it could hurt. I kiss his neck and leave my teeth against his skin a long time. I try to think of something else to say. I suddenly want him there, sitting up. I want to see his face and feel the force of him. I wish he'd pull me under him and make love to me. I want him to shout, to move around, to grab my hair like he did in the bathroom. Anything. But he is motionless. Already he is asleep again—his arm limp around my middle.

Here's the problem: I'm not at all tired. I am very alert, charged up, almost dizzy with energy. Maybe it's from the ammonia. I can't sleep and I know my pacing the apartment will only disturb Victor. I've been thinking of things to do around here that won't make noise.

I go into the kitchen and stand over the counter with a Magic Marker. I paint an orange border on the telephone message pad that we never use. I find Victor's cigarettes and smoke a bunch, trying to blow one smoke ring through another. I rip a page of advertisement from a magazine and tear the smiling face of a Maybelline woman into pieces. Then I try to puzzle her back together. I clean the mud from my sneakers and dry the rubber bottoms with a paper towel. I hear the loud rumbling of jets and go to the window. I watch them storm past, their lights forming two diamonds that fade with each mile.

I decide I'll go on a walk. I'll go to the beach and be incredibly cold and walk along the cold sand with a flashlight, looking at the long strands of dried kelp, the broken shells, the rocks that will appear at first to be crabs. I'll breathe in frozen air, exhaust myself with this.

I quickly pull on my coat, jerk the television cord from the wall, and slip out of the apartment, the television packed under my arm. I fly down the three flights of steps to Mrs. Birkle's door and then, suddenly shy, am afraid to knock. I find a pencil stub in my coat pocket and write a note on the back of a grocery receipt. I write, "Mrs. Birkle, Victor and I got a new television and don't want two of them cluttering up the apartment. Could you find a use for this one? We would appreciate it."

I put the television next to the door and go outside. It is cold, killing cold. Mrs. Birkle's bedroom light is on and I get suspicious because why would someone that old be up so late? Maybe she's sick or maybe something bad has happened. I haven't talked with her in over a week. I feel a clobbering of guilt and also an urgency to make sure Mrs. Birkle is alive.

I decide to have a look in, duck under the porch banister, and get between the house and the bushes. I edge along the wall of the house, making way too much noise, trying to keep the twigs from spearing my face. I brace my hands on the ledge and kick against the house, lifting myself up to the window.

Her bedroom is a green box with a high, narrow bed and several round hat cases stacked in a corner next to a chest of drawers. There is white, embroidered cloth covering each table, nightstand, bureau. Mrs. Birkle, in a saffron bathrobe with flower designs in blue stitching, sits on the corner of her bed, hands folded, back straight, staring into the array of photographs that form something of a pattern on the wall. Her thin neck is stretched forward and the granny-type glasses she wears sit low on her nose. Her hair falls in planks of gray and black. Toward her face it is held back with bobby pins. For as long as I can hold myself up to the window, she is perfectly still.

*T*he sea makes so much commotion. I walk just outside where the water sweeps over the sand, aloof to it but listening. I watch the abandoned shore and am able, however briefly, to believe again the folklore of a long-ago planet, an unsuspecting world without people. Far ahead and on the left is a dark mound and I think for a moment that there is a person lying dead on the sand. It turns out not to be a person but a seal, its tail hacked up by a shark's jaw. What is left of its dark body is swollen and putrid. I walk far around it. The ocean is always washing in dead things, especially in the winter when storms are bad. I've smelled fish, days dead and half buried in the sand. I've reached for what I thought was a shell and found instead the bill of a seagull. You'd think it would be nice to live by the beach, relaxing. And I suppose it is. But the beach is mostly full of fish that lost a crucial fin, beer bottles, and plastic tampon applicators that floated many miles to reach Hull's shores. I pass splintered boards from lobster traps, snags of fish netting, a short coil of broken rope.

Still, at nighttime it is quite beautiful. I am awed by everything, every speck of starlight, the white sea foam that runs against the sand, the dark curls of waves. Shadows of seagulls swoop against the sky.

The moon is high and marbled. We've sent men there and watched them come home, crashing into the sea by Nassau Bay as the world lay motionless. My birthday one year was obscured by this event, as my family piled around the television, watching the spaceship Apollo 11. I grew up around the promise of such ventures, in a world with satellites and computers. It is interesting to me that now, as we near the final stages of the twentieth century, only the blast-off of a rocket draws viewers. And this, I cynically suspect, is attractive merely for the possibility of an on-ground disaster as the great explosion sends up billows of fire clouds at the rocket's base.

But in 1969 I burrowed through cereal boxes to find the prize: glow-in-the dark stickers from an educational series on space. On my bedpost was nearly a complete collection: The Saturn V, the Eagle Lunar Excursion Module, and the Satellite Explorer. I watched them illuminate the dark like fireflies. I watched the iridescent face of my alarm clock tick off the hours and wondered where the spacemen were on their orbital adventure a hundred and six thousand nautical miles away in a place where there is no atmosphere so the stars can't even shine.

The earth, just as a satellite or rocket, makes its own slow rounds through the Milky Way. I am supposed to be learning, collecting information like the astronauts do moon rocks. I should be building something, moving forward. Instead I concentrate on Victor, on his experience, on his death. I don't think being with Victor has helped me understand anything more about death—only about Victor, who is dying.

Lately, I can barely talk to him. In the middle of a sentence his looming death will silence me. I feel my words yanked away, astronauts pulled from their spacecraft and tumbling miserably through space. Everything seems lost and larger than me. Everything foreign and unnatural, like the barren white of lunar soil.

I walk past the dockyard and envision Gordon standing aboard his sailboat, winding rope into a neat circle. I walk the pier, listening to my footsteps hollow against the gray boards. I imagine the summer crowd, their tanned limbs dangling over the sides, stoning jellyfish with clamshells, laughing into their ice cream cones. I walk to the pier's farthest point. This is dangerous, I know. The sea is overpowering. It could sweep me off this sturdy perch and cast me out like a fisherman's line. It could send me off, bobbing through the waves. For a long time I watch the blinking lighthouse and try to make sense of the blasts of light. I look for the moon's reflection against ocean's many plains. The ocean is charming, like a friend who chides you into mischief. I am standing at the corner of my life.

Finally I leave the ocean and make my way inland. I follow the bends of a sleepy street. It is sparsely lit by short yellow lamps and ice that makes the road's surface shine like many mirrors. Something races across the pavement. I think it is a cat and then see the thin wire of a rat's tail. I think about Victor's rat gun, the antique he has had forever, that he has oiled and shined. Now it is lying in the damp earth rusting. This, in my quiet way, I asked for.

At an intersection I kick up a frozen puddle and then am sorry. My feet get wet and the ice is bruising, it's so hard. Most of the houses here are abandoned for the winter, boarded and left to weather the season. The snow of many weeks lies heavy over the rooftops. What will have happened to us by the time these houses are again occupied? When the boards that blindfold the windows are dismantled to allow the salt breeze to blow past curtains, to disturb the papers on desktops? Where will we three be when the sun bakes the shore's white sand and all the woods behind Gordon's house burst green with plants, clogging the pathways and capturing the humid air between wet leaves?

When I was very young I went late one afternoon through a parkland with my best friend. We waited by a creek, pulling clay from the banks and capturing salamanders in our hands. We packed rocks and clay to make traps for fish. We tried skipping stones. Then it was dark. Our faces were no longer reflected in the water. The familiar trees that lined the pathways were no longer familiar. The sounds of the woods grew strange. We stood by the edge of the creek and decided. We decided we would hold hands and run through the darkness— never pausing. Never letting go. I remember afterward thinking that this is what is meant by loyalty. That loyalty is something that resides deep between two people, only surfacing amid struggle. The way my life is now, it's as if I am running through the woods again—this time with Victor. Except I have paused. I have let go his hand and am no longer sure of the decision. I see now that I never understood what he wanted from me. I never understood that I, too, had to allow him his decision to die.

And now I'm standing outside of Gordon's house, where I suppose I have been heading all along. Here, inside this box of rooms, is the material of my disloyalty, my lover asleep. I walk the front path, toward the light that brightens the white planks of the house's front landing. Then I step off the path, my shoes crunching over packed snow, and look through a window.

A living room. The curtain is drawn but I can see the vague pattern of furniture. I work my way to the right side of the house and try to find Gordon's bedroom window. I stand on top of an iron bridge that holds a garden hose in the summer. Inside I see a bathroom with its nightlight that glows like a match in the corner. I hop off the bridge and move farther down, pressing against the sharp branches of bushes. They make a wild sound against my parka but I can see, yes, this is Gordon's bedroom. I am staring right down at his digital clock. The numbers spell three thirty-eight. I can make out Gordon's long frame beneath a down quilt.

Gordon moves, creating a whole new set of shadows across the covers. He brings up a knee and then pushes it back. In his dream, he must be walking.

I go around the back to where the kitchen window looks onto many acres of woods. The wind wraps itself around the house and my hands are cold inside my pockets. I can't feel my face at all. It's as if I am faceless, mummified, like I have been transformed into a spirit that now haunts houses.

I stand on the tips of my toes, straining to see into the kitchen. A fluorescent light, beneath a bank of cabinets, shines through the mason jars that line the window ledge. Dishwashing soap, in a cheery yellow bottle, makes me think of spring. The window isn't locked; I could easily scurry through. And this is suddenly what I want. I want to be inside the house that Gordon lives in. I want to walk around in there.

I'm standing in the quiet of Gordon's kitchen, reading the labels of spices in a wooden rack. There are rosemary, white pepper, cloves, mustard seed. Then I hear Tosh's nails on the hallway floor and she comes in snarling like a dragon and gives one low, hollow bark. She stops at the doorway, recognizes me, and wags her tail. She ducks her head and comes creeping over, burying her face in my knees. I turn on the flashlight that I remember is stowed in my pocket. It's just a little flashlight, a disposable one, but I can see inside the pantry with it. I glide the beam over rows of soup cans, boxes of noodles, various mixes for gravies and sauces, cans of asparagus and hearts of palm. On the bottom shelf are cleaning detergents, all with the word "bright" on their labels. There's a package of blue sponges and a new mop head, still encased in plastic. Everything is so much like I imagine homes should be, so ordered, that I feel I'm inside a commercial.

Also, I feel the way I do when I steal things, though I wouldn't even take a pencil of Gordon's. It's just something about breaking the rules, some desperate inner calling that I behave toward. It's just sneaking through the living room, listening to the tinny vibration of the glass tables as I walk by them, seeing the living room as it is—not *my* living room and for the moment not anyone's. Just a place that looks like this.

I find the linen closet in the hallway. There are pillows and extra blankets and stacks of clean sheets. They are folded, box-shape, and arranged by color. I seek a hint of Gordon that the washing machine has missed. I go into the bathroom and gently pry open the medicine cabinet. I look with fascination at the short rows of deodorant, toothpaste, razors, and aspirin jars. At Gordon's parents' blood pressure medicine, at the nitroglycerin that belonged to his now dead grandmother. And then I stand outside of Gordon's bedroom. I listen for his breathing, stare hard through the darkness for the shape of him beneath the covers. I look outside his window and imagine how I must have appeared out there, my face against the glass. I *know* this is crazy. But it's like when I parked outside to watch Gordon leave his house in the morning. Just a means of grounding myself, just a way of seeing how other people live.

This type of transgression is also my escape. Living with Victor's death means being constantly responding to it. His death, always so imminent, so available, demands both of us to challenge and oblige it. The dread of death enters us like a spirit and transforms every experience. We confront it again and again, at mealtimes or while walking up staircases. And now I wonder if Victor is dreaming of it, even longing for it. An agoraphobe won't look out the window of a tall building. Even driving across a tall bridge has its own special terror. But when presented with an open window and a landscape he will stand nervously at the ledge, sweating and mumbling, feeling the pull of the horizon, and his body will lean out, risking everything.

I walk toward Gordon in quiet, spaceman's moon steps. Somehow Victor and my apartment feel too far away, somewhere I can never get back to. A car drives by, sending a moment's light across the bedcovers, flashing blocks of light against the wall.

"Hilary?" Gordon says. He pulls himself onto one elbow. "Hilary, is that you?"

"Uh-huh," I say, stepping back, timid. Tosh appears at the bedroom door and whines. Then she slouches off.

"Did something happen?" he says. He switches on the reading lamp and squints at me. There are marks across his face from the sheet. His hair tumbles into his eyes.

"Victor was sick," I say.

"Something else?"

"Sicker than usual. He vomited blood."

Gordon sits up. The blankets spill onto his lap. He props a pillow behind him and leans against it. He looks very young like this, his naked torso rising from a nest of covers. "Is there something I can do?"

I shake my head.

"Do you want to get in bed with me?"

"No."

"Hilary, why are you here?"

I don't have an answer. I shrug, feeling foolish, wishing I could slink away.

"I'm worried about you," Gordon says, leaning toward me. He puts his hand on my wrist and pulls me to him. "Get in bed with me."

"No, Gordon . . ." I begin.

"Then what are you going to do?" he says like a challenge. "Look, you go through this all the time. Just own up to the fact you love two men and get in bed. It's four in the morning. You didn't come over to talk."

"I'm going to go to Victor's father's house," I say, recalling the address to which I sent that short letter. "I know the address. It's on Commonwealth Avenue. I'm going to tell him to come get Victor, to take him to the hospital."

Gordon lets go my wrist and leans back against the pillow. "Victor won't want that," he says softly. "That is exactly what Victor is trying to avoid."

"Well, someone has to do *something*," I say. I'm shaking. My words come out in spills and stutters. "He doesn't even weigh himself anymore. He won't let me take his temperature. He makes recipes from that book you gave him and he can't eat. He sweats and shakes all night. I found him searching through the medical supplies and it was the morphine he was looking for."

"Shhh," Gordon says and pulls me onto the bed. He unzips my parka and I discover very suddenly that I'm hot. Real hot. My mouth is dry. My parka comes off and then my sweater and then I hear my shoes drop to the floor. Gordon is wrapping the covers over me. He cradles me beneath him and talks to me. He whispers, "Okay, get his dad if you think that will help."

I make Gordon promise me everything. I make him promise he won't tell Victor about us, he won't tell Victor where I went tonight or where I'm going. I make him promise to stay awake while I sleep, to get me up in an hour, to go to the apartment in the morning and make sure Victor is all right, to see that he drinks juice and salt. The last thing I remember was saying something about the dangers of dehydration, something weird about heat prostration and mountain climbing and astronauts who squirt water into an amorphous

blob that glides weightlessly across the inside of their spaceship.

I fall asleep fast, all the while fighting it. I dream that I
am awake again, gifted suddenly with an awareness of precisely what to do. In my dream I get up, put my clothes on,
and rush outside to tell Victor what I know.

ELEVEN

*G*ordon makes me take his heavy sweater and gives me a cup of hot coffee. He sits at the breakfast table, wearing a white terrycloth robe. His feet are wrapped in wool-lined slippers and he needs a shave. Gordon is cute like that. Adorable and accessible, more like a big teenager than an adult.

He reads to me from Hull's newspaper, the Hull-Nantasket *Times*. The paper issues police reports on a weekly basis: Officer Breaveman reports unopened mail with a resident's address found in an envelope in the trash. There is a report of men in a boat off Point Allerton shooting ducks. A Hull woman reports a domestic problem; a C Street resident reports a stray cat in the basement. Gordon reads these to me as I put on my coat, my gloves. He reads, " 'Oceanspray resident reports broken potted plants; Officer Breaveman questions youths sighted on nearby street corner, reports finding pot breakage in pockets of same. Youths promise to replace damaged pots. . . .' Don't you feel secure knowing we live where even the houseplants are duly protected?"

"What'll I do if his father isn't home?" I say and Gordon shrugs.

Dying Young

"You know, if you'd be mine we could have breakfast together every morning," Gordon says. "I'd read to you from the paper. I'd make you worldly." He laughs.

The Hull-Nantasket *Times* is a slim paper with big type. World leaders collide on major international issues without ever making it into its pages.

"Look here," Gordon says. "They're telling us that more deaths occur from car accidents than from anything else except heart disease and cancer."

"I've been thinking lately that I ought to drive more," I say.

"Hey, don't joke about it," Gordon says, handing me a scarf.

"Who's joking?"

I am going to be on the six-ten to Boston and I haven't lost my nerve. I can remember one dream from my brief sleep and it was enough to provide any extra motivation to see Victor's father. Actually, it was so short that it was more like an episode in a dream, but there was nothing following and nothing that came before. In the dream I was standing in our apartment. Everything had been painted a deep blue and there were crests of light playing on the walls, like the shadows of waves. I was rooting through Victor's clothes, handling all his collection of jeans and flannel shirts. I lifted his clothes over my face; I could smell him perfectly. But he was gone. He'd vanished and left me only the empty apartment and stacks of his possessions, bearing his mark and scent.

At the parking lot, Gordon switches off his headlights and asks again if I want him to go with me.

"No," I say. "I want you to see Victor."

And what should he tell Victor about where I am?

"Tell him I've gone to Boston, that's all. Don't tell him why. Just that I've gone." I realize this is no answer. Or rather, that Gordon can get away with saying nothing but that when I return I had better have some reason for my excursion.

Gordon walks with me to the end of the pier and we kiss at the boarding stair and then I climb into the ferry. I go below deck to where they have a coffee bar and some tables. It's still too early for the commuter crowd and there's hardly anyone aboard. There's maybe thirty people in the large hall, all commuters reading newspapers. The water is very choppy today and many of them look up when there is an especially annoying shift in the ferry's position. Some fold their papers and head down the stairway to the lowest deck, where the ride will be smoother.

The coffee bar isn't open yet. Too bad, because my stomach is roaring hungry. I sit down, overheated in a parka and Gordon's heavy fisherman's sweater, and peel off some layers of my clothes. The gloves get shoved into a pocket with a hat that Gordon lent me. I lay the parka out on the table like a medical patient and throw the sweater on top of it. I search my jeans for my wallet and fish out a five-dollar bill in anticipation of when the coffee bar opens. Then I rest my head on top of the pile of clothes on the table and, almost instantly, am asleep.

I wake up with a face in front of me, a brutish ruddy face with fat, heavily pitted cheeks, uneven lips, and a solid flat nose. He is awful in front of me—a horrible fact of public places. Whenever you go anywhere a face like this will appear in the crowd like a blemish and a reminder of all the people you might have been but, thank God, aren't. I don't mean to be unkind but he is spitting something at me, some warning, I can't tell. I'm sitting up, leaning away from him, and he's grabbing my collar and pulling, the way you lead a dog.

I think, What a stupid way of mugging someone. What an utterly incompetent criminal.

My doughnut money is still in my fist. I push the five bucks at him but he ignores it and keeps badgering my shirt collar. Then he lifts me out of my seat. The hall is empty. The passengers have dispersed, leaving me with this filmy-eyed criminal with a severe speech impediment. I feel an odd rocking, like the ferry isn't going forward at all but is, instead, riveting from side to side. It's hard to tell, though, because I am fighting against the mugger, hitting him across the chest and pummeling his massive, creased neck. He has me in a headlock and pulls me out of the hall, my legs kicking. He keeps saying something but I can't hear. I'm screaming. I'm yelling for anyone to help me. This guy is strong and he is hurting me, the way he holds my head bent under his shoulder. Then I see that in his other arm he has my parka and sweater and I stop screaming and try to imagine why he is carrying my stuff along with me. Then it occurs to me that he isn't trying to mug me, not trying to hurt me at all. I stop kicking and he loosens his grip. He lets go enough so I can get both feet on the ground.

"Lady!" he says, breathless. He begins a long string of stutters, trying to get out the word "this".

"Th . . . th . . . this ship is s . . . s . . . s"

He stops, smacks his hand against his mouth, punishing himself, and then tries again.

"This sh . . . sh . . . ship is s . . . s . . . s . . ."

"Sinking?" I say. "This ship is sinking?"

"Yeah," he says, relieved. He is a giant, maybe six foot five. And he's artful, the way he pushes the door open and holds open the collar of my sweater so that I can duck into it. He extends a glove out for my hand to slip into. I push my hat down to my eyebrows and we exit the hall to the side deck. He walks along the outside of the deck, allowing me the safer position away from the splashing sea. Outside is the sound of the gulls and ocean, radio transmitters, and men with stern voices giving orders over a bullhorn.

"They c . . . c . . . called everyone out. B . . . b . . . but you didn't hear."

A lot of noise from the front of the ferry; the passengers' animated voices, a rope being thrown. A flashing light reflects across the surface of the water and as we walk I see that a Coast Guard boat has been pushed against the ferry's side with a wide plank bridging the two. In the distance is an identical Coast Guard boat, packed with commuters who now wear yellow life preservers over their winter coats. There is a girl in blue jeans struggling with her life preserver, which is apparently too big. Her hair flies in a dark sheet and she picks strands from her eyes. The boat circles eastward, turning back to Hull, and gets smaller as the sun rises cagily from the sea.

The man I thought was a mugger keeps looking at me while we are walking, as if I am some special package he has to deliver and that he wants to be very careful with. I think, Why did this guy come in after me? He's not Coast Guard.

Dying Young

He's got no uniform. He's wearing a hooded sweatshirt beneath an orange poncho. He has a cluster of moles beneath one nostril. Also he walks strangely. He leans way over from side to side with each step. It hits me, suddenly, that the guy is somehow *off*—not that he is retarded but that something is wrong with him. I stiffen with this realization and am all at once embarrassed. We reach the front of the boat and an officer hands us life preservers and tells us, in a competent nautical voice, to watch our step onto the short bridge.

I hardly need the bridge but I step into the Coast Guard *Rescue Vehicle* (that's the name that's been stamped on the supply boxes and on the low edge of my life preserver) and find a place to sit. I look up, waiting for the guy who took me from the ferry. I want to thank him and ask him his name. I want to make up for all my kicking and fussing. But another Coast Guard boat zooms to the ferry's side and begins to board passengers. The boat I'm on disengages from the ferry and floats several feet back, I rush to the front but one of the officers tells me to sit down. I wave at my mugger but he doesn't see me. Then we're off.

We get back to Hull, cold as hell, and are herded into the Coast Guard station. They tell us to have a seat and give us—guess what—instant cocoa in cone-shaped paper cups secured by plastic holders. Cocoa, as if we were the third grade just gotten back from a day of ice skating.

The Coast Guard station is painted kind of dead-leaf brown and has very official-looking cabinets and great blocks of walnut shelves against the walls. There're several closed doors, probably offices for the big brass, and a long row of

benches upholstered in a scratchy, taupe fabric. A few captain's chairs have been thrown in for decoration. On the walls
are many colored prints of various types of Coast Guard ves-
sels. They explain about the origin of the Coast Guard in Hull,
the many gallant lifesaving efforts they undertook early in
Hull's settling, when merchants and fishermen made daily trips
to Boston to buy and sell goods. They tell of the very first
lifeboat, called the *Nantasket,* which is on display at the Lifesaving Museum in town. An ancient sexton sits beneath glass
by the office window. The main office, a tiny room partitioned
from the waiting room by a series of windows, looks too small
to house the enormous radio that occupies a good third of
the available floor space.

There are police. They were here when we arrived, crisp
in their starched blue uniforms, with walkie-talkies chattering
at their hips. Police scare the hell out of me. Since I was a
kid I've been petrified. I'm always worried that they are going
to put me in jail. That there'll be some mistake, some casual
error, resulting in my incarceration. And that, through a series
of similar logistical errors, I will remain in jail for months,
perhaps years, until the prison cell becomes a home in the
sad way that any place will become home if you stay there
long enough.

There's a bearded man in a raincoat, standing board-
straight against the wall. For a moment I think he's a flasher.
That he isn't flashing *these days,* but there was a time in his
past . . . Here, in the Coast Guard station, surrounded by uni-
formed men, he worries, as I do, about his previous crimes.
All my thefts, all the stolen objects with which I've filled my
coat pockets, drift through my mind in an anxious parade. A
woman, maybe my age, wears a smart-looking wool coat and

fingers a glass bead necklace. She looks at the clock, thinking . . . thinking what? About the workday she is missing because of the sinking ferry? The woman returns my stare and for a shocked moment we lock eyes and I wonder—God, would I like to know—what it is she sees when she sees me.

We are told to fill out an accident report but there aren't enough pens to go around and also nothing to write on. I wait my turn for a pen and then try to fill out the form using my knee as a surface. I've sort of hidden myself away in a corner to avoid the cops and I huddle over my report form, checking the appropriate boxes for gender and height and civil status. The form is typed with these incredibly minuscule letters. A Xerox of a Xerox. It's hard enough to read, let alone find space enough in the short blanks for the required information. I am already considering a means of escape when the police, as if they read my mind, tell us no one can leave until the reports are filled. They also want all of us to go to the hospital—I don't know why. And I hear ambulance sirens in the distance, so I know they mean business.

I can't remember my zip code at all and am struggling to recall it when I look up and there's my mugger, a report form on his broad lap. He has the pen stuck in his mouth and looks as baffled as I am over the whole thing. So I slide down the long bench to where he is sitting and he looks up at me with the sort of welcome you give an old college chum. Over his shoulder I get a glimpse of the report form. He hasn't filled in a single blank.

"Stupid form, huh?" I say. "What is your name?"

"David," he tells me. "I c ... c ... can't r ... r ... read without my g ... glasses."

"Here, I'll read it for you." I tell him my name and he says it with a grin, no stutter, just a perfect Hilary.

His name is David Alexander Kennedy, an impressive name. Among the rest of the information I learn as I fill the report is that he is a resident of Hull, single, twenty-six, which is sad because he looks much older. His next of kin is his mother, Sybil, whose office phone begins with an 800 number. He has suffered no injuries and doesn't know his Social Security number.

"I don't know my Social Security number either," I lie. I decide David's face doesn't look so bad, at least not horrifying, when he's grinning.

$\mathcal{P}$eople are lining up by the exit sign and the police are collecting forms and then sending the passengers off with some paramedics, who arrived with the ambulances. "I'm not going to get into one of those ambulances," I tell David. He gives me a mournful look, like maybe I ought to. "I feel fine," I tell him, "you saved me."

I go to the window and count seven ambulances, big ones, the size of vans. They load people fairly quickly. Then a guy slams the back door and the ambulances take off, one by one, their sirens flashing but soundless. No one is hurt anyway. But outside there is some commotion. There's a small gathering and a television crew waiting, their cameras in black piles.

David taps me on the shoulder and points to the line

where people are handing in their forms. I nod and tell him I'll join him there in a second.

I am not going to the hospital. I don't even know where a hospital is around here. There's an exit sign on the far side of the office window and I amble over nonchalantly, making it look like I'm still reading the accident report. I tap the pen against my cheek to show everyone how much I'm concentrating. I furrow my brow. I get to the door and stand with my back against it, as if I don't know that it is an exit. A young guy behind the office window smiles at me and I smile back and then stare into my report. He keeps watching though. Whenever I glance up he looks away suddenly. He has a shadow of crew-cut hair and a tiny nose, like a neat little package. He wears glasses, thick froglike lenses. He can't be more than twenty.

Lucky for me an older officer tells him to find something in the file cabinet and so he goes digging through one of the metal drawers that are stacked against the wall. Soundlessly, I turn the doorknob and then back out, ashamed at myself, guilty over my inability to just go along with things, the way other people do. I give the door my most gentle closure, guiding the knob silently back into its fastenings. I am a fugitive. A delinquent. Reprobate, polecat, insect, worm.

I'm standing on a cement staircase with a damp, cellar smell and iron rails leading eight stairs either direction and then twisting and going eight more. I fly down the steps, balancing myself on the railing, letting my feet do magic against the stairs. I stop finally in front of a metal door painted a strange light aqua. It has an alarm just above its handle with a sign that says ALARM WILL SOUND WHEN DOOR IS OPENED. I get my face close to it, trying to figure the exact mechanism that sounds the alarm. I think maybe I can disengage it in some way, the way they do on "Mission Impossible," but I can't come up with a convincing plan. I think maybe I should go to the hospital. They could see there was nothing wrong with me and then I could head out again to Boston to get Victor's father. The only problem is there would be all those wasted hours and Victor home the entire day, alone and sick.

Reluctantly, I climb a few steps back to the Coast Guard office. I feel very defeated. The events of last night haunt me: Victor throwing up, the mound of our possessions piled like a trash heap, Mrs. Birkle in her bedroom, the parachuter. Then I think of past months, historical months before Victor became so apparently ill. I see Victor and me under a silver maple, the autumn leaves showering us and snapping beneath our shoes. I see him dragging a crate of books up the stairway to our apartment the morning we moved in. I see him at the coin-op laundry, folding my underwear into careful piles.

Then I turn, jump down three stairs at a time, and shoot right through the aqua door.

I'm almost deafened by the shrill scream of the alarm. I thought the door would open to the outside but instead it leads into a narrow cement-floored hallway, barely brightened by a tube of light. The sound of the alarm chases me down the hallway and then I'm running to another hall that bends right. There are doors every ten or so feet. I try them, twisting the knobs hard either way, but they are locked. I'm thinking, Oh, shit, oh, shit, shit.

Dying Young

Then finally I see a stairway and a short patch of light on one of the gray steps. It leads outside. I push open the door and feel a cold blast of air inside my lungs as I scramble out to the bay side of the Coast Guard station. I upset a crowd of sea gulls who fly off, squawking in a huge noisy cloud.

I can hear people on the other side of the building so I head to the dock and squat by one of the Coast Guard boats. The alarm is finally silenced. Everyone who was in the station is now standing in the parking lot and a fire truck makes its way down the street, dodging ambulances as it turns into the driveway. The police are still calling for their accident report forms. The siren lights flash blue and red across the shining snow.

A television guy calls orders to his crew as they balance their cameras at their shoulders, trying not to miss anything. The crowd of observers has thickened. Some have takeout doughnuts and coffee. I leave my place by the boat and walk boldly across the snow. I feel like they are all looking at me, like I'm the first soldier on enemy lines—but no one pays any attention.

I stand in a crowd that watches the Coast Guard station as if it might at any moment crumble into dust. I ask a woman in a fake fur coat what happened and she says a boat sank in the bay and that they've been pulling people out of the water all morning. The man standing next to her, probably her husband, says, No, they didn't pull anyone out of the water. There was a fire on board the ship and people were being asphyxiated from smoke. A kid in a motorcycle jacket says, No, it was a bomb.

We stand like that for a while. I suggest maybe the engine quit or they hit the underwater edge of a cliff, which is what happened. I say maybe the ferry suffered some minor damage but they sent out the Coast Guard even so.

That doesn't go over well. The lady in fur puffs her cheeks and says no. Okay, I say, maybe someone hijacked the boat and the captain wrestled him to the ground while crew members ushered passengers aboard the rescue boats. The motorcycle kid pinches his lower lip between two teeth and considers this.

After a few more minutes I begin my walk home.

J turn the corner of our street and finger my car keys. It will take me a good hour and a half in rush-hour traffic to drive to Boston. Maybe longer. I've walked now for forty minutes, watching my breath cloud the air and feeling my toes freeze inside my sneakers. My car is rusted so bad on this side that it looks two-toned. I approach it as if it were someone else's car and discover all over again how ugly it is. A mobile dump. An embarrassment you can sit in. The rat over the wheel has a grimace like someone has just poisoned it. The rust is so bad in parts you can see daylight.

I'm about to get in when I see a movement by the hedges. There's a raccoon in the garbage pail. His hind legs secure him to the top of the pail while his head burrows deep inside. His ringed tail swings up and down, and his sharp raccoon nails create a metallic scrape against the aluminum. I know I've got to chase him out, but that round butt and funny tail are so pathetic, balancing on the thin rim of the trash can, that I fight an urge to give him a teasing push.

I walk from the side of the car and get close enough to the raccoon to get a sense of the texture of his long, winter coat. After a minute he swings his head around, an eggshell crunching between narrow jaws. He's hunchbacked, his face half hidden in black fur. Seeing me, he jumps down from the pail, anxious over my presence but at the same time hesitant to give up his prize. There's a scattering of trash he's pushed out of the pail and he makes one more attempt at a pizza box before waddling off. Then he disappears into a stack of bushes.

I pick up the trash he's strewn on the ground—empty tuna cans, scattered Kleenex, a greasy strip of aluminum foil. There are chicken bones from what we ate three nights ago and an empty applesauce jar. Then, beneath a vile chunk of molded cheese, I find a ball of adhesive tape, the size of a silver dollar. I peel back the tape, ripping it and getting its glue on my fingers. Inside is a thin cluster of shiny needles. I pick one up, hold it carefully between two fingers, and stare into its hollow tip. Then I break it in two and fold it back into the tape. These are morphine needles. Victor has been giving himself injections.

I run into the house.

"Victor!" I say when I burst through the door.

He is sitting on the bed, a coffee mug in his hand, watching the morning news.

"Mrs. Birkle won't take the television," he says. "She told me to tell you to come see her."

On TV they show clips from outside the Coast Guard station. The camera follows the people as they climb inside ambulances and then wave goodbye before the doors shut. I stand in front of the TV, my fists clenched, and yell into Victor's surprised face.

"Victor, you didn't tell me about the morphine! You didn't say anything! That was wrong; I have a right to know!"

He stares at me blankly and then looks away, as if he'd never even seen me. He takes a sip of his coffee.

"You're a bastard!" I say. "You're a bastard and you hide things. Important things. How could you? How could you not tell me?"

I take a handful of his shirt and pull it toward me.

"You went to my father's house," Victor says. His jaw is clenched. One of the muscles in his cheek twitches and then is still.

"I didn't go anywhere," I say.

"Gordon was very worried. He came over this morning nearly frantic. We called the Coast Guard station and the hospital. They didn't have any record of you."

"That just proves I didn't go," I say.

"The engine on one of the Coast Guard boats blew up. I thought you drowned in the Atlantic," Victor says, "on the way to my father's house."

"Well, I didn't."

"I wish you had."

I jump him. I pound his chest and he pushes me hard beneath the chin so that I bite my tongue. I knock his arms away. Then he smacks his coffee mug against my cheekbone and I am blinded, temporarily, by the hot coffee. It isn't so hot that it scalds, but it sends me running into the kitchen for the faucet. I stand by the sink, my head ducked under the running water, and feel a trace of blood in my mouth and the hot tears being washed away by water. Whenever I get a breath, I yell insults from the corner of my mouth.

Victor comes into the kitchen and puts the coffee mug by the side of the sink, inches from my nose. I reach over and knock the mug off the counter so that it shatters on the floor.

Dying Young

Victor stands behind me and I kick him hard in the ankle. He puts his hands beneath my coat and I jerk forward away from him. He untucks my shirt from my jeans and wraps his arms around my bare middle. He leans over me, his face at the back of my neck. The water cascades from the faucet in a noisy jet and I can hardly hear what Victor is saying. He keeps repeating the same sentence; his body shakes, and he presses against me. I straighten up and begin to turn in his direction. But he pushes me back around. I feel his tears wet against my neck and I freeze in awe of this. He says, "Baby, you're safe," again and again.

TWELVE

*M*rs. Birkle tips the pitcher and pours juice into a tumbler. Then she disappears farther into the kitchen and I can't see her from where I sit. I listen to the sounds of cabinets shutting, of the tearing of packaging and a cookie plate being filled.

Already she has said exactly why she wouldn't take my television when I offered it to her. She told me she knew I was lying and that I didn't have another. She also said that it was the kind of lie that God forgives.

On the table, next to an elaborate crèche, is Mrs. Birkle's television—the old one. Gordon delivered it today with all new color tubes and circuits, a dusting of each of its parts, and a smooth face of new glass. When he brought it in Mrs. Birkle cried.

The refrigerator door opens and she bends over, her spine prominent, her legs awkward beneath the raised edge of her dress. She replaces the pitcher. In careful, slow steps, she brings the tumbler of juice and her offering of cookies into the living room, where I sit on the couch.

She rests the tray on the coffee table, sits down, and

smooths her dress over her knees. She says, "There, Mary," and then covers her mouth. Mary is her daughter's name.

*T*oday is like many of the recent days Victor and I have spent together, hardly leaving our apartment at all except to buy a newspaper, take the mail from the basket by our mail slot, or replace a souring carton of milk. We are quiet around each other. Our time together isn't what you would call full. Mostly Victor stays on one side of the mound of our possessions, which still occupies a large portion of our front room, reading in his chair. I lie on the bed with my head over the edge and a newspaper and some magazines on the floor. I scout through the paper, cut out articles that interest me, and save them in a shoe box marked "To be read." I decipher anagrams from the comics page and make Christmas ornaments for our tree out of glue and magazine ads. Drying on the kitchen counter is an assortment of Santas and candles and snowmen and sleighs. Of wreaths and Shetland ponies and angels.

Little by little the pile on the floor diminishes as Victor and I put away a few more things. While I was in the shower yesterday Victor brought in my canister of hair combs and jewelry and placed it along the sink edge. He hung some of my blouses in the closet and folded a stack of jeans. Last night he mixed a salad dressing and I dug out the rack of spices so he could add cilantro. I lined the shelf with his books and put a fresh pad of paper near his chair. The nights are hard and Victor often wakes up in chills and sweats. We change the sheets each morning and I take them to the launderette with a few stray socks and a towel or two. Things are better between us.

In three days the phone has rung only once and Victor answered. Gordon, of course. They talked briefly and then Victor hung up and asked if I wanted to go to Gordon's house to watch a movie. Today, Victor is napping when the phone rings. I know it's Gordon. I turn on the sink water so that Victor will have a harder time hearing our conversation if he wakes up. I keep the phone close to my mouth as I speak.

"I can't see you right now," I tell Gordon. "It's important that I stay with Victor for a few days."

"You are always with Victor," Gordon says. "When have you *not* been with Victor?"

"You know what I mean," I say.

Gordon sighs into the phone. "Are you still angry that I told him you went to Boston to speak with his father? It's not fair, Hilary."

"No," I say. "Of course it's not that."

"We were all terrified that you'd drowned. We were going to call his dad and see if somehow you had gotten there by another means. We didn't know what had happened."

"I know," I say. "I know all that."

"Meet me at the launderette tomorrow morning," Gordon says. He is trying so hard. His voice has a sad tone of false confidence. "I'll sit with you during the spin-dry cycle."

"How do you know I go there?"

"Because I've been watching you," he says. "Please don't get mad but I followed you in my car."

Gordon calls back at six o'clock, a little drunk. Victor is awake now, in bed with a book. Because the nights are so bad for him, we've been injecting tiny amounts of morphine in the evenings and it makes him strangely distant and peaceful. He nearly grins into his book and he reads each page a long time.

"Tomorrow," I tell Gordon. "I'm busy right now. I'm doing something."

"What are you doing?" Gordon says. I hear pub noises in the background, chattering people and orders for beer.

I tell Gordon that I am cooking dinner, which is not true. I don't cook any dinner because Victor is still working on a glass of wine and the rest of his lunch. I'm taping cardboard to the back of more Christmas pictures I cut from magazines. The kitchen counter is covered with glue, scraps of slick magazine paper, and drying paper ornaments. I've tied ribbon through the finished ones and hung them on our tree.

"What if I told you we have an emergency on our hands?" Gordon says.

"We always have an emergency," I say. I poke a hole through the top of a picture of a toy bear and tie a bow with gold ribbon.

"What if I told you Victor's father was in here asking about him?"

"When?" I say. I put down the bear and scrape glue from my fingers with a fork prong. "Where are you? Cappy's?"

"The Tavern."

"How do you know it was his father?"

"I know, Hilary," Gordon says. "He said he was looking for Victor and that he knew Victor was somewhere in Hull."

I think about that note I sent to his father and realize that, of course, it been stamped at the Hull Post Office and probably had the name of the town on the postage mark.

"This is my fault," I say.

"Everything's always Hilary's fault," Gordon says, breathy and drunk. "If I go to bed early would you break into my house again?"

"Gordon . . ."

"If I fell from the roof would you come take care of me? If I get drunk and crazy and beat you up, would you want me like you want Victor? Would you, Hilary?"

It's very dark, deep night, and the doorbell rings, two rings. I stand at the door frame, watching Victor. He shrugs his shoulders and gives me a baffled look. He has one of my books, a book about space travel and UFO sightings, face down over his leg.

"You think that's Gordon downstairs?" he says.

"No, Victor," I say. "No, it's your dad, I'm pretty sure."

I sit on the edge of the bed. On the bedside table is wine, a prescription bottle, half a glass of milk, and a mound of used cotton balls, each with its speck of Victor's blood. Victor holds my hand and traces circles over my knuckles.

"I want to learn about what interests you, Hils. Yesterday I read your book about skeletal problems in canines. Very interesting stuff about Great Danes. This book on space is a little more complicated," he says. "And the morphine and wine make it hard to concentrate. I can't see anything right anymore. Even your face, Hilary, has a ring of light around it—a sort of yellow aura. Wouldn't Estelle be proud of me, reading auras?"

The doorbell rings again.

"Does everything have yellow around it?" I ask.

"No. There's blue sometimes, or rose."

Dying Young

The doorbell rings once more and I wince.

"Man is born free, and everywhere he is found in chains," Victor says. "Do you know who said that, Hilary?"

I shake my head.

"Rousseau. *The Social Contract.* 1762. Rousseau thought man was born innocent and good and that if a person followed his natural feelings and sentiments he would stay just and good. What do you think, Hilary? What happens when a person follows his natural feelings?"

"Do you want me to get the door, Victor?"

"Does Gordon follow his natural feelings?" Victor says.

"You'll have to ask Gordon."

"Who called my father, you or Gordon?"

"I wrote a letter," I say.

"One more question, Hils," Victor says. He takes my face in his hands. "Would it be easier for you if I left? My father is going to want me to go home, or somewhere. You have to tell me, Hilary, because there's going to be a fight here tonight and I just want to make sure that it's worth it."

Victor's face models a whole attitude. The tone of his voice offers everything. I start to respond, knowing that the stutter of my message cannot be understood. Words rattle through my mind and I pluck out acceptable ones. Outside, I hear an owl and I wonder if that is good luck or bad.

I tell Victor that what I want is to be with him.

"Everything here is very beautiful for me," Victor whispers. He smiles like a Buddha and brings me up against him. We listen to the incessant ring of the doorbell. Then Victor stops and lets go of me. He turns his head, listening. "The room is humming," he says.

. . .

Downstairs, Mr. Geddes stands beneath the orange light of our porch front. He's in a long wool coat and heavy gloves. He's a sharp-featured man, with gray curls circling his head and, like his son, an elegant narrowness about him. I notice he has a smart-looking BMW parked on the street. Also, he has a dreadful cough.

He smiles politely and sends an explosion of coughs into his glove. He says, "I am looking for Victor."

I lead Mr. Geddes up the three flights, listening to his coughing and the sound of his shoes against the tired wood of the steps. He is red-faced and breathless by the time we reach the apartment. I tap the door before opening it, just to let Victor know we are there. Then I swing the door open and take a look at the apartment with its heap of belongings by the bed and the oversize Christmas tree in the corner, half decorated with strange paper cutouts. Victor has turned his chair so that it faces the front door. He is sitting with one leg draped over the other, a cigarette dangling from his lips. He stands, inhales a lungful of smoke, and then, because there is no ashtray, grinds out his cigarette on the heel of his shoe. He takes four long strides across the room, his hand outstretched. His father and he share a firm handshake.

"Am I interrupting? Was it a bad time to . . ." his father asks softly.

"No, Dad," Victor says. "Have a seat. You've met Hilary?"

"I'm Hilary," I say. Mr. Geddes stares at me. His mouth opens and he looks at me as if he were suddenly noticing me for the first time.

"You're familiar," he says. "Were you going with Victor before . . ." He pauses abruptly and undoes the top button of his coat. He steps toward Victor anxiously and then hesitates. "How are you feeling, son?"

I go into the kitchen and take two wineglasses from the cabinet. The phone lies uncradled on the counter. I didn't even realize it, but I left it that way after Gordon's last phone call. The line is dead. When I put it to my ear all I hear is a faint static crackling. I hang up the phone and have a pang for Gordon. Then I fill the glasses of wine and give one of them to Mr. Geddes, who finishes the first third of the glass in a single swallow.

*V*ictor and his father go at each other like two pros. Top-speed minds; the words cannot come quickly enough. They play out the conversation with fast, strategic sentences, constantly sizing each other up for the next line of defense. They dodge each other's questions, twist statements into unreasonable demands. Victor is impressive, the way he tackles his father's reproaches. But it's hard for him. He loosens himself from his father's fast grasp only to become pinned and carried again into the topic of his father's choice and tone.

But Victor is a decent player here and eventually he gains the lead. Mr. Geddes is trying to be serious, warding off his son's responses with well-timed blasts of rigid curtness but again and again he finds himself presented with all of Victor's laughter.

Victor succeeds in joking his way out of a straight answer about what he is planning to do with his illness, and then everything changes and he succumbs to the threat of his father's yet unleashed tears. Then Victor takes control again, clowning his father into silence. He goes to the bookshelf and removes a thick volume of English poems.

"You have heard of J. B. S. Haldane, right, Dad?" Victor says. "Because he wrote a poem called 'Cancer's a Funny Thing' that I would like to quote from, if you don't mind."

"There is nothing funny about . . ."

Victor stands, one leg in front of the other, and recites from the book. He coughs, holds up one finger, and readies his audience. " 'I wish I had the voice of Homer/To sing of rectal carcinoma . . .' " he begins.

"Stop that, Victor," Mr. Geddes says sourly. "You don't even *have* rectal carcinoma. I wish you did have rectal carcinoma."

" '. . . provided one confronts the tumour/With a sufficient sense of humour./I know that cancer often kills,/But so do cars and sleeping pills; . . .' "

Mr. Geddes goes to Victor, slaps the book out of his hands, and they start at each other again: Mr. Geddes firing questions and Victor fielding them with confidence. Finally Victor calls a halt to what he refers to as the "interrogation," reminds his father that he is many years into adulthood, and then drops his offensive line as his father stoops before him, pleading with him to be sensible.

"Please!" Mr. Geddes says, his hands raised with open palms. Victor turns away.

"Can't you forget for a moment about our particular brand of family politics and talk to me as if I had some hint of objective reasoning?" Victor says. He runs his fingers over the coffee table, searching for cigarettes. His hand grazes magazines, a coffee mug, ashtray, wallet, keys, before finding the pack of Marlboros.

"Fine," Mr. Geddes says and stands straight in front of Victor. "Let's do that. Let's reason our way through this. You are going to reason your way into the grave."

"It's boring, Dad," Victor says. He lights a cigarette and blows a stream of smoke over his father's head. "All the treatments, all the sickness . . ."

"This is a very strange society, where people kill themselves out of boredom," Mr. Geddes says.

"I've had a decade and a half of this disease. You've never been sick like this . . . you aren't even qualified to make a judgment."

"You're killing yourself," Mr. Geddes says, holding out a shaking finger.

"I'm a lot sicker than you think. Besides, I've been dying for over a decade."

"No. There was hope."

"I'm tired," Victor declares, dragging deeply on his cigarette. There's something in his voice I've not heard before. A desperate, sad tone that makes me remember again that Victor's decision was not made easily and that he has spent hour after hour in bed, alone, listening to the sounds of each day opening and closing around him. He turns to his father and says in a soft voice, "I'm tired of this 'hope,' as you call it."

"God damn you!" Mr. Geddes says and doubles over as if he'd been struck in the stomach. "God damn you for being tired!" He nearly dances in front of Victor, shaking the mop of gray curls on his handsome head and hardening his lips in a way that reminds me of Victor. In his face I see Victor's chin and Victor's wide, lined forehead. He has a concave back, like the gentle inward slope of a canoe, making him appear somehow hollowed out, but also very young. He swoops in on his son, echoing the same arguments he began the evening with.

I bring out the rest of the wine bottle and leave it on the coffee table. Then I rush back to the kitchen and sit on a stool, feeling nervous. I pull the laces from my sneakers and relace them into a strange pattern. I rearrange the magnets on the refrigerator.

Victor's voice booms. He says, "Don't tell me I don't want to live! Sure I want to live. If I could live without this disease, then I would, wouldn't I? If a suicide could escape certain horrors without killing himself, don't you think he would do so? Suicide, and I don't think that is what I am committing, is the expression of a sort of concealed will to live."

"Who told you that?"

"Arthur Schopenhauer. A nineteenth-century philosopher."

"What did he know? He was living before we even had chemotherapy!"

I hear a sigh and imagine Victor rolling his eyes.

"Frankly, Father, I think that I am handling this in a very civilized way," Victor says. "You might not know this but people in other cultures would find my approach not at all extreme. The Iglulik Eskimos, for example, believed that a death by violence was the only way into paradise."

"What Eagle Eskimos? I don't know any Eagle Eskimos."

"*Iglulik* Eskimos. The Igluliks would see a death, by nat-

ural causes, as a condemnation to an afterlife of eternal claus-
trophobia."

"There is nothing natural about dying so young," says
Victor's father.

$\mathcal{F}$inally there is a pause in the yelling and I peek out.

I see Victor in his chair, his legs splayed, drinking slop-
pily from his wineglass. The skin beneath his eyes is blue, as
if he'd been given a double whammy in a fight. Sweat forms
over his lip and slicks the hair around his face. He is feverish
and probably nauseous. The tiny dosage of morphine has undoubtedly worn off. It is enormous effort to fend off his father,
who has all the bounciness of a Little Leaguer at his first ball
game. The air is hazy with cigarette smoke and the window
is clouded with steam. Mr. Geddes talks quickly in a low voice.
He explains how easy it will be at the hospital, how glad Victor
will be that he didn't give up.

"All you need is four years of remission to be considered
cured," he says.

"Dad," Victor explains slowly, "I have never had even
two years of remission and I am not, I repeat *not*, going to
the goddamned hospital."

The phone rings and Victor goes into the kitchen to
answer it.

"Mr. Geddes," I say, "would you like something to eat?"

"I'm Richard, please," he says. "Do you have any bourbon?"

I hear Victor's voice in the kitchen. He says, "Buddy, I
don't have time to talk to you. My father is here making a
scene. Talk to Hilary. . . ."

"Excuse me," I say, and go into the kitchen. Victor is standing with the phone away from his ear. Gordon is yelling something; I can hear his voice coming strong through the receiver.

"Talk to Gordon," Victor tells me. "He's drunk. And don't give my father any bourbon."

Victor stands in the kitchen doorway and leans into the front room. "Dad!" he calls. "You aren't getting any more to drink over here! The bar is closed after that glass of wine."

"You're going to tell me not to drink? When did you become so health-conscious? Look what you live in! Look at this pile of junk on the floor. I don't suppose you have a proper toilet?"

"In there," Victor says and uses his whole arm to point to our bathroom.

"Gordon," I whisper into the phone. "Gordon, are you okay?"

"This isn't any good what we're doing. It isn't right," Gordon says. He slurs his words and can't keep a consistent volume to his sentences. One minute his voice is trumpeting into my ear and the next it's distant, as if it had been swept up by the wind.

"Gordon, I can't hear you. Keep the phone next to your mouth."

"I'm going to tell Victor," he says. "I have to. He's my friend. He called me 'buddy' just now. I was trying to tell him that you and I are having a . . . what do you call it anyway? But he wouldn't talk to me."

"Gordon," I say. I look into the living room and see Victor standing by the window, looking out. I whisper, "Gordon, you can't do this. You can't tell Victor. . . ."

"I haven't had a friend in . . ."

"Gordon, where are you?"

"I'm at Cappy's now. But he's going to throw me out. I don't even know why I came here. Hey, Hilary? Hilary, you know we have a date tomorrow?"

"I'm coming right now, Gordon. Stay at Cappy's, okay?"

"We have a date for the launderette. A passionate laundry date."

I make Gordon promise to stay at Cappy's and hang up the phone.

In the living room, Victor smokes a new cigarette and pitches his wine around his glass before swallowing. He glances at me with a conspiratorial look, as if I'm supposed to be as disgusted by his father's efforts at persuasion as he is. I don't like all the commotion, but I sort of hope Mr. Geddes is working magic on Victor, changing his mind so that Victor will go to the hospital where he can get treatment, where he can recover. But I know this is out of the question. One look at Victor tells me that.

Victor walks toward me and pulls me close against him. I put my arms around him. Every day he is smaller in my arms, shrinking with illness, taking on the frailty of an old man or a tiny, precious boy.

Mr. Geddes comes out of the bathroom and says, "Oh, Hilary," as though he has forgotten all about me. Victor sits down and I perch on the arm of Victor's chair and put my hand in his hair. I sneak a feel of his hot forehead.

"I'm going out," I tell Victor. "I'm going to make sure Gordon gets home safely."

"That's fine," Victor says. He squeezes my hand. "Dad,

you want to leave now? Because if you do I know the last ferry leaves in a half hour so you could just make it."

"I'm not leaving," Mr. Geddes says.

"I'm going to bed, Dad," Victor says. "Dying men need their sleep."

"GOD DAMN YOU!" Mr. Geddes yells. "You're just like your mother; the same maddening sense of humor."

"Quit flapping your arms, Dad. I once asked Mom why she married you and she told me that it was because you were such an intelligent, open-minded, compassionate fellow. She said you could search the world over and never find another man more receptive to new understanding."

"She said that?" Richard says. He nearly smiles.

"No," Victor says.

This starts a new round of screaming. I gather my parka and scarf. I am down the third set of steps before Mr. Geddes's voice pauses. I stop at the door leading to the street and listen for Victor. Whatever he is saying is delivered quietly; the whole house is silent.

Cappy's pub is full. I wander through the crowd, looking for Gordon. I can't find him sitting at any of the tables or talking to the group in front of the bay window. He isn't sitting at the bar and he isn't outside, so I take a bar stool and order a beer from Robert, who works weekend nights.

Cappy is playing darts. He stands in the center of a half circle of men, most of whom wear caps with fishing emblems on them. I swing my stool around to watch Cappy and he gets lucky with a triple nine. He goes to the board and pulls his darts from the cork.

I say, "Pretty good, Cappy."

"Hilary!" Cappy says. "Victor's dad find him?"

"Oh yeah," I say. "Hey, I'm looking for Gordon. Wasn't he in here?"

Cappy's face clouds over. "He's here okay. At least he was. I told him to go home."

Cappy holds a fistful of darts and shoots them one by one into the board. "Told him to get the hell on home," he says.

I swing back around on my stool just as the bartender puts a tall beer on the counter. I give him a couple of dollars and wish I hadn't come. On the other hand, I couldn't easily have stayed at the apartment, waiting for Gordon to call Victor again. I drink fast, trying to decide what to do.

I watch a couple at the end of the bar. She has dark Cleopatra hair and from my clumsy angle I can see she has a dimple in her left cheek that her date keeps kissing and teasing with his tongue. She giggles and slaps him away. Her earrings are the sort that dangle and glitter in strands. When she tucks away her hair she reveals such a pretty ear that her date abandons the dimple and begins nipping the spot above the earring. She laughs, tips forward, then looks up straight at me with a level, lipsticked mouth that shows suspicion before curving into a smile. Then she points and claps her hands and I realize she is Annabel, out of her gray workday uniform and dazzling in a white blouse with a long V running down the front. She waves me over and I obey, balancing my beer in one hand and my coat and scarf in the other. She greets me with a hug and I feel the flatness of her narrow back and the strange cushion of her breasts against mine. I smell hair spray, perfume, the faint odor of face powder, the perspiration at the base of her neck. And I am indebted for this hug.

"This is Lenny!" Annabel says. She points to her date, a large, square-faced guy with eyes so green and so surrounded by thick black lashes that they almost look girlish. "We're getting married in the spring and everyone is coming. You, too!"

"Married?" I say and shake hands with Lenny. "I didn't even know you were engaged."

"We weren't—I mean not formally. But Lenny just got a job in Los Angeles and he wants me to move out there with him and so we're getting married."

"That's great. A lot of movie stars in Los Angeles," I say. Lenny laughs, showing a space where his front tooth should be. The gap gives him a sort of rugged appearance that offsets his pretty eyes and makes them more beautiful by contrast. He and Annabel together are adorable.

"I'm quitting at Estelle's," Annabel says. "She's giving me a bonus for Christmas. And you know what else? I'm going to her Christmas party tomorrow night as a *guest*. You better be there. You and Victor."

"Sure," I say, remembering now the invitation that was so pretty I hung it on the Christmas tree with the other ornaments. "Listen, have you seen Gordon?"

"He always comes to the Christmas party."

"But do you know where he is *tonight?*"

"He said he was going to the launderette," Lenny says. "I told him that was ridiculous." Lenny has a Boston accent so heavy that it sounds odd to me, the way my accent must sound to Victor, for example. But I like Lenny's voice. He reminds me of the kids I grew up with, and he kind of personifies the city. Lenny looks like he should be an ice hockey player. He's got thick hands, like ice hockey mitts, and somehow I can't imagine him in Los Angeles, where there is no ice hockey or even a true winter, and where no one will identify his accent or really very much about him at all.

It has started to snow. There is still ice on the road and the addition of snow makes it especially slippery. I drive carefully through the streets, being cautious not to brake too fast. The launderette is in a cluster of other stores, all of them closed. They are dark except for the sparse light from their burglar alarm systems. Gordon's car is alone in the lot, collecting a dusting of snow. I park next to his car and can see him through the glass wall of the store. He is slumped on one of the benches that line the front of the yellow laundry room. I see his blond head and the overcoat that he wore to Estelle's house that afternoon we all met for tea.

The management has tacked a "Merry Christmas" sign to the front door and a strap of braided leather with three sleigh bells that jingle softly when I come in. Gordon looks up, opens his mouth to say something then closes it again. He stands, loses his balance for a moment, and then steadies himself against one of the washers. The washers sit back to back in a long white row. Inset in two walls are the dryers. One of them spins a full load of many-colored clothes. They go round and round, blending into each other, like the colors on a pinwheel.

"You found me," Gordon says. "I was sitting here waiting to be . . . I don't know . . . rescued."

"Annabel and Lenny told me where you were."

"Cappy threw me out of the pub," Gordon says. He stoops his shoulders and puts his hands deep in the pockets of his coat, as if he is cold. Then he cranes his neck to the ceiling and asks me to sit down, which I do. He paces in a small circle in front of me, clearly troubled. He looks as though he might say something, then catches himself short. He pouts, screws his eyebrows together in concentration, and leans into his coat pockets so hard that his back is rounded.

On the opposite end of the launderette, Alien Turf generates absurd synthetic sounds. It boings and beeps and makes electronic whispers. I feel sorry for Gordon, having to listen to its embarrassing noises as he searches for words. There is the metallic scrape of a zipper against the interior of the dryer and the sound of coins cascading against the dryer wall. But Alien Turf chides with the most effect. Every minute there is a blast-off noise and some electronic voice that says, *"You are now on Alien Turf. Destroy or be destroyed. . . ."*

Gordon grimaces, squeezing his eyes nearly shut. The muscle in his jaw flexes in spasms and he tugs on the front of his hair.

"See those clothes?" he says finally, and points at the dryer.

"Yes," I say.

"I don't know whose they are. I came in and they were drying. They've been dry for over an hour. I put in quarters anyway so they would keep spinning."

"Why?"

"I don't know, Hilary. I wanted them to keep spinning. It made me feel better if I was sitting in here and something was happening. I've been acting very weird lately. Freddie sent me the divorce papers. I was signing my name and I signed "Hilary." I drove around in my car today—all day—going, like, nowhere. Then I packed my stuff and put it in the car. I drove north all the way to the roundabout in Quincy where you turn off to Boston. But I couldn't turn. I just kept going round and round."

I look over my right shoulder and stare outside, past the glittering snow, where our cars become identical under blankets of white flakes.

"Hilary, don't turn away!" Gordon says. He brings me around to him and I look into his red face and the strained tendons in his neck. "Look, I know how it is supposed to be— that you are supposed to be able to freely give love and that you aren't supposed to be possessive. You may think this is primitive but I don't even know how to love someone without . . . *having* them. Why do you want Victor so much? What's the matter with me?"

"Nothing's the matter with you, Gordon," I say.

"Well, we have to tell him," Gordon says. "He has to know."

"Know what?" I say. Suddenly my shoulders feel too heavy, as if someone has dropped a beam across them.

"About us!" Gordon says. He squats down in front of me, balancing on his ankles. He holds both my hands and rubs them under his, as if he were washing them. He goes into a long speech about why we should tell Victor everything, why we should go to him right now and have a long talk. "It's only fair . . . we want to do the right thing . . ." Gordon says. "We have to be honest. . . . He shouldn't die without knowing . . . if we are really his friends. . . . I can offer a future together that he cannot. . . ."

His speech is eloquent and full of the type of reasoning on which we were all brought up. The decision should be easy: the logic on his side is so clear. Gordon is a catch, I guess you would say. He's done with his life what we all hope to do: has created a business that is profitable, demonstrated the ability to love a woman completely, given to his parents all that a son can. He is young, but wholly mature, and he's settled into a man I should admire.

Still, I have my own unnameable logic, something inside me that demands custody of my decision.

He waits for me to speak. He waits, as always, with patience but also with the eagerness of one who is confident of his persuasiveness.

"I don't think so," I say finally.

"What?" Gordon says, his eyes widening.

"I don't think that would be the right thing to do, that's all," I say. "It might make *you* feel better, but I don't think it would make Victor feel better to know that we were having an affair."

"An *affair!*" Gordon says, nearly spitting the word. He stands and walks along the row of washing machines. The dryer gives a final turn and then stops, making the sounds from Alien Turf seem even louder. The blinking lights get Gordon's attention. He stands in front of the video machine and picks a wooden hanger from a basket of other hangers. When Alien Turf's computer voice comes on saying, ". . . *Destroy or be destroyed* . . ." Gordon bashes the face of the screen. His first stroke hits the machine just as it boings. He crashes the hanger again and again against Alien Turf. He bends over, looking like an ax murderer, beating the hanger down onto the game screen, sending glass shattering to the floor. The machine protests in buzzes and peeps. Then, after several more clubbings, the electronic visage blackens and is silent.

"I'm sorry," Gordon says and drops the hanger on the floor. His hands fall to his sides and his face shows an open-mouthed bewilderment and then relaxes into a nearly blank expression. "Would you like to go to my house?" he says.

Gordon is still pretty drunk, so I drive, perched on the edge of my seat, trying to see clearly through the snow. The storm becomes so heavy that I can only see ten feet of road in front of me. When we reach Gordon's house I turn off the car and lean back in my seat. I half expect Gordon to reach over and hug me but he is already out of the car. He opens my door and pulls me out by the elbow. He huddles over me as we run for the porch door. Even so, the snow flies into my eyes and I squint and rub the wet flakes away. By the time we've gotten inside, our hair is white with snow and our faces are fresh red as if we'd been slapped. The kitchen is dark, except for the frail light from beneath one cabinet. The radio is on, loud, with a discussion about how to shop for safe toys for Christmas. I kick off my wet shoes and slip my parka from my shoulders. Gordon drops his coat into a chair and leans against the wall, his hands folded across his chest.

"Spend the night," he says.

I turn on the stove. The gas flame burns in a ring while I fill the teakettle. The radio show lists the top ten safe toys of the year and then five that were responsible for at least one injury last Christmas.

"Spend the whole night," Gordon says. "Just once. You can tell him I was so drunk you were afraid to leave me."

"He'd never believe you got that drunk."

"Tell him anyway," Gordon says.

I put the kettle on and take two mugs from a cabinet.

"Just tell him," Gordon says. He stops leaning on the wall and comes over to stand behind me. I watch drops of water trickle down the side of the kettle and evaporate as they near the flame. Gordon turns me around and takes me by the wrists. He looks at me, pulls my sweater over my head, and then undoes the line of buttons on his jeans. He crouches on the floor and then pulls me under him, onto my belly. He hikes my jeans down and holds my shoulders still.

The radio show speaks of the dangers of dolls' clothing that kids can swallow. Gordon reaches under me and squeezes my breast while someone named Dr. Beedelhan describes an unfortunate incident with a girl and her Kiddie Cook oven. Then I don't know what happens on the radio. Gordon pins me under him. I feel his breath at my ear, his arm under me, his hand across my pelvis, pulling me against his hips. Then we roll together on the floor, knocking against the sturdy legs of his mother's breakfast table, slapping twice the broad aluminum of the refrigerator. We slam into the breakfast table again and a sugar bowl comes down; glass breaks across the floor. We hit the telephone stand and sent the phone flying toward the pantry. At some point there is the recorded voice of an operator saying, *"Your call cannot be completed as dialed. . . ."* The teakettle steams and whistles above and the dog comes in, barks in a circle around us, and then runs back into the living room, afraid.

Dying Young

Under normal circumstances it would be funny.

Under normal circumstances, I wouldn't be struggling to get on top of him.

We slow down. By his left shoulder, littering the floor, are flecks of blood and a thin line of red forms under his arm. I sweep the glass away from him with the side of my hand and see that my palm comes up spotted red, with a glistening from glass.

Finally we are still. I stand up and turn off the burner, putting an end to the screaming kettle. Gordon lies on the floor, watching me as I hang up the phone and close the door to the kitchen so the dog stays out. I throw my sweater on the floor and sit on it, so that I won't get any more glass. I sweep Gordon's hair back from his eyes and look down at him. I say, "Did you ever think that maybe Victor already knows?"

Driving home, I try to not to think about the particulars of Gordon's and my relationship but, in spite of myself, all I can think of are things Gordon and I have done together, of the way we have felt. I wonder how love affairs evolve into such complicated happenings. I wonder why I feel such deep regret. If I had met Gordon before Victor, I would understand a simple dimension of what constitutes love and undoubtedly I would be happy with it: love that is rooted in the notion of its own immortality.

But Victor has renegotiated the terms of love for me. He has made it seem that the future of a relationship is not as important as I once imagined. To love Victor is to save nothing for tomorrow. With him, the territory of love is limited to immediate interactions within a hovering realm of emotions. I've learned to love him for what he can give me and also for what he cannot give me, for that future he cannot provide.

After Victor, Gordon seems a tremendous compromise; because Gordon's and my relationship is domesticated with a logic that pertains to survival and common sense. It's true that at the moment when I began with Gordon, when I first became infatuated with him, I was investing heavily in this issue of survival and security. But survival has taken on a new meaning for me. If there is anything to learn from Estelle's long parade of speeches concerning spiritual matters, it is that the spirit, to survive, must disregard our customary logic of survival, must challenge our ordinary perception of what is right. If I love Gordon it is not the sort of love he wants or even that he can imagine. And, in any case, there is Victor, my fragile Victor, whose life has become fused with mine and with whom love just *is*.

I drive down Nantasket Avenue, past the pinball arcade, now closed for the winter season, the great span of beach, Hog Island, the cemetery, the hill commanded by an ancient watchtower. I feel compromised by the necessity to explain to Victor my late arrival. I can say that I spent several hours looking for Gordon and then met up with Annabel and Lenny and went off with them somewhere. I can take Gordon's suggestion and claim Gordon was so ill that I didn't want to leave him. I can say I drank too much and had to wait out the effects of the alcohol.

Or I could say nothing. It seems lately that Victor is willing to believe nearly anything I say, that he doesn't want an excuse, that for him the issue of truth has taken on far greater scope than determining whether or not I happen to tell a lie.

As soon as I walk in I know that I won't need any excuse. All the lights are on but Victor is asleep, lying on top of the covers. I go around the room, turning off lights. I go to the window to pull down the shade and am startled by the presence of his father, who slumps in Victor's chair, drooling over one arm. In the closet are army-issue blankets and I pull one out. It smells like mothballs and cedar. The blanket drapes nicely over Richard but he nearly wakes from the weight of it. He snorts and moves; then he settles back into the chair.

When I get in bed, I am so wary of Victor that he feels to me like a minor wound that I want to protect and accommodate. I am careful of my movements so that I don't disturb him. I am comforted by the slow procession of his breathing, by my place next to him in this small room where I have learned everything that seems important to me now. As I fall asleep, I feel the weight of new knowledge. It seems as if all secrets rumble toward me, their answers unfolding.

THIRTEEN

Richard Geddes hasn't given up, despite Victor's battery of reasons, despite threats from his son that he will move to another state unless he is left alone, despite even Estelle's attempts to quiet him. It has been six hours of arguing about what Victor should do about his illness. We are in a cherry-red Jeep of Estelle's, the kind with a soft top and no back seat. I am cross-legged on the floor, facing Victor, and feeling every bump on the roadway. Estelle is driving, awfully fast, to an antique auction in Cohasset, a town that Victor reports is more offensively bourgeois than any I am likely to encounter in a lifetime. At nine o'clock this morning she appeared at the apartment.

"Aren't we going a little fast?" I say.

"First time in years I've slowed down this much," Estelle says. The Jeep kicks up snow, gravel, mud, behind it.

"Victor, about this hospital business. You realize you really have no argument," Richard says.

"What do you know about it anyway?" Estelle says. "It's his disease, it's his life, it's his choice, simple as that."

Estelle swerves to the left, honks at another driver, and tells Richard to buckle his seat belt.

"Can you *see?*" I ask Estelle.

"See? Sure I can see. I see too much."

"After this auction," Richard says, "we are going back to the apartment, gathering your things, and heading straight to the hospital, aren't we, Victor?"

Victor doesn't answer. He makes faces at his father instead. His new tactic is to thwart his father's efforts by acting as absurdly as possible. Richard keeps looking over his shoulder at Victor, who puts his thumbs in his ears and flaps his hands at his father.

As we plow past a yellow Volkswagen Estelle yells, "Get off the road if you can't drive!"

"Stop acting like a child, Victor!" Richard says. "Get your hands out of your ears."

"Dad, I am not going to the hospital. You've forgotten the limitations on your role as father. I can do what I want after a certain age. Even the law supports me on that."

"Did you say something about the law?" Estelle says. "You see any cops? Nothing works in this car—not the radar detector, not the telephone . . ."

"If I want to throw myself from this Jeep I can," Victor says. "Estelle, drive faster so I can hurl my body onto the road. Hilary, help me with the back door."

". . . not the four-wheel drive, not the security system . . ." Estelle continues.

Victor balances on his knees in front of the back door of the Jeep, which is not a proper door at all but the sort of thing you find on a pickup truck. He unlatches one of the metal stays and begins on the next. I'm sure he's kidding because he winks at me and smiles. But it bothers me anyway. It bothers me so much that I welcome Richard's resonant voice saying, "Would you stop it, Victor? Get away from that door!"

"No throwing yourself from my vehicle," Estelle says. "My insurance man would go mad. Besides, you need to help me at this auction. You promised."

"Did you ever think of what this does to your girlfriend?" Richard says. "Look at her! Poor Hilary is petrified."

"I'm fine."

"She's ghost white," Richard says.

"Leave her alone, Dad."

"I'm not saying anything. Just look at her face. Look at it, Victor."

"Hang on, folks, we're going over my favorite hill!" Estelle says. The Jeep's engine roars and we top a hill, flying. My stomach lurches as we drop down the other side. The rear of the Jeep skids to the right and then straightens out. When we slow to a normal speed, Victor refastens the stays on the back door.

The auction is held at an elementary school in the center of Cohasset's postcard-perfect village. Nine classrooms of furniture. Estelle has a booklet listing all the items to be auctioned. She's stingy with it. Victor tags close to her, peering over her shoulder at the pictures and descriptions of coffee services, wardrobes in Spanish mahogany, dressing tables with mirrors built on elaborately molded walnut legs, Rockingham saucers, game tables with chessboards inlaid.

Victor grabs at the booklet, but Estelle pulls it away.

"I am trying to decide on a decent wedding present for Annabel and Lenny!" Estelle says.

Victor says, "If you want my advice, you have to let me *see* the thing."

I follow, lingering. I look at the bulletin boards of artwork. Kid stuff: finger paints, collages on construction paper with the themes of each printed in bold marker. Many are some variation on Christmas, or "What Is a Home?" or "Animals in a Zoo." Someone named Penny in the first grade labeled hers "Beauty," and has plastered pictures of little kid models showing off little kid fashion. Craig, in the third grade, has magazine advertisements of liquor bottles lined up in perfect order, none touching. He has drawn borders for each ad. I worry for Craig.

Richard keeps stopping to take water from one of the fountains that dot the hallway. The fountains are grade school height. He has to bend way over; I'm surprised he can drink from that angle. He wipes the water from his mouth and I wait for him to catch up to me. He jogs forward, then stops and fills his hands with coughs.

There's a crowd in the hallway, lots of nicely dressed couples pointing into the booklets and nodding their heads; people ducking in and out of classrooms stuffed with furniture. They make room for Richard, who coughs a full minute and then finally joins up with me.

"Hilary, don't worry," Richard says. He slings an arm over my shoulder. "We'll have Victor back in treatment tomorrow."

Each classroom features different types of antiques. Estelle leans into Mrs. Cushing's fourth grade class, eyes a roomful of tables, overhigh for their spindly legs. To Victor she says, "Could the sideboard be saved?"

Victor looks into the room. He pushes his glasses up on his nose and turns to Estelle.

"With an ax," he says.

Everybody at the auction has killer clothes, killer perfume, and killer watches. Some have dogs. Puny French dogs and Yorkshire terriers with barrettes in their combed bangs. Pampered, artificial little dogs you don't buy for protection. They have armed guards at home for that.

I pass two women, both with identical strings of pearls and hair set in broad curls over their heads. They are trying to decide on whether to buy a chest of drawers.

"There's no way Donald won't find out about it," one of them says. "I used to buy what I wanted and say Mother sent it to me. But now she's dead. I lost a lot when I lost her."

Her companion has overenameled lips in a rich burgundy color. She holds a fidgety toy poodle, fresh from the grooming house, trimmed to its little dog toes and looking like a sculpted tree.

When I pass them they give me questioning glances, as if afraid I might overbid them on the chest or as if I don't belong here, I can't tell.

I am nervous and I steal. I steal from each classroom in turn. Nothing big, nothing I can't hide in my coat. Except a beautiful bowl with an ornamental design. I walk right out with that.

Dying Young

.   .   .

The auctioneer is a snarly-faced man with a big tuft of yellow-white hair and dry, nicotine-stained lips. He wears his collar too tight. His Adam's apple jiggles just above the knot in his tie. He calls out item after item, revving up the bidders.

He says: "We've got earthenware tiles by William de Morgan. We've got a collection of stoneware jugs, we've got a Norrington flagon in silver, a copper gravy saucepan, English stoneware, brass milking jugs from Holland, Staffordshire spaniel mugs, butter molds in sycamore wood . . ."

Estelle won't let Victor out of her sight. Not to drink water, not to pee. She grabs his arm, pushes the auction booklet up to his face, and says, "What about the easy chair in the bergère shape?"

"Ugly and in poor condition," Victor says. "They've got it roped off as if it were worth something. Horrendous bad taste."

"When did he learn so much about antiques?" I ask Richard.

"His mother talked endlessly about antiques."

"Shoveled it down my throat," Victor says.

"Pay attention!" demands Estelle. "They're starting."

"If I throw up, can I be excused?"

"If you throw up, you're going to the hospital," Richard says.

"Nazi," says Victor.

There's a break at noon. In the back of the cafeteria, in the area where kids buy their school lunches, you can buy croissants, good black coffee, juice, and fruit cocktail. Everything costs two dollars. The croissant, the juice, the fruit cocktail, the coffee. No distinction. Easy arithmetic.

"I'll have two dollars of your juice, two dollars of your croissant, two dollars of your coffee . . ." Victor says.

"Will that be all, sir?" the counter woman asks. She has on a restaurant hat that looks like a shower cap.

"Now quadruple that order and divide it in half," Victor says.

"Don't give her a hard time, Victor," I say. I lean toward the counter woman and wonder if, indeed, the hat really *is* a shower cap. I say, "Give us two of everything, please."

The woman hands Victor an eggshell-colored paper tray. RECYCLED PAPER, it says in raised letters.

"Victor, is this for Estelle and your dad, or are you hungry?"

"Are you kidding?" Victor says. He knocks at the croissant with his fingertip.

"Where's Victor? The auction's starting again," Estelle says. "Richard, find your son. He's escaped."

"He's probably in the bathroom," Richard says. He has taken Victor's seat and is rummaging through the auction booklet, trying to give advice to Estelle. He says, "Hey, I know something about this. I can help."

"He might be ill," Estelle says. "Of course he gets sick at *my* auction."

"How in hell can you say that?" I ask. Pissed, too. I'm ready for an argument. Estelle drops her jaw and Richard puts down the booklet and looks around at me.

Dying Young

"I assure you, Hilary," Estelle says, "I am Victor's first fan. He is not going to die. He's just playing around with death the way young men will. Richard ought to buy him a motorcycle; that would do the trick. Twenty hairpin turns at ninety miles an hour, his leg grazing the ground, trees in his vision, that would change his mind."

"He's got leukemia," I say.

"Oh, he's had that for years," Estelle says. "Hasn't he, Richard?"

"Since college," Richard says. He's got his nose in the auction booklet.

"As soon as he goes back into treatment he'll be fine," Estelle says. "I indulge him in all this death talk only because I know nothing serious will happen to him. Don't get me wrong; I really do have philosophies about the afterlife. But I only let him *pretend* that he's going to kill himself. He'll get bored with it soon enough. Don't you think so, Richard?"

"I hope so."

"And many days he's perfectly normal, isn't he?" Estelle says. "As if all he had were a mild flu."

"Today for example," Richard says. "But I don't trust it."

"As soon as he feels some real pain he'll go running to the hospital, you'll see," Estelle says, patting my hand.

"I've seen him cry with it," I say. "I've seen him pound the mattress while I fumble with the needle."

I try to find Victor, but he's nowhere. I steal more stuff. A statue of an eagle, a cut steel brooch, a Christmas ornament in gold wire. I take these things outside to where the Jeep is parked. Behind the front seat I have the rest of my stash, stuffed into a Hefty bag.

I find Victor spread horizontal in the back of Estelle's Jeep. Eyes open, his elbow bent over his forehead. Somehow he must have gotten Estelle's key out of her purse because the engine is running. There's Stravinsky from a classical station and the heater's on full blast.

He is surrounded by the things I've stolen: a small mid-nineteenth-century copper kettle, a half dozen sterling and crystal perfume bottles, a Staffordshire cider mug, two brass candleholders, and a scattering of sterling pins. I unload my new findings and settle into the Jeep.

"You are crazy," Victor says. He picks up the kettle and swings it by its handle. "What's going to happen when they auction this stuff? They're going to say three cider mugs from the 1860s and there's going to be only two. Why do you do these things, Hilary? It's only going to embarrass you someday. Hilary? Hilary? Don't leave, honey. Aw, come on. Hey, I'm glad you took it. You hear me? I'm tickled."

I shut the door again and pull myself inside. Victor laughs and says, "I threw up on an Ernest Gimson cabinet. I swear to God I didn't mean to. . . ."

"Estelle and your father have no idea how sick you are," I tell him.

"This is news to you? Good job, Hils, to cop this sterling pin. It's pretty and it's you."

"I wasn't going to wear it," I say. "I just wanted it."

"You know, you need direction. Something to do, something legitimate to make you feel better. Maybe you should get a job," Victor says. He positions the pin next to my chest, deciding how it looks.

"Are you as sick as I think you are?"

"Sicker, honey," he says. "Listen, if you ever want to rob someone, rob my father."

"I don't do people," I say, "only stores. And auctions, I guess." I lie down with my feet propped on a spare tire and play with Estelle's car telephone. It's a great gadget. You dial the number and then send it out. It makes a sound like it's transmitting, although it is broken, as Estelle said.

Victor takes it from me and pretends like he's a police sergeant, commanding orders to a team of squad cars in a stakeout. He presses in a collection of random numbers, pounds the "Send" button, and says, "Okay, Units 23, 10, 4, I want you to close in on second and third grade. Cover the music room, Unit 12. I want careful surveillance of the kindergartners. Check all their lunch bags and pencil boxes. Search the book bags on the sixth graders . . ."

We curl up together and fall asleep to Bach. I don't know what piece, but the notes are so light that they ring as natural as the sounds from an ocean, the easy rhythm of night crickets, as constant as weather.

We're awakened by the sound of the car next to us starting up.

"Where are we?" Victor says. Then he says, "Oh yeah."

On the radio, they do an advertisement for the Boston Pops. The cellular phone is kicked onto its side.

I look through the plastic windows on the Jeep and see Estelle and Richard. She steps down a stairwell, past a jungle gym and a set of swings. Richard staggers behind her, carrying two cardboard boxes, stacked on top of each other, an embroidered stool, and her purse.

"You are terrible!" Estelle announces when she's reached the car. "Abandoning me like that!"

"You had my wonderful father," Victor says. "Dad has terrific period sense."

"I paid way too much for everything and hate it all," Estelle says.

Richard pushes the cardboard box into the Jeep. Victor kneels in front of it, picking through the purchases.

"Good on the pottery, bad on the oriental porcelain," Victor says. "Good on the mirror."

"It's all overelaborate, isn't it?" Estelle frowns. "Overdone, dead styles. I just can't help myself at an auction. There's all those people, calling out numbers, and I just can't stand to lose."

"You never had a chance. There were a half dozen dealers in there scooping up the good stuff. But look at what Hilary got," Victor says. He points to one of the antiques I've stolen.

"Where did you find that darling junket bowl!" Estelle says, marveling. "Oh, Hilary, it's superb."

$\mathcal{T}$he fog comes in, smoke-gray and sitting squat against the ocean. Estelle drives slow on the way home, sharing a silver flask of brandy with Richard. They are like two teenagers, giggling as they hand off the liquor. She's driving too carefully to be drunk; and even if she were drunk I don't think I'd care.

The ocean is a two-hundred-foot drop from the roadway.

Dying Young

The evening is falling quickly. There is only fog, dim road lamps, a heavy sky. A flock of sea gulls burst into flight and I watch as they become black dots against the horizon. Victor is curled up with his shoulders balancing against my knee. His hand occupies the space between his cheek and the carpet of the Jeep. He is asleep through all manner of traffic and conversation. He stays asleep over potholes and sharp curves.

"Victor thinks I should get a job," I say.

"You have a job taking care of my son," says Richard.

"You know what I mean."

"Do you know the story about the field mouse who thought he wasn't a good mouse because he couldn't harvest the corn in the fall and couldn't make a good field mouse home and wasn't very good at alerting the others if a cat or a snake were near?" Estelle asks. She takes a swig from the flask and hands it back to me.

"I don't know any story like that," I say. The brandy sends a fire into my stomach. Outside the Jeep's plastic windows the Atlantic Ocean opens and closes against coastal rocks. Far off a lighthouse blinks its coded message.

"When winter came," says Estelle, "and all the little mice were huddled in their mouse home and all the corn sat waiting by the oven, the mouse who thought he was useless told them stories by the fireplace. He told them all about the days of the harvest, all about the construction of the mouse hole. He told each story with perfect clarity to all his brother and sister mice. And that was his job."

FOURTEEN

*R*ichard leaves us at
the apartment and goes hunting for flowers to take as a gift
to Estelle's Christmas party. It feels better at home when
there's just Victor and me. I like the messiness of the apartment, how there is an order to where we keep things that
only he and I know and that we live unself-consciously in the
clutter.

I spread a dishcloth over the floor and iron a blouse.
Between ironing strokes I pick Cheerios out of their tall
yellow box. The fireplace smells like gutted houses and tree
bark.

At only six o'clock there's a midnight sky.

On the radio a choir of young boys sing "Silent Night."

Victor comes out of the shower, a towel draping his
middle. He shakes a cigarette loose from a pack on the mantel
and stands over me, looking down.

"You know what's missing?" he says, beneath a halo of
smoke. "A feeling of plenitude."

.   .   .

Dying Young

We start dressing for the party. Victor goes to the closet and pulls out a bow tie, a joke, with horn-tooting cherubs, printed all over it.

"They don't look like cherubs," I tell him in the mirror. "They look like little dogs."

I yank on a pair of panty hose. Color: Nude. Size: Medium. Direct from the store, they are clean and snag-free. I work them all the way to the top of my thigh, admiring the smooth job they do on my calves. I put on heels and stand on a chair so I can see how I look in the bathroom mirror.

Victor runs his cheek along the back of my knee.

"Splendid," he says, fawning.

Richard returns from the flower shop with a crop of lilies clinched in a lavender bow. He barrels in asking if we are ready. We are not. The stockings, the bow tie, everything is in a heap next to our unmade bed. Richard leaves again, pouring out apologies and turning off the light as he shuts the door. We hear him race down the stairs. Victor touches me—with emphasis. We try to make love but can't. Instead, Victor gives me a neck rub. He marches his fingers up and down my spine. He tells me jokes so that I have to laugh.

We drive between the line of sycamores that leads to Estelle's house. The trees have been laced with white lights and stand large above us, shadowing the moon. The lights add a touch of the fantastic, a tiny reminder of the paradisiacal virtues of Christmas. Victor leans over the car seat, watching the trail of decorated trees behind us. In one hand he holds his cigarette. In the other he balances a silver box with a floppy pearl bow. It's a set of six pewter beer mugs, with handles shaped as hunting whips. Richard bought them privately at the elementary school. He paid way too much for them so that they didn't go to auction. So that he could surprise Estelle, who had admired them.

The car is filled with Christmas music. There's a faint smattering of snow.

"You know," I tell Victor, "your father is after Estelle."

"Why do you say so? Because he went to the party early?"

"Well, that too."

"Hils, he was probably so pleased we were in bed. He wanted to get to the party ahead of us so he could drink in peace before I got there."

"Christ," I say, "*my* father's an alcoholic."

"We're all alcoholics."

There are cars all over Estelle's looped driveway. Nice cars, fat Mercedeses and boxy Volvos with their sort of utilitarian, Protestant snobbishness. Cars from Hingham and Cohasset and Beacon Hill, There's the Geddes BMW, in desperate need of a waxing, and then there's the rest of the cars—just normal.

"None of them have the élan of your Oldsmobile," Victor says when we park.

I say, "How come your father can be an alcoholic and my father can be an alcoholic and my father is disgusting when he drinks and your father is . . . aesthetic?"

"Do you want me to answer that?"

"Yes," I demand.

Dying Young

"Do you want me to be callous?"

I nod. Victor curls a lip and rubs his thumb against his first and second finger. "Money," he says.

Estelle's house is beautiful with people. I don't know who they are, but they are as colorful as a royal flush. The dresses range from a shimmering gold and crimson gown to a simple floor-length wool skirt and lacy blouse. The men's jackets seem more stationary and lend a stabilizing element to the chaos of bright dresses and Christmas bulbs. Victor and I are a little underdressed. My skirt is barely made tolerable by a silver and jade belt that Estelle bid for, won, and then couldn't make small enough to stay on her skinny waist. Also I have the pin that I stole and that Victor insisted on my wearing. Victor has on a jacket and a pair of fancy, mustard-colored corduroys. But they're his father's and way, way big.

White candles burn on tables and three fireplaces glow with comfortable flames. There's a band two rooms over doing jazz tunes. Someone plays a heavy sax. So much chatter, so many smiling faces, that for a moment I am lost in it, floating through the room with Victor's hand at my elbow, guiding me through the gatherings of people.

We are besieged by waiters bearing silver trays of steaming hors d'oeuvres. I am afraid of them. They come at us and at us with food I can't identify. Victor has no problems. He takes a toothpick and spears a block of artichoke heart with crab and hollandaise sauce. He slips down an oyster. He is crazy over the smoked salmon. He eats something brown and fried, something fleshy pink in the shape of a curled star, and something that I think really was a bug and that he shouldn't have eaten. He can tag all cheeses with their proper names and goes for the smelliest, most formidable type. He tries to get me to eat, explaining the mysteries hanging at the ends of toothpicks. I slap his arm and plead for him to be quiet, that he is embarrassing me.

He laughs, says, "Snail!" and holds up something I have to close my eyes for.

Belinda McCann, who went to the sister school of Victor's prep, has her eye on Victor. She slides right between us wearing a vermilion dress with an absent front, shakes the pendant on her necklace so it disappears between her breasts, and says, "Don't be such a tacky person, Vic, tell me what you're doing."

"I'm not *doing* anything," Victor says. He gets a new gin and tonic from the barman. It comes with a red sword through the lime.

"You're just living off your daddy's money, aren't you?" Belinda says. She smiles to lighten the sting of her words. She calculates their effect on Victor. "No, you aren't. I can tell you aren't. You lie!" she squeals.

Victor looks at me. I reach for his drink and draw the red sword from the lime. I stand behind Belinda, who is a good half foot shorter than me, and pretend like I am going to stab her head with the sword.

"You devil!" Belinda says to Victor. "Talk!"

"I can't," Victor says, and shrugs deeply. "I've run out of words."

I hold two fingers in peace-sign fashion over the top of Belinda's head. I make a face and Victor smiles.

"Never! Are you one of those tacky people who has secrets? I've told *you!* I sold our West Coast house when I got divorced from the polo player. I'm thinking of, you know, my own little business. Like maybe a clothing line or a cosmetic company. Now you know everything. It's no fair, Victor, I haven't see you in years!"

"I didn't want to admit this," Victor says, mocking honesty. "I'm a guerrila. I work in Central America. I have a banana garden on the side."

"Don't *do* this to me, Vic!" Belinda wails. She gives him an inviting dip with her eyes.

"Okay, I'm a pathologist. Want to smell my hands?" Victor watches Belinda's face fall. "There's nothing to say. I'm really not doing anything."

"Dance with me," breathes Belinda.

Estelle has adopted Richard as her date. No, as her slave. She orders him around, saying, "Richard, find my wine! Richard, ask the band not to play so loudly . . . Richard, tell the cook that whatever is on this platter is completely unsuitable and have one of the staff destroy it."

He's good at all these chores, but drunker by the minute.

Gordon pulls me backward sliding between the backs of two elderly men, and hugs me from behind, saying, "Guess who?"

"You smell wonderful," I say.

"You look wonderful. I've been watching you since I came in. For twenty minutes I've been stalking you. Mistletoe," he says, pointing up. "Let's dance."

He pulls me onto the dance floor, spins me around, and

sends me under his arm for another whirl. Victor and Belinda aren't close enough—at least for Belinda. She keeps pulling his jacket and he gives in—you can tell—reluctantly. So close to the band that the sax moans just above their heads, Annabel and Lenny sink into each other. The music speeds up but Annabel's head remains dreamily on his shoulder.

Gordon and I knock into several couples as he reels me forward, spins me around, and yanks me back behind him. My shoes are no good for this and I'm hardly able to keep up. Gordon's such a hotshot that people gather around and watch us. The band obliges by throwing out some true swing. Estelle claps her hands and urges Richard to whirl her, which he does in a clumsy, cute way. For a fraction of a second, as I am sent springing into a double pretzel, I see Victor's face, smiling at me. I catch the colors of Belinda's dress.

"Be careful now, Hilary!" Victor calls. "Stay within the laws of physics."

Between directives by Estelle, Richard finds the time to hound Victor about his being ill.

"Can you leave me alone, just for tonight, Dad?" Victor says. "I feel great tonight. I feel perfect."

"You do?" Richard says, his eyebrows rising.

"Never better."

"What do you think, Hilary? How's my boy?" Richard asks me.

"Charming," I say and Victor squeezes my hand.

"Christ, son," Richard says, and slaps him on the shoulder, "maybe you have this licked."

Estelle orders Richard to dance with her. Richard raps

Victor's shoulder again and smiles broadly, showing stained, crowded teeth. When he's gone, Victor says to me, "I have so many drugs zipping through my veins that I couldn't feel bad even if I wanted to."

I frown because I, too, was feeling hopeful.

*A*nnabel drags Lenny through jungles of Christmas gowns. He mutters "Excuse me's" all the way toward us.

"She's going to get me arrested," Lenny says. "The big-butted lady in the super-short skirt said I was *trying* to bump into her."

Victor says, "I heard the news, Lenny, congratulations."

"In May," Annabel says. On her hand is a modest though beautiful diamond. "You're coming to the wedding, aren't you?"

"Wouldn't miss it," Victor says, reaching to kiss her.

*C*appy won't dance with Estelle, but she's going to make him. She takes his plate of Christmas pudding, his pipe, his drink. She puts these things on the edge of a tea table and pulls him by the belt buckle onto the dance floor.

"This is humiliating," Cappy pleads.

Estelle claps in a circle around Cappy, who bounces feebly and then claims exhaustion. We urge him on. Gordon says he looks like a bear in a circus and Victor says he looks like he just went through shock therapy.

"How about you and me again?" Belinda says to Victor. She's half hooked up with a tall thick-haired man with a catcher's mitt face. He stays within earshot of her at all times. He brings her drinks once or twice and he stares.

"Belinda, I'd like you to meet Gordon," Victor says. He presents Gordon as if he were the prize behind door number one. "You'll like Gordon. He'll be able to tell you what he does for a living. He's real humble. He says he makes video games, but don't believe him. Gordon's just waiting to increase the speed of light and thus reduce delays in extraterrestrial and metadimensional paging. Isn't that right, Gordon?"

"I'm in love with your girlfriend," Gordon says.

"You have a girlfriend?" Belinda sighs.

"What is the matter with you?" I say, loud. No one can hear us, I know, except for the fake deer and the hedgehog and the squirrel. We are freezing outside. Estelle's garden is shrouded in snow.

"I don't see why you're so upset," Gordon says. "He didn't pay any attention anyway."

"You told him," I say. "That was enough."

"He thought it was a joke."

"Funny," I huff. I'm shaking. Cold and mad.

"Victor is going to have to know eventually."

"Yeah? When? When you tell him," I say.

"I'm not threatening anything," Gordon says.

"The hell you aren't."

The snowflakes, thicker now, rain into Gordon's champagne glass. He stands on the incline of a small hill. Next to him I feel childish and short.

"Look, I know you love me but this is hard," Gordon

says, his sweetest expression on his face. His hair falls into his eyes and he pushes it back. Thick, shiny hair. His hands are immaculate.

In the dark, Estelle's ground animals are somehow made frightening.

"You do love me, don't you?" Gordon says.

"Not if you tell Victor, I don't."

"But now, you love me now, right? Right, Hilary? Hilary?"

I dance with Lenny, I dance with Richard. I look around to dance with Victor but he isn't in sight. I check the bar but can't find him. I ask Belinda, who looks at me rawly and shakes her stupid, pretty head. I lunge through a gathering of people, young couples. A dazzling gray-eyed woman stands in front of a guy with a seemingly pregnant stomach, explaining, "She's fine, I suppose, just boring. People are all like commercials and I'm waiting for the *movie.*"

"Oh, sure, I know," the young man says. His thin fingers, pianist's fingers, blot a dab of makeup from the woman's gray eyes. "It's just the same with my brother. Sure, he's eccentric, but only in the most convenient way."

I reach Annabel and tap her on the shoulder, asking for Victor. But she doesn't know. And Estelle doesn't know, nor Cappy. I check the kitchen, but he's not there. I go upstairs, opening doors shyly, and closing them with disappointment. Outside there is nothing but more snow.

Downstairs again, I see that the hallway has a line forming outside one of the bathrooms.

A woman in a silk dress and shoes decked in rhinestones stares impatiently at the bathroom door. She looks more than annoyed. She looks like she's in pain.

"There's another bathroom off the kitchen," I tell her.

The entire line races down the hall.

"Victor?" I say, knocking. I push open the door and he's there, leaning against the wall, head tilted up, eyes closed. The toilet is full of vomit. His tie and shirt are in bad condition.

"What happened?" I say.

"Dunno. Four guys did it. They took everything. My wallet, my watch, my shoelaces, my hair comb. Bastards," he says, "they stole my pocket lint."

"Let's go home, Victor," I say. I feel bottomless misery. "I've had enough of this party anyway."

There's a spray of vomit across a low end of the wallpaper. Rust-colored blood.

"No, you haven't," Victor says. "I've never seen you more happy."

"I just stopped being happy," I say. "You look awful."

Victor stands, pale and long, against the wall, his clothes hanging loosely on his body. For the first time he looks old to me—not like thirty-three but more like sixty-three. He looks sick and old and like someone who might die.

Richard's voice: "What's happened?"

He pokes his square head through the door and gasps. "Jesus H!" he says. "Is that blood? Well, that's it, Victor. You're going to the goddamned hospital! God damn it."

He pushes his way into the small bathroom—just a toilet and sink. He moves me aside and works over Victor with his handkerchief.

"Oh, Mother Mary. Oh, Judas Priest," he says.

"Dad, leave it, okay?" says Victor, pushing his father away.

"You're going to the hospital. I've had enough of this nonsense," Richard says. I know he's drunk but there are tears in his eyes. He's trembling. "If it were your mother asking, you would be at the hospital right now."

"Mother wouldn't have asked," Victor says. He looks at Richard, whose desperation contorts his face, making him look foolish. Making him look ineffectual and small.

"All right," Victor says. He leans into the sink and spits a puddle of brown. "Okay, Dad. I'll go. Tomorrow morning."

We leave the bathroom, splitting in two the new line that's formed outside. Victor has his arm around me. He smells awful and knows it and is embarrassed, which kills me. We hear a guy's voice, "This is disgusting!" and Estelle saying, "I have a half dozen bathrooms, dear. . . . Richard, get one of the maids."

Victor and I go upstairs. We find a guest suite, two rooms, neatly furnished with antiques. There's a quilt over the couch and a lace bedspread; by the window is a stiff chair with a woven seat. Next to it are three books in a pile. One is open to a page that shows a nineteenth-century map of the world. You can tell no one sits in the chair and no one reads. The lamp next to the chair is so dim, it couldn't even support reading.

"Half-tester bed," Victor says. "Adam wardrobe, very nice. Uh-oh, mistake. Estelle's put a drawing-room chair in a bedroom."

We go into the bathroom and find a big round tub with copper fixtures and a dish of clover-shaped guest soap with a perfume smell.

"Do you like all these antiques?" I say, turning the soap over in my hand so it foams.

Victor leans against the bathroom mirror and says, "If I had my own house, all the furniture would be dumpy and mismatched, just like where we live now. Or there would be none. We would live on floors and pillows."

"You'd need a desk. How could you do your work?"

"I wouldn't do any work," he says.

He pulls off his tie and loops it over the towel rack. Then he undoes the buttons on his shirt. On his knees, he presses against the side of the bathtub, his head beneath the faucet spray. I lean over him and soap his shoulders, neck, and chest. He swallows water from the faucet and spits. He dunks his head deeper, wetting his hair. He takes the soap and scrubs his face. He leans away from the tub and runs his hands over his wet hair. I give him a towel and he shakes it over his head. He blots his face dry, sits on the edge of the tub, and digs in his pocket for a cigarette. His pants are spotted with water. He is bird-boned. His skin papery. He puts his arm in front of him and runs a hand down it, as if it were someone else's arm. His body has become alien to him and alien to me. He drags on the cigarette, staring into the bare tile. When I ask him what is wrong his eyes close and he is silent.

"I would have gone home with him," I say to Gordon. We're dancing. The band changed and now there are five guys doing

Dying Young

delta blues. The lead singer, with a beer gut and a heartbreaking harmonica, wrinkles his forehead, stepping forward and back in time to the music. "I told him it was silly but he said no, he'll take a taxi home. He insisted. I couldn't convince him."

Gordon dances slow, right against me, putting his shoulders into it.

"I love you," he says, asking for something.

I'm trying to find my coat when I see Richard. He's in the library, alone in a chair, holding a napkin to his mouth. He's dreaming through the bay windows.

"Will I see you later tonight?" I ask. He shakes his head as if it were a sad thing that he would be here with Estelle. Or that his condition will not allow for driving even short distances.

"What do you see out there?" I say and take a half step inside.

He puts down the napkin and sighs long and noisily. "Snow. A maze. One of Santa's reindeer," he says.

I've said goodbye to everyone except Gordon. To him I feel I cannot say goodbye. But he sees me by the door and pulls me toward him.

"It seems to me that you are always leaving," he says.

"That's not true," I tell him.

"Every time I see you go through a door I wonder if you'll come back. Don't go away from me," Gordon says. His blond hair has curled up away from his ears, loose ringlets, delicate gold bands. Never has he seemed so solemn and so wise. He looks young and sad and irreparably damaged.

"I have to go home," I say.

"Let me dance with you again," he says, his hand on my waist. "Let me . . ."

He pulls me against him. He kisses beneath the ledge of my jaw.

"You're trying to seduce me," I say, smiling.

"Maybe, but not in the way you think," he says. "I want to seduce you with the memory of our being together, of having loved in just this way. I want you to wake up one lonely night with your ears full of the sound of skin against my bedsheet and for you to want me."

I touch his lips with my fingers. I look at this man who has spent himself on me, who has been my best friend. I am full of unsaid apologies. "Gordon . . ." I say, trying to be tender. But something in my voice slides. I search for words, but I see already something inside him collapse and be still. He looks away from me, staring down at his shoes. He breathes out heavily.

"You have somewhere you think you ought to be," Gordon says, letting me go.

Getting home is hard. Bad roads, bad visibility. Snow thickening in the spot where my wipers won't reach. The windshield fogs and I have to wipe it with the wrappings from an order of fries. Nine miles feels like ninety and I'm exhausted even though it's only midnight. The dancing has worn me out. The heel of my right shoe snags on the car rug. When I stop the car it takes all my will to get out onto the sidewalk. I'm so tired that I walk slowly to the front porch, even though the snow on my bare legs makes them burn with cold.

Up the steps is drudgery. I'm drunker than I should be. I get my key in the door after three tries. At first I think it's my fault that the lock won't turn. Then I see that the lower lock is open. It's the bolt on top that won't move. I knock on the door and wait for Victor but nothing happens. I knock some more and then I pound. I call his name. I put my face down the space that runs between the floor and the bottom edge of the door. It's what I think it is. It's gas. I'm screaming now. I'm drumming on the door. I kick it with my knee and lose a shoe down the hallway. I lean my body into it and shove so hard that I'm not surprised to see the door bow against its frame, or to hear the creaking of separating wood.

"You can't do this!" I yell. "You can't do *this!*"

I nearly lose my voice calling him. Finally I collapse against the door, crying, shaking, slamming my heels on the floor, biting my fingers. I keep saying his name. I keep saying, "No . . ." as if anyone were listening.

Then I hear something inside. I screech like a monkey.

Victor opens the door slowly. The smell of gas enters the hallway like poison. Victor stands, naked torso, his father's corduroys strapped up by a belt.

"I'll kill you!" I scream and I jump him. He backs into the apartment and we land on the floor, me on top, hitting him, pulling his hair. He fights some and then gives in. He takes a blow to the stomach without even tensing. I sit up and grab a wineglass off the coffee table. I smack it twice on the floor. The first blow shatters the cup and the second sends the stem into a thousand tiny daggers of glass.

"We break a lot of things," Victor says. I hug him and

he rocks me toward him. He races his hands over my back as if he were looking for something.

"I'm sorry, Victor, I'm sorry." I reach to his belly, where I've hit him, where earlier tonight he felt so sick. I kiss his soft skin, the freckles I've memorized, a flat, dark mole. In my mind there's a river of images of Victor, memories of exactly how he looked once while I was watching him, while I was loving him. A thousand angles of Victor turn in my mind like a prism. I brush my cheek against him, going lower. With my arms tight around his hips, I burst into a single moment of the deepest pain, one long wail.

"If we stay in here, we will *both* die," Victor says.

On the hallway stairs, we sit together, knees touching.

"I almost hoped you'd run off with Gordon eventually," Victor says.

He's not looking at me. He's staring, with concentration, somewhere he occupies alone.

"When did you find out about that?"

"Oh, I don't know. Not a specific time, really. Just one day we were over at his house and I looked up and you were standing with him, I don't know, fixing a sandwich in the kitchen. And you looked at him with an expression I'd seen you give me. I thought, Oh, yeah, they're lovers."

There's a fluorescent light supported by two hooks on the wall. It blinks and it buzzes, like an insect lamp. I have a palmful of coins that I hurl one by one at the light, missing.

"You're not mad?" I ask.

"Mad?" He turns to me like I've grown gills and says, "Hils, do you know what I've done to you? After all the things that have happened to you and I have to love you and die and break both our hearts?" He looks away. "You want me to be mad at you? Oh, God, Hilary. I couldn't be."

"If you knew about Gordon, then why didn't you say something?"

"I was afraid you'd stop," Victor says, and then more quietly, "or that you'd leave me. I was afraid of both, exactly the same amount of afraid."

I turn the coins over in my hand: nickels, pennies, dimes. I look at them not like they are money at all, but as if they come from some foreign place, somewhere I've been long ago but can hardly remember.

"You could go to the hospital," I say.

"Baby, I can't. I can't go to the hospital."

"Wait until Christmas, Victor, why can't I have a Christmas with you?"

"Leukemia," he explains, "is in the bone marrow."

"Christmas is nine days."

"They can do marrow transplants but they don't usually work. And it hurts, Hilary." Victor closes his eyes. He winces. "Already it is hurting."

"I got you a present. I put it in Mrs. Birkle's apartment. It's nothing. It's a first-edition *Beyond Good and Evil.*" I wipe my eyes on his shirtsleeve. I say, "Bone marrow?"

"They try to remove all the cells, both normal and leukemic, in the bone marrow. They lock a needle inside your pelvis and draw out the marrow," Victor says. He glances at me, pitching up an eyebrow. "You got me Nietzsche?"

"What were you planning to do? Have me walk in late tonight and find your corpse? God damn you, Victor!" My voice rises. It whines. It sounds as if it comes from just behind my teeth.

"What do you want me to do? Go to the hospital and have them suck the marrow out of my bones so that the replacement marrow instead of my own can kill me? Is that a good idea? A great fucking idea," he says.

I chuck the handful of coins at the light fixture. They ricochet off the wall, bringing paint. The ones that hit the light make a pinging noise and send the bulb into a spasm of blinks.

"Did you leave me a note?" I say quietly.

"Don't cry," Victor says, crying.

The morning comes and Victor helps me put my stuff into the car. He wants me to take all his books. Between the hours of 2 and 4 A.M., when the apartment became sufficiently aired out, we took volume after volume from the shelves. He made me write my name next to his on the frontispiece of each one, so that I would truly own it.

He told me facts about suicide. Victor's beautiful facts. He told me most self-destructive behavior stems from guilt associated with the Oedipal situation, though, for him, this was not the case. He said that in classical Greece the magistrates kept a supply of hemlock for anyone who came to the Senate with a convincing reason for wishing to die. Also, that doctors use poison more often than the rest of the population and that psychiatrists kill themselves much more often than other physicians. He said that gas wasn't working. It was only making him sick. But he's got tranquilizers and painkillers.

Dying Young

Lethal mixtures and hours and hours before anyone will find him.

"Look," he said when I protested everything, when I laid myself across him and begged, "even Pascal says that it is easier to die than to have to think about death without dying."

"I don't know Pascal," I said. "I don't even know why he's so famous."

"You will," Victor said, smiling, promising, holding a book.

We made a plan for my future. I'm not going back to Boston; I'm not going to my mother's apartment or work as an assistant somewhere. I'm going to school. I'm driving this day to Pennsylvania, straight to the university to fill out an application for veterinary school and demand an interview.

"You speak beautifully," Victor told me. "You're brilliant, just relax."

We practiced what I would say. He told me not to be afraid. And for the first time I am not.

The morning is a winter painting, thick snow with a crust of ice. Shadows of tree branches and rooftops. The sky is so blue.

When I get inside the car to go, I find I cannot see. The tears come down in streams. No sobbing. But it goes on a long time and Victor stoops down level to the car seat, one knee in snow, and hugs me. We wait for the crying to stop and it does.

"Your dad is going to miss you," I tell him. "It's going to break his heart."

"His heart has been broken and broken, Hils," Victor

says. He means it, too; he speaks quietly like a doctor giving a diagnosis.

" 'Cause of your mom?" I ask.

"Because of her, yes. Because of everything. You want to know what my mother would do today? If she were standing here in front of me she would take both my hands in hers and say, 'Son, don't tell your father anything. Just do it. Leave him to me.' After it was over she'd perform her magic with him. She'd tell him exactly the right way; she'd hold him together. She might even get a smile out of him, who knows? And then, much later, she'd wander off to the woods like a dying cat and cry until the stars came out."

I say, "Tell me, honest, Victor, how I should have acted with you. Should I have been different than I've been? Funnier or smarter or more serious?"

"You should have worn more blue," Victor says, teasing. "It makes your eyes stand out. See the color of the sky right now? That is your color."

Above us the sky is clear of clouds and blue, stratosphere blue, the color of everything beyond.

He kisses me dozens of times, all over my face. He kisses me so much I can't kiss him. He hands me the note he wrote last night. It's folded four ways and taped at one end. I take it from him, making a point of touching his hand.

It's not me driving, it is someone else. It's not Victor I see in the rear-view mirror, waving. It is someone else. I drive through Hull like a stranger or like someone who knows the place so well that the thought of leaving it has become strange.

Dying Young

I think of Victor, turning back to the front door, kicking the snow from his boots, and taking each line of the staircase in his easy way. I can envision him pulling a cigarette from his shirt pocket, sitting outside our apartment, and smoking it on the landing.

I think of Gordon, too, closing up his parents' house, returning to his life in Boston. I imagine him hammering plywood over each window, shutting off the water, pulling sheets over the living-room furniture. I wonder if he will drive by my house later and look up at the spiraled roof to our apartment, thinking that I am there with Victor. Thinking that he would like to see me, if only I would just come down.

And what I would do to be with Victor, to remain always inside our home with its uneven floors, the peculiar lamps that shed only vague light, the sloped ceilings I've stared at with Victor sleeping next to me. I wonder if I'll ever know a home like that again; if someplace else will ever feel as familiar.

In my mind I see Victor, stubbing out his cigarette, staring at our apartment's oak door. He is wearing an expression I have never seen before, a private face, vivid, nervous, not to be shared. He is taking an awful long time to stand and go inside, but he is going.

Book Mark

The text of this book was set in the typeface
Perpetua and the display in Weiss
by Creative Graphics, Inc., Allentown, Pennsylvania.

It was printed on 55 lb Glatfelter,
an acid-free paper,
and bound by Berryville Graphics, Berryville, Virginia.

Designed by Marysarah Quinn